The Divine Formula

A Sam Buckner Adventure

By

Leo J. Audette

This book is a work of fiction. Names, characters, places and incidents either are products of the author's imagination or are used fictitiously. Any resemblance to actual events or locales or persons, living or dead, is entirely coincidental.

Edited by Dolores Garon.

www.leoaudette.org

Dedicated to

This novel is dedicated to the memory of my father and mother, Claude and Theresa.

They supported me in any and every endeavour I wanted to take on. They never criticized my decisions, but were always there to help me pick up the pieces. They fostered my love of travel and allowed me to dream.

Though they have passed, their influence is still felt and cherished.

With Thanks

I need to acknowledge Dolores Garon, who expended so much time and energy in editing this novel. She kept me on the straight and narrow, checking and double-checking, not only the spelling and grammar I used, but also some of the statements I made, in order to ensure they were correct and accurately reflected my intent.

"God doesn't play dice with the universe."

Albert Einstein

Other books by the author:

The first of the Sam Buckner Adventures:
The Osiris String
> (Available now at Amazon)

The third instalment to the trilogy: **SlipTime**
> (Available October 2015)

The Divine Formula

Prologue

Mohammed Al-Kammin had been on the run for four months.

He was also on the hunt: looking for the men whose names were on his list. He had already *visited* two of his former investors, including Sheikh Wadi Al-Kabir, the mastermind behind what would become life-shattering events, and leading to the death of the people Mohammed cherished the most.

Having twice taken care of business, he now had to deal with the remaining eleven members of the board of directors of the Foundation for the Promotion of Islamic Culture: They needed to pay for their sins.

Mohammed was, or had been, Ra'id Al-Eissa's partner in developing an invention that promised to cure HIV. Ra'id conceived of a way to excite, with harmonic microwaves, the HIV genetic code to the point of combustion, without affecting the infected host cell. It wasn't a far stretch of the imagination for the Sheikh to see the potential of the invention. He used his tremendous resources to manipulate Ra'id's life in order to persuade him to convert his invention into a weapon able to kill anyone, anywhere, in order to control world politics through intimidation and assassinations and clear the way for him to establish an Islamic federation.

Two laboratories had been set up, the primary one in Frankfurt, Germany, and a backup lab on the small island of Kamaran in Yemen. However, both had been destroyed during raids by German and Israeli Special Ops teams, led by Homeland Security.

Before Ra'id was killed, under orders from the Sheikh, he had learned of the latter's betrayal and involvement in the deaths of his parents and that of his beloved Samihah. As a result, he had asked Mohammed to take up a *jihad* to punish those responsible, a request which Mohammed had accepted without hesitation.

Going *underground* for almost three months before surfacing and taking out the second person on his list, Mohammed was now on his way to Saudi Arabia to find the third.

Still driving what looked like an old, beaten-up Mercedes van, he maintained the pretence of being a used-furniture vendor.

The vehicle was nothing like it seemed to be. Both sides had large motifs of old furniture painted on them, with the company's name, "Mustafa's Pre-Owned Furniture", written in Arabic in the lower-right corner of the signs.

When he and Ra'id had originally used the vehicle to avenge Samihah's death at the hands of an elite Israeli commando team, the van also had the name posted in Hebrew, considering they were *visiting* their targets in Israel.

A few scratches and dents on the bumpers and sides completed the look of a well-travelled vehicle. The four rear tires, two on either side, seemed to show the stress of the vehicle's age. In fact, the tires were rated for the additional strain of a series of lithium-ion batteries hidden within the frame of the vehicle, adding nearly twelve hundred kilograms to its weight.

The interior of the rear cab was just large enough to accommodate a variety of old pieces. Two antique tube-type radios, an Art Deco Grunow World Cruiser Tombstone radio and a larger floor model antique Philco AM radio were secured by bungee cords to the front wall. There was a single bed with box spring and mattress lying flat on the floor to one side, with an assortment of boxes piled on top. A Louis XV armoire stood against the right side wall, next to a Crystal Ice Box from Freemont, Nebraska. There was barely room for anyone to move within.

These items too, were not what they seemed to be. Hidden under and within the old furniture were the components of the portable version of what was the deadliest weapon ever created: not as deadly as a nuclear bomb or the Ebola virus, but more like a *designer* weapon, able to target anyone, just for being who they were, using their DNA.

The drive to their destination felt that much longer without music because the truck's radio functioned as the control unit for the equipment in the rear. Cleverly camouflaged within the pieces of furniture were the different parts of the weapon. The two radios had working dials and control knobs, but, hidden inside and crammed tightly within the speaker cavities were the oscillators and capacitors for the maser. In a false back at the rear of the armoire were concealed the components for the computer which coordinated the process. The coil assembly in the box spring below the mattress was actually the antenna array. The maser which created the microwaves was itself in parts, hidden inside the walls of the metal icebox. As for the boxes piled on the mattress, they were filled with dishes and pots and pans to add a final touch of realism.

When in close proximity to the target and with the switch flipped on, a pulse of incredibly complex harmonic microwaves would be emitted and would simultaneously excite every cell in the victim, literally frying him, or her, within a matter of thirty-odd seconds.

The target he had just killed had recently been appointed chairman of the Supreme Council of the Armed Forces of Egypt, after the upheaval that had been caused by

13

his predecessor's demise: all part of the Sheikh's master plan.

Colonel General Mahmoud Hassim was one of the thirteen members of the board of directors of the Foundation for the Promotion of Islam and had been groomed by the Sheikh for almost seven years. He was to assume the new position and prepare the *coup d'état* which would let the council reclaim the power it had been forced to relinquish by the president.

Mohammed smiled to himself, thinking *that* would never happen now.

Part One

Chapter 1

President Alexander was sitting behind the Resolute desk, quietly reading a summary which the Democratic strategists had prepared for the upcoming presidential election, a year away to the day. The President knew he had to begin politicking if he hoped to remain in power for another four years. It wasn't the type of activity he liked, but he knew it was part of the job and, more importantly, what the electorate expected.

He sat back in his chair and rubbed his temples as he contemplated *why* he had gotten into politics in the first place. He remembered his stint in Political Science at Harvard and how he had come to see the American experiment in governance as one of the great stories in history. After all, when the Declaration of Independence was proclaimed, the rest of the world still held to the archaic notion of the monarchy, believing in the divine right of kings.

As much as he thought the pomp and circumstance surrounding the monarchy could be good for tourism, he was happy with the knowledge that if he wanted to experience it, he could simply go to England. And yet, thinking twice about the subject, it struck him that many Americans also yearned for a little of the institution. Had they not had their own version of *Camelot* with Jacqueline Bouvier and JFK?

Most of all, he had embraced politics hoping, naively, to change the world for the better.

Just then, the intercom next to him beeped, pulling him back to reality.

"Yes, Mildred."

"Sir, Secretary Fleet of Homeland Security has arrived."

"Good. Send him in."

Alexander closed the folder holding the report he had been reading, rose from his chair and walked around the desk, all the while fastening the button of his suit jacket.

He got a shiver up his spine thinking about how Secretary Fleet's predecessor, Carl Broom, had died down in the war room below the White House. He could still picture Broom's agony as he was targeted by the devil's own weapon. Broom's entire DNA had been excited to the point of combustion. The President, as well as everyone in the room, had been caught completely dumbfounded, unable to react. Alexander understood now that nothing could have helped Broom. That still wasn't much consolation for a man who prided himself on being a person of action, always in control of events around him.

Wilson Fleet walked into the Oval Office and was greeted by President Alexander's outstretched hand followed by a friendly greeting and warm pat on the shoulder.

Quickly pointing to the sofa, the President continued, "Make yourself comfortable, Wilson. Can I get you some coffee? Tea?"

As he sat, Fleet smiled. "No, thank you, Mr. President. I've already had my two daily cups of Java. Please have one yourself, if you wish." Then, flashing his pearly whites, "I hear you tore up the greens the other day."

The President had just turned to walk over to his intercom. Pressing it, "Mildred, can we make it one cappuccino, half teaspoon of sugar?" The disembodied voice responded immediately, "Yes, Mr. President. Give me three minutes."

Looking back at Fleet and in turn sporting his own grin, "You heard about that. Yes, it was probably the best game I've ever played."

As he walked over to the sofa opposite Fleet and settled in, he continued, "Let me tell you, the Prime Minister mumbled a few expletives under his breath every time I parred the holes. He wasn't too pleased to honour our wager either. He said I was trying to launch a new period of diplomatic frost between the UK and us."

Fleet responded, "I would love to have been there to see the look on his face."

Alexander's demeanour changed ever so slightly. "It was a good day. We did a lot of business during the game. And I like the guy. However, for the moment, let's get down to this business, shall we?"

As Fleet was opening the folder on his lap, clearly labelled *CONFIDENTIAL*, Alexander thought that he liked the new head of Homeland Security as much as the former. He was so easy to talk to, unlike Carl Broom.

And there was that chill again.

Yes, Carl was all business and though socially awkward, he had been an incredibly competent man. Fleet was just as capable, but he had a swagger about him. Tall, handsome, prematurely grey at fifty-one and still single: The only thing wrong with the guy was that he was a Cambridge man. Well, there was also the question of his sexual orientation, one which was discreetly discussed in some circles and confirmed during the vetting process for his current position. Alexander didn't care about his *tendencies*, provided he produced the results he had been hired to deliver.

"Well, sir, the first item deals with the security around our embassy in Athens. With the economy being as bad as it is there, we're getting wind of a small faction of radicals who believe *we* are at the centre of a conspiracy to keep them on the brink of bankruptcy."

The President suddenly looked miffed. "They must be kidding. It's so easy for them to blame everyone else, ignoring their own unwillingness to take responsibility for years of corruption and overspending. And, they'll do anything, *anything*, not to pay taxes."

He paused a moment. "Do you have any indication that some action against us is imminent?"

"No, sir. I believe we need to raise the state of readiness a notch in order to prepare for the protests these groups are pushing for. And, as you've seen, most of these protests turn violent and fiery."

Alexander stared at Fleet for a moment. "I believe you're right. It wouldn't be prudent to think they can keep their cool once a protest begins. Let's raise the security level to *Elevated*."

"Thank you, sir. Next on my list is a status report on Under Secretary Gordon's search for Dr. Al-Kammin."

Just then, Mildred stepped into the room from her office area and brought the President his coffee.

"Thank you, Mildred. By the way, can you schedule a telephone call with Ambassador Lucas in Athens? See if he can take it in an hour."

She said nothing, nodding in the affirmative and exited as quietly as she had entered, closing the door behind her.

The President sat back, took a sip of his coffee and leaned into the sofa. "OK, let's hear it."

"Well, sir, Gordon made good progress in tracking down the names of all the board members. I have to admit it was a complicated task, especially with the secrecy surrounding the group."

"How did she do it?" asked Alexander.

"Well, by filtering thousands of flight plans across Europe and the Middle East, she and her team were able to link the group of thirteen individuals by using the flight plans logged for them and having as common denominator Sheikh Wadi Al-Kabir, his villa on Capri and the compound on Kamaran Island."

The President smiled. "Let her know I think she's doing a good job."

Taking a sip of his coffee, "God, if the Europeans have anything right, it's their coffee." Setting the cup down on the table in front of him, he resumed the discussion. "How close is she to finding the doctor?"

"That's a little more problematic. We assume he is using a truck or van of sorts. Beyond this, little is known. Now, we understand the weapon was used to kill the Sheikh and two days ago, General Hassim in Egypt was reported to have died mysteriously. Our contacts confirmed it was spontaneous combustion, though that fact is being kept confidential by the regime. Because this is the second case they've experienced, they have been sending out discreet feelers to see if similar deaths have occurred elsewhere. As you know, they have not been informed about our mission to Kamaran Island."

The President interrupted Fleet. "And the general *is* on the list?"

"Yes, sir, he *was*."

"Have there been reports of others dying in the same way?"

"No, sir, which leads us to believe the doctor is avenging the death of his partner and is travelling to find each of the board members."

"So, isn't it possible to get ahead of him and stop him?"

"Yes and no, sir. The logistics in setting up stakeouts for every one of the individuals on the list are daunting. First of all, trying to follow them without tipping them off would be difficult if not impossible, especially when we consider some of the countries involved, Iran being the stickiest."

The President nodded in agreement.

"Then, there's the issue of how wide a stakeout we set up and for how long. A more immediate issue, however, is that from Egypt, he could be going in any direction: south to the Sudan, north to Syria, or east to Saudi Arabia. They are all on the list of probable destinations."

"So, what do you suggest?" asked Alexander.

"Well, considering no one else has been targeted, we assume Al-Kammin is single-mindedly trying to use the weapon on each and every board member . . . at least for the time being. As well, because we want to obliterate the same targets for their part in the Osiris String, I think we should let the doctor do the job for us."

The President shifted in his seat, saying nothing.

"I propose we let the doctor go ahead and take out as many of the targets as possible. The greater number of individuals he kills, the fewer targets we will have to stake out, thereby reducing the resources we'll need. This should increase our odds of getting him because, now that we know who he's going after, we can keep track of the path he's taking. When he is down to three targets, we'll pull out all the stops and swoop in to get him and the weapon."

"Above all," interjected the President, "we can't allow him to disappear with the weapon. I've seen what it can do, and I refuse to allow it to fall into the wrong hands. Even if a few members of the board survive, we can take care of them on our own terms."

"Understood, sir."

"Good. Is Under Secretary Gordon on board?"

"Yes, sir, she is. Actually, the idea is hers. Before she came to see me with the plan, she had drawn up a complete description of the procedures and resources required."

The President stood, picked up his coffee cup and took another sip. "Good. You have my approval to move on this."

Picking up on the hint, Fleet nonchalantly said, "Thank you, sir." As he rose from his seat he added, "So, if you have nothing else for me, sir, I'll take my leave."

A big smile lit the President's face. "Only a Cambridge man would dare use that type of language."

The two shook hands warmly, and Fleet exited using the same door through which he had entered.

Chapter 2

Sam was sitting at a table inside the *World's Biggest Bookstore* in Toronto, surrounded by copies of his book. Before him was a long lineup of people, waiting to get him to sign their copy. He had been at it for three hours and, every now and then, he had to shake his right hand to relieve the cramping. When the last person whose book he had signed was about to leave, he leaned over to the pile of books on the floor to his left and got a whiff of the perfume worn by the individual next in line. He knew that scent and before he even turned to see who it was, a wide grin came to his face. Still not looking up, he announced, "I'm sorry, but I think it's time for a break. You'll have to come back later."

Only then did he raise his eyes to meet Melinda's. But, she wasn't smiling. "I paid good money for a book I probably won't understand. So I would suggest you *take* the time." Then she smiled back and slowly deposited her book in front of Sam, opening it to the dedication page. "And make sure you don't sign it 'To a fan.'"

As he rotated the book toward himself and set about to start writing, he paused and looked up thinking, God, she's beautiful.

Melinda was striking: tall and slender, reminding Sam of pictures he had seen of Maasai women, with a Swedish elegance. And, she had all the right curves.

He loved the way she pulled her hair back into a ponytail, accentuating her high cheekbones and perfectly straight nose. And her smile, well, it just melted him.

Most of all, he was mesmerized by her clear blue eyes. He had never known an African American with such eyes, and he thanked her Acadian ancestor for that. Jean Pelletier had been deported by the British to New Orleans back in 1757, as had, coincidentally, Sam's ancestor. That's when he had met Melinda's great-great-great-grandmother, Murielle Montpetit, a beautiful black woman, and had taken her on as a mistress, a common practice for some of the wealthy entrepreneurs of the time. Each generation that followed had produced at least one black child with blue eyes.

Shaking his head to come out of his reverie, he asked, "And where have you been lately?"

"You know I can't say exactly where. I've been more on the go than not. Now, sign the book."

He looked down and wrote, "To my one and only. Love, Sam"

Spinning the book back to her, "Will this do?"

She read the inscription and slowly closed the book, holding it up to her heart. "Do you think you will be much longer?"

Sam leaned over to glance behind her and seeing the lineup was only about twenty deep, he looked back at her. "Give me about ten to fifteen minutes. Are you hungry?"

"Very," she replied with a wink.

Picking up on the *double entente*, Sam retorted, "Make that eight minutes."

Shortly after, the two were walking out of the bookstore. "Seriously, are you hungry?" Sam queried Melinda.

It was about four p.m., and she hadn't had anything to eat since before her flight at eleven a.m. "I have to admit, some Thai could almost feel like foreplay."

Sam squeezed her hand and suggested a small restaurant, a few blocks up Young Street. The late November air was quite nippy and the sidewalks were somewhat slippery with snow, even though they were continuously shovelled by city maintenance crews.

Sam was dressed for the season, sporting a casual white linen shirt, jeans and a caramel suede sport coat, under a long black cashmere overcoat, and a double-wrapped grey wool scarf around his neck. His warm polar boots and alpine gloves would keep him nice and toasty, no matter how cold it was out there.

He couldn't help but chuckle at what Melinda was wearing and half-heartedly felt sorry for her. Typical of so many Americans, he thought. They either believe we have snow all year and live in igloos, or they are clueless about how to dress for our winters. Her tight jeans were indeed nice and her leather boots, with their three-inch heels, did exactly what they were meant to do for her behind, though they did little to give her stability on the ice. To her credit, she wore a down-filled bomber-style jacket. Her silk scarf and thin leather gloves were no match for the cold wind which was chilling her to the bone.

Sam quickly removed his scarf, and wrapped it around her neck and over her head to cover her ears. He put his arm over her shoulders and held her tight, rubbing her arm every now and then to increase the circulation.

By the time they got to the restaurant, some fifteen minutes later, Melinda's eyes were watery, and she couldn't feel her cheeks, all due to the freezing Young Street wind-tunnel effect.

Looking through her tears at the sparkling lights and feeling the warmth of the restaurant, she chattered to Sam, "Tha-that, wa-was, the co-coldest, d-damn walk I have ever t-taken."

She paused for a moment, her entire body shaking, and said with a *brrr*, "There's no way in hell I'm walking in that again."

"Don't worry," said Sam, "it will be warm taxis from here on."

Sitting in their private booth, Melinda refused to remove her jacket for another five minutes, something Sam tried to convince her was the wrong thing to do if she wanted to warm up more quickly. "I have a cure for the cold," he said.

He called the waitress over and ordered some drinks. Two minutes later, she returned with two shooters of Sang Som Rum and two bottles of Tiger beer as chasers. Sam picked up the shooter glasses and handed one to Melinda. They downed the drink in one gulp, quickly followed by a swig of beer.

"Ooh, that's better," she said. "It warms me all the way down. How about another?"

Sam laughed out loud and waved to the waitress for two more Sang Soms.

After ordering Pad Thai loaded with chicken and shrimp for both of them, Sam looked lovingly across the table to Melinda. "Are you warm enough now?"

"Yes, thanks. I think I reacted more dramatically to the cold because of where I've been the past week."

Sam had waited patiently to ask her again, "OK, now that we're alone, where have you been?"

She quickly glanced around. "North Africa. To be more precise, in Egypt and Saudi Arabia."

Not having to say who she was talking about, "*He* struck again in the latter. We think now that he will either head to the United Arab Emirates or Yemen. The next attack should give us the circuit he is following. The list of names we have isn't useful because there are so many possible directions he could choose. That in itself makes it difficult to know or predict exactly where and when he will strike again, and at what point we need to take him out."

Sam responded, "Sounds like the Heisenberg Uncertainty Principle to me."

Melinda looked at him quizzically. "Pardon?"

Sam explained in his best professorial tone: "The uncertainty principle is the concept that precise, simultaneous measurement of some complementary variables, such as the position and momentum of a subatomic particle, is impossible. The more precisely one is calculated, the more flawed the measurement of the other will be."

She shook her head and chuckled. "Only you would come up with that type of comparison. Yes, I see your point, and you've clearly described why I'm so frustrated. I'm worried I may not make the correct call as to when and where to stop this."

Sam reached across the table to hold her hand and said, in a soothing voice, "I'm not worried at all. So far, you've made all the right decisions." Pausing a moment, he continued, "And what about the weapon when you get him?"

"The President hasn't given the final order. My directives were to make sure Mohammed doesn't disappear with it."

"Do you have an idea of when you will try to zero in on him?"

Melinda responded, "My gut feeling is that he will head to Somalia, then to the Sudan and on to Lebanon. That's where I think the showdown will take place. From there, he could go on to Iraq, or Iran, or Syria. With the last two countries, he's as good as gone."

Just then, their Pad Thai dishes were brought to them.

Happy with the slight diversion and a chance to change the subject, Melinda smiled and said in a perky voice, "So, tell me about your book."

As he laid the napkin on his lap and picked up his fork, Sam began, "Well, there isn't a whole lot to say. I'm really pleased with its reception in the academic world."

Spearing a shrimp, Melinda said, just before popping it into her mouth, "Tell me everything. We have plenty of time right now."

With a twinkle in her eye, "I won't be ready for dessert until we get back to your place."

Not knowing if he was more excited about sharing his work with Melinda, or the thought of sharing his bed with her later, he attacked his food and the subject matter with eagerness.

"Let me explain it as simply as I can. Jalal and I are investigating the possible effects of gravitational waves on genetic combinations at the moment of conception. We know the moon has a strong impact on the oceans on a daily basis. We know women carry babies in amniotic fluid, which is the substitute for the salty oceans our oldest ancestors came from. So we hypothesized that at the very moment of conception, gravitational waves might affect those RNA molecules, which when combined, give rise to our physical makeup and things such as eye and hair colour."

Melinda listened and nodded in a show of understanding and agreement.

Sam continued, "Because the moon has been there since well before the beginning of life on our planet, it would be impossible to prove our hypothesis, simply based on the lunar pull. We needed to find a direct correlation between gravity and genetic changes on earth. That's where Jalal comes in. His area of expertise is in computer programming of celestial bodies, such as planets, stars and even galaxies."

Melinda interrupted him, "Are you saying we come from out there?"

Sam smiled. "No, well, not to the extent that it couldn't be where the initial ingredients for life came from. I wanted to know if there was a correspondence between the flyby of stars and planets close to earth, which might have precipitated major genetic changes in life here, due to increased gravitational waves, above and beyond those of the moon. If we could show that, we would have proof of the slow and constant impact the moon has had on all life on earth and an explanation why there have been great shifts in the types of life on earth through the eons."

Melinda cut in again, "And you found the proof you were looking for."

"Yes, we believe we have. It will be up to other scientists to prove us right or wrong. I've had dozens of calls from scientists around the world saying they agree and from others who disagree. All have said they are planning to investigate our hypothesis. That's exciting and the reason why we published our findings and the book."

Melinda responded, "God, and I thought my reputation was on the line."

"Anyway, to get back to the story," Sam said without missing a beat, "we first focused our attention on a star named Gliese 208, which flew by about four hundred and ninety thousand years ago. We compared the date with the earliest evidence of our species, which most call Homo sapiens, some hundred to two hundred thousand years later. Then we looked for other stars that came close to earth and found a similar correlation with several others such as Zeta Leporis and Gliese 710. We found more relationships to major changes in human evolution in roughly the same time lag.

"For example, we worked our way back to the time Homo erectus and Australopithecus were the dominant hominid species, and found similar flybys a little more than a hundred thousand years earlier."

The look in Melinda's eyes told Sam that the names didn't mean a whole lot to her, but the nod of her head indicated she was interested. "Quite the coincidence. Have you found your theory fits changes in other species?"

Sam grinned, as though he was keeping the best for last. "The clincher," Sam said, "was the discovery of the Sagittarius Dwarf Elliptical Galaxy."

Melinda's facial expression displayed confusion and wonder.

"OK, OK," Sam continued. "We went back some two hundred million years, and found a correlation with the early Jurassic period and the birth of the first dinosaurs."

Still not seeing the reaction he was hoping for, Sam thought for a moment. "Let me shorten this up a bit. Believe it or not, the Sagittarius Galaxy crashed into our Milky Way Galaxy, and ours, being the larger of the two, began to cannibalize it. And it's still doing so. As our galaxy is stripping the other of its stars and as the Milky Way's disk is spinning, our solar system and its planets are flying through the millions of stars in the other galaxy every two hundred twenty-five million years. Can you guess when we last did?"

Melinda's puzzled look turned to one of understanding. "At the time you say the first of the dinosaurs emerged."

"Bingo. Give the lady a cigar."

Melinda chuckled. "So what you are saying is that you have proof of why the different species have evolved, and that it's due to the influence of the gravitational pull of all these stars we come close to?"

"I wouldn't say proof, but rather evidence. I've been able to come up with a formula that seems to account for the number of estimated individuals who would mutate into a new direction of evolution and ensure its dominance. It looks like it takes about a hundred to two hundred thousand years for the number of individuals with the mutated genetic material to be in a dominant position, relative to the older group."

"So, this formula of yours is the one God uses to create new species?"

"You could phrase it that way, and it's one of the reasons I called my book *The Divine Formula*. The formula would seem to account for about eighty percent of the known changes we've seen in flora and fauna in the past, including our own."

"I thought one species would take over when another died off. Isn't that what happened to the dinosaurs and mammals?"

"Yes, to a point. There have been five mass extinction events in our past, one of which came at the beginning of the Jurassic. Another happened about sixty-five million years ago, ending the dinosaur age. Both seem to have been due to meteors striking the earth."

"OK, so chance events need to be factored in," Melinda said smugly.

"Ah, not so fast," Sam responded with a mischievous smile. "Where did the meteors come from, and why then?"

Melinda shrugged her shoulders.

"The rogue stars we claim are responsible for the changes in genetic combinations at the moment of conception are also the reason why thousands of comets in the Oort Cloud, which circles our solar system, or asteroids in the asteroid belt between Mars and Jupiter, were knocked out of their orbits and sent flying every which way, some toward the inner system and, ultimately, earth."

Melinda looked pensive for a moment. "I can see what you are proposing, though I'm trying to understand why something so straightforward and scientific, could explain why there has been such a reaction to your theory in some areas around the world."

It was Sam's turn to look puzzled.

"Homeland Security has seen an incredible increase in cyber activity revolving around your book."

"Why the hell would my research be of interest to your organization?"

"You know we monitor chatter across all information media, keeping on top of developments which could possibly pose problems to our national security."

Melinda looked directly into Sam's eyes and said, in a serious tone, "There has been quite an increase in the volume of info traffic coming from religious circles, and none of it is pretty. Normally, I wouldn't have taken note of it but because your name came up in the briefings, I checked into it further."

Sam was shocked. "You've got to be kidding me. I know genetic researchers have shown interest and, for the most part, it's quite favourable. Why would . . ." Sam stopped mid-sentence.

He mentally raced through the pages of his research and stopped on one topic he had originally speculated could be controversial, but never thinking it would generate interest beyond academia. "Does it have anything to do with my suggestion that our species should not be called Homo sapiens but rather Homo symbolicus?"

"I don't have the particulars. It was included in a report I read on my way back from Egypt, concerning pressure from a mufti in Iran, to ban your book because of its blasphemous conclusions. Is there anything to this?"

"It shouldn't, though it almost proves my point."

"Huh?" was all Melinda uttered.

"If you remember, I mentioned one star, Zeta Leporis, which flew by about eight hundred and sixty-one thousand years ago?"

Melinda nodded.

"Well, Jalal and I were a little confused because that was about the middle of the Paleolithic period and, true to the formula, not long afterward several branches of our kind, including Homo erectus, appeared. Most other species died out, such as Neanderthal man or Peking man, and nothing substantial seemed to happen until the arrival of Gliese 208, about four hundred thousand years later.

"During all that time, what we call ourselves, Homo sapiens, evolved into being and ultimately overpowered or outnumbered the older species. With more analysis, we realized that archaeologists had shown that our ancestors from that particular time period had indeed begun creating art, ritualistically burying their dead and showing signs of more advanced cultural traits. It started during the time the Neanderthals were disappearing and the time we took over."

Melinda looked somewhat lost. "And this relates to the reports I spoke about, how?"

"Who we are, from a purely physical point of view, has not changed much since then. What has changed has been mostly societal or cultural in nature, as a result of an increase in size of the frontal lobe of our brain. For example, Cro-Magnon Man is us, without agriculture and all the differences that engenders."

Seeing Melinda was still struggling with the concept, "Well, one hypothesis we proposed was that the core of who we are, that which has driven humans from the middle of the Palaeolithic period to modern times, is symbolism.

"Our brains were evolving in such a way that the frontal lobes were growing much larger and becoming increasingly able to process the thoughts or instincts generated by the other two parts, call them the mammalian and reptilian portions of our brains. This led to an effort to interpret what and why things happen: who we are, where we come from and our purpose in life. In other words, what we call religion and God."

"Oh boy," commented Melinda. "I think I can see why the Muslim Brotherhood wants to ban your book."

"You're not kidding. We never imagined there would be a major upheaval over a simple suggestion that we should be called Homo symbolicus rather than Homo sapiens. It reflects the reality we live, how we tend to react and why. But we have seen evidence that the evolutionary process toward our becoming *sapiens* is still happening."

Melinda sat quietly for a moment and then said pensively, "Wow . . . I think I get what you tried to do and the position you are in. I'll keep monitoring the chatter, though I'm hoping this will just blow away."

Looking at Sam, she smiled coyly. "This has been too serious a discussion for my time off. How about we lighten it up a bit? I think I'm about ready for dessert. Aren't you?"

Sam smiled and quickly put his hand up to get the waitress's attention. "Check please."

Chapter 3

Two days later, Melinda walked into her office, bright and early, coffee in hand. She hated the times she was away from Sam. On the other hand, who was she kidding? She loved her job, and she had to admit that she enjoyed the perks her promotion had also provided.

First, there was the increase in salary which allowed her to move into one of the long-term suites at the Watergate Hotel, similar to the one she and Sam had shared when he was last in Washington to meet the President. Although her apartment in the Naylor Gardens District had proven to be quite adequate, it was rather small. The Watergate was so much more grand and closer to work. It offered security and all the amenities she could want: pool, exercise room and interior parking.

Not that the inside parking was a big deal. Yes, her small Toyota was safe and out of the elements, but she had not used it since her promotion. She had returned to work after a two-week trip to French Polynesia with Sam, which had allowed her to recuperate from the injuries sustained during the mission to destroy the weapon Dr. Al-Eissa had created. For security reasons, she was chauffeured to and from work, and to any and all of her official outings.

As she walked by the staff room, she noticed she wasn't alone. Three agents sat at the small table in the centre of the room, engrossed in a low-volume discussion. Melinda stopped at the door and said in a pleasant, professional tone, "Good morning, gentlemen. I see I'm not the only one who gets up with the sun."

Then, focusing on one agent, "John, could you meet with me after your coffee to bring me up to speed on our dossiers?"

Agent John Doyle looked back at her and in his North Carolinian accent, responded, "Yes, ma'am. Be happy to, though there hasn't been much action. How was your time away?"

Feeling the question wasn't all that sincere and a little intrusive, Melinda dropped the smile. "Relaxing, thanks for asking."

Then she quickly headed for her office, fully aware there would be additional conversation at her expense. She shrugged off the thought, knowing some of the male agents were somewhat jealous of her promotion, both because she was female, and because she was African American. In this usually reserved-for-white-males-only domain, she was a bit of an oddity. Truth be said, she was the boss, and they would have to grow up and deal with it.

She was right about her first impression. No sooner had she left than Doyle turned to his two partners in crime. "Some debutante. You'd think she'd been with the company for years, the way she orders us around. Only a few months ago, she was just one of us grunts."

One of the other agents looked over his shoulder toward the door and then back to the others saying, "I've been asking some discreet questions, and it seems she was involved in some really hush-hush mission and somehow, the order to promote her came directly from the President."

Agent Doyle scoffed at the comment, pushed away from the table and took a sip from his coffee cup. "Shit, she must have slept with the man." This provoked a chuckle from the others. "Gotta go and report to the bitch, so she can look good to the Secretary, too." With that, he stood huffily and walked out of the coffee room.

It wasn't that Doyle was a terrible person, though he did have issues. The son of a very wealthy entrepreneur from Charlotte, North Carolina, he grew up in the shadow of several highly decorated ancestors. From his father to his great-great-grandfather, all the men in his family were volunteers in major military campaigns ranging from the Civil War to the Second World War. Even his brother was an Iraq war hero.

Like his brother, Doyle went to West Point and graduated at the top of his class. Unlike his brother, he was not allowed by his father to remain in the military. Rather, with his training and further studies at Elon University, a private school ranked the top southern university, Doyle's father mustered his contacts to have the doors of several federal institutions open to him. It was the CIA that appealed to Doyle, and he was appointed agent only weeks after graduating.

He knew his father loved him and worried about him, but he hated the fact his life was being planned and controlled, especially because his brother, or rather, his adoptive brother, was allowed to make his own decisions about remaining in the military.

Doyle's adoptive brother was the product of a dysfunctional family and had been a problem child. His parents had divorced when he was eleven, and his mother had died of a drug overdose six months later. He was put into one foster home after another by the courts, never quite fitting in the normal family setting. When he turned fourteen, he found himself in a military-style, church-run secondary school programme for troubled youth.

It was there that he found his sense of self. He excelled in every subject and became one of the most disciplined students the school had ever seen. For that reason, the headmaster had contacted his superintendent who in turn had reached out to a close friend of his, the school's benefactor, Oliver Doyle, who then had taken a personal interest in the boy who was the same age as his son, John.

Soon, the lad was visiting the family and participating in its gatherings and festivities. He and John bonded quickly and became best friends: John, never once showing any sign of resentment or jealousy.

Somehow, Oliver Doyle saw a little of himself in the boy and, after consulting with his wife, petitioned to adopt him, allowing him to keep his name, due to his age. Later, when they graduated from college, Oliver pulled strings and the two boys entered West Point. The rest was history.

John's personality wasn't that of his brother, and he accepted the differences. He capitalized on his demonstrated capacity for analysis of events concerning world issues and soon moved up from the rank of field agent in the CIA, to Homeland Security out of San Francisco, and eventually, to the main bureau in Washington.

He was there when Melinda was hired on in the same capacity. In her, he found his competition. Though he would never admit it, he knew she was quicker than he was in reaching a position on particular issues referred to their department for analysis. Plus, her reports were just that much more elegant and precise than his were.

However, when she was promoted to the position of Assistant Secretary, the very position he had coveted, it soured him and moved him further into the boys' club state of mind.

Even so, he was a patient man, and he believed Melinda would screw up at one point or another. He would do the best job he could and would be there in the wings waiting for her to drop the ball. He would be the obvious man to replace her in the position.

Chapter 4

A month later, the day before Christmas, Melinda stopped in at the office at her usual time to check on the current security situation across the nation. She first looked in on the staff that had picked the short straw and had to work through the holiday. Seeing they were diligently monitoring their computer screens or reading reports sent up from the data-gathering units located on the lower floors of the building, and realizing there were no alerts, she decided she could put in a few hours of work before heading off to the airport to catch the three p.m. flight to Halifax and then on to Moncton to meet Sam.

He had decided he would do something special with her this yuletide. Well, he hoped she would find it special. He invited her to visit his family in Moncton and celebrate Christmas the Acadian way.

Melinda had four older sisters who had married and moved with their families to the four corners of the country. She would fly out to see them at least once each year and each in turn for Thanksgiving. Rarely, however, would she get together with them at Christmas, believing it was almost an intrusion on their family time. Besides, she had more than once been one of the unlucky agents who had to work during the holiday season.

So when Sam decided to take a break from the lecture- and book-signing tour his publishers had arranged, he had invited her to come along with him to Moncton. She thought it was a perk no longer having to work the holiday shift. It could also be a treat meeting the other

Buckners, though she didn't quite know what she was getting herself into.

Sam met her at the arrival gate with a huge hug and a passionate kiss. He then led her to the pickup parking area toward the rental car he had reserved and stuffed her suitcases into the trunk along with his own. Gallantly opening the door for her and letting her get into the vehicle, he jogged around to the driver's side and hopped in. He leaned over to give her another kiss and said, "Get cozy. It's a bit of a drive."

The farm was about forty kilometres outside of town, and it took them about an hour to get there. Heading in a south-eastern direction from the airport on the Trans Canada Highway, they quickly made ground, but then he turned off the main roadway at Sackville and onto a secondary road for about five kilometres before again turning onto a series of narrow country lane ways. Some nine kilometres further, just before reaching a junction in the road called Johnson's Mill, Sam turned the car right onto a long driveway leading to a farmhouse overlooking the Petitcodiac River.

Melinda kept somewhat quiet during the ride, letting Sam concentrate on his driving. It was about nine-thirty when the vehicle came to a stop at the head of a lineup of about twenty cars and pickup trucks. It was her turn to lean over to Sam to give him a kiss and then commented, "I don't know how you found this place. We're out in the middle of nowhere. However, judging by the number of cars, your uncle is either a car dealer, or he throws quite the party."

Sam smiled and responded with, "My family may not be like the Washington in-groups you are used to, but I think you'll enjoy yourself."

As the two walked together to the front door, Melinda looked around at the scenery. It was eerily silent, with only the crackling sound of their boots on the snow breaking the stillness.

The full moon's indirect lighting softly illuminated the snow-covered fields which sloped toward the river. It was so beautiful, she thought.

And though she could see their breath in the air due to the cold, she felt warm, both because she was with Sam and because she had learned her lesson and had dressed to suit the Canadian winter.

About ten feet away from the front steps, she quickly glanced at the house, only to realize how large it was. Before she could make a comment, Sam interrupted her train of thought. "Oh, did I tell you most of what you'll hear will be in French?"

Surprised by the comment, Melinda replied, "Say what? I don't speak French, well not much. Why didn't you warn me before?"

As they reached the door and Sam pressed the doorbell, he turned toward her and added, "Don't worry. They all speak English very well."

He bent over and kissed her tenderly. "They will love you. I promise."

The door opened and there stood a slightly stocky man with a ruddy nose and a huge smile. "Samuel, mon p'tit. Bienvenue!" Though a head shorter than Sam, he wrapped his arms around Sam, giving him a bear hug and almost lifting him off the ground.

Sam couldn't help but let out a grunt, feeling the air being squeezed out of him. Only when he was released did he catch his breath and respond, "Bonsoir, oncle Pit. Joyeux Noël."

His uncle looked around Sam to see Melinda, who was standing a little behind him. "Et qui est cette belle demoiselle?"

Sam reverted to English when he answered, "Uncle Pit, I would like to introduce Melinda. Melinda, this is Uncle Pit, my father's younger brother."

Melinda confidently extended her hand to shake the uncle's hand, but before she knew it, she too was swept up in a bear hug of her own.

After letting her go, the uncle kissed her on both cheeks and turned to Sam, saying in a slight Acadian accent, "My God man, where did you find her? She is definitely out of your league."

Sam looked at Melinda, and sporting a broad smile added, "That is the truth. I don't know what she sees in me."

The uncle turned to walk back along the hallway toward the kitchen at the rear of the house, passing the stairs going up to the second floor on the left side and the double-oak doors leading into the parlour on the right.

As Sam and Melinda slowly followed, she looked at him, again showing some surprise, but this time with a smile and whispered, "I didn't know you could speak French."

Sam smiled back, winked and said, "Guess it never came up. Besides, I have to have some secrets, don't I?"

By then, they were entering the kitchen. It was a typical country kitchen, only much larger than the average. Along the rear wall and extending about eight feet along both adjoining walls were seasoned pine cupboards. Melinda had almost expected to see a wood-burning stove, but instead, there to the left of the large apron sink, she spied a commercial size, six burner stainless steel range with griddle and double ovens. The huge vent system above assured visitors and family members alike, that serious cooking took place here. On the right wall stood a massive side-by-side stainless steel refrigerator-freezer unit while at the heart of the room was found a large country table, capable of seating sixteen people.

And tonight, there were about that many people sitting around the table, with the same number sitting on chairs all around the periphery of the room. All were engrossed in lively conversations with one another, sipping at their wine or beer.

No one seemed to have noticed another three people walking into the kitchen. Sam's uncle simply said in a loud voice to his wife and the crowd in the room, "Hey, Marie-Laure, tout le monde, Samuel est arrivé." Switching to English, "And, he is here with Melinda."

The crowd cried out, "Allô Samuel! Hi Melinda! Joyeux Noël."

The next fifteen minutes were a blur for Melinda. All she could remember later was that several uncles, aunts and cousins rose to greet her and Sam. Smiles, pats on the back, the offer of wine, beer and food galore were all part of the welcome.

Sometime during these introductions, Sam brought her to meet the older relatives, including grand-papa François, now ninety-four years young. He lived there with his son Pit and his family. Though his face was heavily wrinkled due to the many years working the land, first with his horse and wagon, then on his tractor, his eyes were still bright and his mind was quick. Sitting in his rocking chair in the corner, he proudly looked upon his progeny, a little like a lord looking over his manor.

Melinda gazed at him and had a strange thought: she could actually picture Sam sitting in the same chair in the future, with her next to him in her own rocking chair. The thought was fleeting, but it pleased her somehow.

Sam found two empty chairs along the left outer wall, close to the door which led down a few steps to the landing at the side entrance or down to the basement.

Being somewhat on the outskirts of the group, Melinda finally felt she could breathe a little, in spite of the number of people who came over to say hello. The teenagers weren't shy about coming to wish the two a Merry Christmas. She hadn't noticed that this group mainly congregated in the large family room just off to the right of the kitchen.

Melinda leaned into Sam and whispered, "OK, can you just remind me who's who again?"

Sam leaned closer to her ear and, looking and pointing to the people they had just met, he named them. "That's Uncle Claude, Aunt Thérèse, there's Marcel and Rita, that's Robert and Édith, Justin and Thérèse, Cajetan, Raoul and Émilien."

She closed her eyes and quickly memorized the faces and linked them to the names.

She was a little puzzled that she hadn't seen any children. She again whispered, "Aren't there children?"

Sam smiled, took her hand and said, "Come with me."

They rose and he took her to the side door leading down the stairs to the basement. As soon as the door opened, Melinda could hear noises coming from below: squeals, laughter and giggling. They went down as far as they needed to bend over to look at the hoard of kids running and playing in the two rooms in which the area was divided. Sam looked at Melinda and said, "I remember behaving like them when I was a kid. It was fun being able to let loose and not have adults tell you to keep quiet."

Melinda looked back at him. "I don't know if I can ever picture you that small." He took her hand and led her back upstairs.

No sooner had they returned to their seats than the music began. It was Uncle Pit, sitting on his chair with a squeeze box on his lap.

He began playing French Canadian jigs to the delight of everyone there. He played and they clapped and tapped their feet to the rhythm. Suddenly, Sam's uncles

Claude and Marcel began playing the wooden spoons and a violin, respectively, adding to the liveliness of the moment.

Melinda couldn't get over the friendly atmosphere of the home and the group. Her family get-togethers were lively and fun as well, but this crowd brought lively and fun to new heights.

Uncle Pit played animated get-up-and-dance songs nonstop for about an hour. At the stroke of midnight, he shifted gears and began playing Christmas carols, such as Adeste Fideles, with all joining in and singing in Latin. This was followed by a host of other holiday songs, many of which Melinda recognized but whose French lyrics were unfamiliar to her. At one point, Uncle Pit yelled out, "This is for Melinda," and began playing Greensleeves while everyone sang the English carol version of the song in unison. She was touched.

Melinda locked arms with Sam and took his hand in hers as she leaned into him. She had tears in her eyes thinking she had never experienced anything like this, and that she couldn't love Sam any more than she did at that moment.

Sam looked over to her, squeezed her hand, kissed it and continued singing with the group.

From his side of the room, grand-papa François looked at the two, winked and smiled in approval.

****

Sometime about three a.m. the music stopped and the children were shepherded to the upstairs bedrooms to get some sleep, while the adults continued the *réveillon*, eating and talking until the break of dawn. They would all go to mass as a group later in the morning and then return to their respective homes to open gifts.

Sam and Melinda decided to leave around four a.m. to head out to their hotel in town, the Chateau Moncton Hotel & Suites, overlooking the Petitcodiac River.

Melinda dozed off for a short while during the ride back. Sam didn't mind. He knew she had been up since early the day before, and she had been through quite the experience with his family. He only hoped she wouldn't just opt to go to sleep when they got to their room.

He had a special little gift for her. He wanted her to see the tidal bore of the Petitcodiac which would come in at nine forty-five a.m. After all, the moon's effect on the oceans had led him to think about the impact of gravitation fields on the genetic evolution of species and the bore was one of the main reasons he had come up with his divine formula.

Most of all, he wanted to make love to her.

He had never met a woman like her. She was intelligent, principled and spoke her mind without being overbearing. She was driven to succeed and willing to take on challenges such as her job at Homeland Security. On the other hand, she was tender and had a warm heart.

He considered her an equal yet far above his level, as his uncle had so aptly stated. She made him want to be a better man, for her. He could see the two of them as a lifelong team, and he hoped tonight was the first of a great number of family celebrations.

They arrived at the hotel at about five o'clock and quickly went to their room. Melinda said she needed a shower to help her wake up, which gave Sam hope.

While he waited to take his shower, Sam pulled out the bottle of champagne he had stored in his suitcase. The time in the trunk of the car had chilled it perfectly. He then took a small wrapped box from a side pocket of his carry-on bag and hid it under his pillow.

Melinda came out of the washroom, dressed in a red eyelet lace trim teddie under a matching cover-up. Sam's jaw dropped. "Wow, now that's what I call the perfect Christmas outfit."

She just laughed and sexily sauntered over to the bed. Then she unceremoniously jumped onto it and dropped down into a seated cross-legged position.

Sam simply put his hand up and out in a stop pose. "Hold that thought." He then ran to the washroom to take a shower.

No sooner had the water turned on than Melinda hopped off the bed and went over to her suitcase. She too took out a wrapped box and slid it into the drawer of her night table. She then resumed her position on the bed.

A few minutes later, Sam was back donning a white T-shirt and blue and black striped boxer shorts. She thought he looked rather sexy as well.

He uncorked the bottle of champagne and poured some in two flutes he had ordered up when he had reserved the room. He brought them over and sat opposite her on the bed. Handing Melinda her glass, he began, "I want to toast our first Christmas together." He looked at her lovingly and choked up a little. "I took a bit of a chance in bringing you here to celebrate Christmas. I've never done so with anyone. I hope it wasn't a mistake because you are more than special to me."

Melinda giggled.

Looking surprised, Sam stopped speaking.

She smiled, reached over and put her hand on his, saying, "Don't worry. I'm not laughing at you. I just can't let you continue to worry about me. I had one of the best evenings of my life. I saw you in a completely different light, and I love what I saw. You usually come across so methodical and scientific-like. Tonight the real you was revealed and where you come from. There's nothing I couldn't love about what I experienced and how I felt."

The look on Sam's face was one of complete relief and love. Unable to come up with a follow-up to her comments, he thought, gift!

"I bought you a gift. I can't wait to give it to you." With that, he leaned over past her and pulled the box from under his pillow. Facing her again, he continued, "This is a little something I found while I was in Québec City giving a lecture on my research. Since I had time to kill before my flight back to Toronto, I shopped. When I saw this, I thought, Melinda." He paused and handed her the gift.

She looked at the box and then at him. Sam was surprised when, instead of unwrapping the gift, she leaned over to her night stand and pulled out her gift for him. "I have a present for you as well. I have to admit, I had a hard time thinking of something I thought you would like or want. Let's open them together."

The two began unwrapping their gifts. Melinda was a little faster than Sam. When she opened the small box, the first thing she saw was a folded card with the letters of the logo Korite embossed on it. Then she looked back inside the box. On a small, white silk cushion lay a beautiful Ammolite column-pendant.

Melinda teared up. "It's beautiful."

Sam explained that he'd been told it was one of the company's signature pieces.

It was a simple, 18K gold column, with a diamond above an exquisite 26 by 5 mm blue-green-red stone. The Ammolite seemed to change hues and colours as one moved it.

"It reminded me of you because it is simple and complex all at once, just like you. And, it's *the* Canadian gem to boot."

Melinda chuckled and said, "I simply love it. Can you put it on me?" She handed him the box and leaned in his direction, moving her hair out of the way. He removed the pendant, attached it to the gold chain that came with it, and placed it around her neck. She sat up and looked down to try to see it. "What do you think?" she asked.

Sam looked at her and then at the pendant, and he couldn't help but think how beautiful she was, and how the pendant with its gold casing, the deep colours of the stone and the dazzling diamond, were enhanced by the dark colour of her skin. "Just incredible. You rock the pendant."

"You're so sweet. Now finish opening your gift."

Sam smiled in a childish way. "Knowing you, this should be good."

He feverishly attacked the wrapping on the box. When he lifted the lid from the cherry-wood box, he saw a strangely shaped band.

Sam took a second to try to understand what he was looking at. Then it dawned on him. "You've got to be kidding me!"

Melinda smiled broadly seeing the reaction she had elicited. "Do you know what it is?"

Sam looked back at her, realizing that she must have had to jump through hoops to get it. "Only the coolest watch on the planet."

Melinda had been able to get an advanced prototype of the Emopulse Smile SmartWatch. Dick Tracy would be envious of this baby. The watch itself was a sleek wide band that wrapped around the wrist. The complete surface was nothing less than a computer screen which did so much more than just tell the time and date: it was a Smartphone, an entertainment and gaming hub, a social network and news feed, a personal assistant which could also monitor one's workouts and the body's vital signs.

Placing it on his wrist, he looked back at her. "There must be only about twenty of these commercially available anywhere in the world. How did you get your hands on it?"

"It's my turn to say that I have secrets of my own to keep. I knew I had to get something different for my special geek."

Sam laughed out loud and pulled her to him. They kissed for a long while and then Sam turned out the lights.

After making love, the two dozed off and slept until three p.m., missing the tidal bore, breakfast and lunch. They didn't leave the room until the next day, preferring to order in supper and breakfast the following morning.

They made it to the airport just in time to catch their respective flights.

Sam needed to get to Philadelphia to continue his American university lecture tour which his publisher had arranged.

Melinda was heading back to Washington to continue the hunt for Mohammed.

Chapter 5

John Doyle flew into Charlotte for Christmas. He had driven home from the airport in his 5.0 litre supercharged F-Type R Jaguar, which he left in storage at the special valet parking area, while he was at work in Washington. He hated taking taxies and refused to have someone pick him up. So it was simpler for him to pay for the car to be parked there weekdays and picked up each weekend, when he came back to the estate.

His father was somewhat irked at the fact that John preferred foreign cars to US-made vehicles. He, himself, drove a Lexus RX 450h and proudly, if not smugly, parked it next to the Bentleys and Ferraris of his peers at the country club, as an overt display of patriotism.

As he passed through the gate at the entrance to the twenty-hectare homestead, he drove up the long, half-kilometre paved and tree-lined driveway, to the front of the mansion. The baronial-style architecture had been inspired by a home Oliver Doyle had seen in Inverness, Scotland during one of his holidays there, forty years earlier.

The two- and three-storey house was built in a basic square "C" formation, with the public rooms to the front of the building, and the eleven bedrooms and eight bathrooms split between two wings at the rear of the house.

Built with natural cut stone, it was adorned with two mini turrets at the second-floor level above the main entrance doors. One would walk into the foyer and then into the long central hallway which separated the major rooms of the home.

If the exterior looked Scottish in nature, the interior was truly Early American, with its wainscoting, high ceilings, heavy wood trim and soft green and yellow pastels throughout. To add contrast to the pale palette, paintings of Oliver's ancestors bedecked the walls, as though to remind him of whom he was. In an area designed to honour two of his ancestors in particular, were hung two framed American flags, one which had been carried by his great-great-grandfather and the other by his grandfather during the Civil War and the First World War respectively.

One could access the formal parlour to the left, next to the large library and by crossing the hallway to the right, could enter the dining room which was capable of seating thirty people comfortably. Also, the hallway led to a wall of paned glass windows at the rear from where one could see the protected courtyard between the two bedroom wings.

True to the style of the house, Oliver had a three-storey space built as his *personal* area. On the first floor was his exclusive living room. A spiral staircase in the far corner led up to the bedroom, continued up to his private study and then on to the roof level. From the outside, the space looked like a medieval tower, such as can be seen at Windsor Castle in England, complete with the sentry area on the roof.

His wife had died of cancer ten years before, and though he found the space quite large for one person, he found solace in the privacy of the three rooms.

This was one of the reasons John had decided to continue living with his father. In spite of being in the same house, the distance between their sleeping quarters and the sheer size of the building assured them both the *space* they needed and the opportunity to be together when they so desired.

As he drove up to the house and parked on the sizeable stamped concrete area to the right of the main entrance, he noticed a large black Mercedes to the left of the entrance. It was a car he knew well.

The vehicle belonged to Pastor Ian Trumbell, of whose church his father was a dedicated member. The pastor had ten thousand parishioners and most showed up at either of the two Sunday services. The pastor's receipts were, therefore, hugely lucrative, but he did something John's father admired: He only kept ten percent of the offerings for himself and his family, and, after setting aside a portion for the cost of maintaining the church, donated the balance to charitable organizations and *causes* dear to his heart, some of which were more political than social.

John got out of his car and went to what he now called the *boot*, as the British did, and removed his luggage. He hopped up to the door and, not bothering to ring, walked right in, dragging his packs behind him.

"Hello! Where is everyone?"

A voice came from the library. "We're here. Come on in."

As he walked along the hallway and through the door to the library, he saw his father sitting on his favourite plush leather chair, a cognac in his left hand and a Cuban cigar from his private stash, in his right. Sitting opposite from him in a similar chair and having adopted the same pose, was Pastor Trumbell.

The library was made up of two areas. At the far end was the pool table section, surrounded by glassed-in cabinets containing part of Oliver's book collection. The other half of the collection was housed in the area where they found themselves. The focal point of the right wall was a large fireplace in which an inviting fire was burning. On the left wall stood the other bookcases while in the centre, four matching leather chairs surrounded and faced the coffee table.

Gesturing not to get up, John walked over to his dad and bent down to give him a short hug. "Hello, Father. Merry Christmas."

Turning to the pastor, he extended his right hand, forcing the man to put his cigar down. "And Merry Christmas to you as well, sir. It's so nice to see you again. How long has it been?"

It had been at least six months since John had last seen the pastor at the house. In fact, he came to the house on a regular basis in order to discuss issues that were important to him and which he thought John's father could help him with.

Oliver Doyle had established himself as a man who could get things done. He had accumulated his wealth by creating a huge sales empire which some would call a pyramid company, in household goods. He had thousands of sellers across the country selling hundreds of articles to their personal clients on a monthly basis.

Remaining true to his patriotic spirit, he believed he was creating jobs and income for his American employees and suppliers, by selling products only made in America, using a model of capitalism he felt captured the heart of the American spirit.

In the process, he had made a huge fortune and incredibly important connections: connections he did not hesitate to use in order to get what he wanted done.

A strong believer in Republican ideals, he had moved more to the right of late, feeling the President had moved too far to the left in his policies. He thought it was a citizen's duty to strive to balance the equation where possible.

As well, he was a staunch Baptist and used his fortune to help ministers that were inspired by the more conservative interpretation of the Bible.

Pastor Trumbell was one such individual. In return for sharing Doyle's convictions, the pastor was able to build his church and his congregation, thanks to a personal donation from Doyle.

Oliver was both pleased with and expected the visits from the pastor. He was able to keep track of issues he would normally not be aware of. Today was just one of those moments.

"John, grab a chair."

Pointing to the brandy snifters on the table, next to the bottle of Rémy Martin Louis XIII Cognac, he added, "Join us, will you."

John did and then settled into the chair. "What are we talking about this time?"

Oliver puffed on his cigar, blowing the smoke high above his head. "Ian is filling me in on the state of the registration at our church-run colleges around the country. It seems there is a slight decrease in certain departments."

"By decrease," John stepped in, "you mean there aren't as many new registrations?"

The pastor responded first. "No, the decrease we've seen, one of ten percent, is due to our students leaving their studies, especially in the sciences."

That surprised John. "Do you have any idea why?"

"Well, we've interviewed almost all three hundred and thirty-two to determine why, and there would seem to be a common thread. They all indicated a questioning, if not a loss, of their faith."

"And this is over how long?" John questioned.

"In the past month or so. That is why we are so concerned. We've never seen anything like this. And if it continues, we will be hard-pressed to stop it or to explain it to the public."

"This has to be triggered by something," John added.

"It might be. A good number of them admitted having attended a lecture series delivered by a Canadian scientist, which deeply perturbed them and got them thinking. Many of them shared their experience with others, some of which have left as well. It went, how do you young people say it, viral? Thank God we have students that are firm in their faith and have the strength to fight off sinful ideas."

John pressed on. "What are you planning to do about the situation?"

Oliver answered, "Why, we are going to fight wrong ideas with correct ideas. I've arranged for the pastor to meet the scientist and take him head on."

Pastor Ian smiled meekly and nodded.

"I've contacted the people at "Welcome To Your Take" on CNN and they've agreed to invite the scientist to present his theories. I've also arranged to have the pastor as one of the panellists. We will establish a good forum to question his theories and debunk them as speculative in nature.

"As well, Pastor Trumbell knows the archbishop of Boston and he has agreed that someone with a strong, conservative bent from within his Church should also be on the panel."

"But wouldn't that come across as ganging up on the scientist?" queried John.

"I agree," said his dad. "That is why we suggested CNN select a historian or an archaeologist to sit on the panel too. We will also mobilize our *call-in group* to support the pastor."

He was alluding to the huge network of young church members they had organized to respond, at a moment's notice, to pressing issues affecting church dogma and politics. Originally created in order to skew local, state and national elections, they had found that the network could be used to influence social issues as well, such as voting in or voting off certain candidates in popular televised singing contests. Gays, lesbians and *rocker types* stood little chance of surviving the elimination bout.

John thought for a moment and said, "It sounds like you might be able to discredit this man, but it could backfire on you if it isn't forceful enough. Who is this scientist anyway?"

The pastor sipped the last of his cognac and said, "A professor named Samuel Buckner."

John's jaw dropped. "I know of him. You won't believe it, but my boss is dating this man."

He looked at his father who raised his hand ever so slightly, to warn him not to go any further.

Oliver turned to the pastor and moved forward in his chair. "So, I believe we have a plan."

Trumbell nodded and then rose, putting out his cigar in the ashtray on the coffee table. "I am sorry, but I have to head home to the family and prepare my sermon for tomorrow. I do like Christmas: It gives me a chance to deliver a sermon that is not all *hell and brimstone*."

He got a laugh from the others and continued, "It's been a pleasure speaking with you Oliver . . ."

Turning to John, he added, " . . . and so nice seeing you again. I'll have to call you to get more information on this professor. It could be useful during the debate."

With a quick, hesitant look at his dad, John responded, "That might be problematic. My position at Homeland makes me privy to some information that is classified. I may have said too much already."

The pastor smiled. "I understand. Pardon me for imposing. I can do this on faith alone."

Then he turned and walked toward the hallway, followed by Oliver, leaving John in the library.

His dad returned from seeing the pastor to the door and sat in his chair again. "That was quite the news you just delivered."

"You're not kidding. If I disliked *her* before, this just drives the last nail into the casket."

His father sat back into the chair and crossed his legs. "Is there anything you can tell us about this man?"

"Honestly, no. I know his name, but she hasn't said anything about him or his theories. I can try, but she's so guarded. I'll have to go through other channels."

"OK. Why don't you settle in and let me know when you're ready. Your brother should be here shortly and we can all go into town for supper."

Both picked up their snifters and raised them. "Cheers."

Chapter 6

A week and a half later, the phone on Melinda's desk rang. Melinda was busy reading reports from the field agents and writing her comments on the borders of the pages. All the pertinent information she was identifying and her own observations would be transcribed by her assistant, Gloria George, for her daily conference with her boss.

Not even looking at the receiver, she reached for it and brought it to her left ear, all the while continuing to jot down her thoughts. "Yes, what is it?"

Her assistant simply replied, "I think you want to take this call. It's from Beirut."

Melinda's eyes grew wide and she dropped her pencil and the report she was working on and pressed the blinking button on her phone.

"Yes, this is Melinda Gordon."

"This is Agent Williams in the Beirut office. We found him." Those were the words she had been waiting to hear.

"Where?"

"He just left the Mar Mikhael section of the port area. We believe he is heading toward the Emile Lahoud highway and then to the Elias El Hrawi highway, which will take him to the southeast of Beirut."

Melinda pursued. "And you know it's Mohammed?"

"Yes, Assistant Secretary. The markings on the van are those we were told to look for. We weren't able to get a clear picture of the driver, but we do know there is only one person in the cab. What we have is a little blurred, but the shot has been sent to you."

"And are you still in pursuit?"

There was a moment of silence at the other end. "Actually, ma'am, we lost him in the evening traffic jam. But if you are right and he is going to Damascus, there are only a few ways out of the city and the route I have just suggested is probably the fastest and most direct one."

This time it was Melinda's turn to pause and think. After about thirty seconds, she continued, "What time is it there?"

"It's 8:30 p.m. local time."

"OK. Tomorrow is the Sabbath there, isn't it?"

"Yes, ma'am."

"That means he will probably try to get out of the city tonight, find a place to stay and complete his mandatory prayers in a mosque tomorrow, Friday. That will give us time to get the teams together and send them to Beirut to continue the search. How many men do you have with you?"

"There are only three of us, ma'am."

The 'ma'am' was starting to irritate Melinda, but she knew there were few terms this man could use to address her without constantly including her title, so she decided to ignore it and accept it as a sign of compliance.

"Let me look at my satellite recognizance maps of the area." She quickly brought the map of the Beirut area to her computer screen, and then zoomed out to get a better picture of the roads going in the direction of Damascus.

Her eyes widened a bit as she looked at the multitude of roads leading in the direction of the Syrian border from Beirut, realizing this was not going to be an easy task. "What would your recommendations be, Williams?"

"Ma'am, I think he will go the more direct route, if you can call it that, through Jamhour, Bhamdoun Al Mhatta and Sofar, over the mountain range and through Bar Elias to Highway One into Damascus."

Melinda looked at the route Williams was describing. "I see your point. But, I have a hunch he will not go the expected way. He's proven to be very difficult to predict."

Pausing another moment, she then said resolutely, "I want you to drive to Jamhour. If he is to stop for the night and go to prayers, I think he'll do it there. From what I can see, the roads from there become treacherous with all those hills, valleys and switchback roads. He won't dare take those at night."

Williams responded, "Point well taken, ma'am. And if we find him there, what?"

Knowing these agents had no idea who Mohammed really was and what was in the rear of the van, Melinda did not want to risk having Mohammed *make* his tail and disappear for good. And she could not explain why the content of the van was so important: This was a need to know situation.

"I need you to find him. Do not approach and do not bring attention to yourselves. I simply must know if he is there. If he is, contact me. Then, you will each travel to a different city on the route you are suggesting. I need one of you to take a position to see the main road at Aley, another at Bhamdoun Al Mhatta and the third at Sofar. If you are correct, he will be committed to that route."

Agent Williams responded, "Agreed. But to be honest, I can't see why he would go in any other direction. The other roads go through some very difficult terrain. It would really slow him down and extend his run by a couple of days."

"That's exactly what has me worried," replied Melinda. "I have to report to the Secretary. Keep me informed." And then she hung up.

Five minutes later, she had an emergency meeting with Secretary Fleet during which he decided she needed to personally head the mission. She had the most contact with the doctor and the Secretary felt she needed to see it through herself.

Back in her office, she picked up her phone and dialled Sam's cell phone number.

"Hi sweetheart," Sam blurted out without thinking.

A warm feeling swept over Melinda and a smile came to her face. "And what if it was my boss calling you?"

"Sorry, I just saw a Washington area code come up and I really only know one person who would call me from there, next to the President of course. And then again, I thought he liked me, too."

Melinda chuckled. "Not like I do. Where are you, anyway?"

"I'm in Syracuse at the Holiday Inn. I have a lecture tomorrow at the university."

"Your publishers have to line up more *fun* towns than that."

Sam laughed. "It's not so bad. The minibar is well-stocked and I'm watching reruns of *Desperate Housewives* on TV."

"Showing your feminine side, are you?"

"What's up, sweetheart?" was all he would say.

"I have to leave for a short while. We've located Mohammed."

"You're kidding. That's great!" A short pause. "Will this be dangerous?"

"I doubt it. It will really depend on him when we find him. I'll have a good team to back me. So I wouldn't worry."

"I can't help it. But, I know you can do it."

"Thanks. I love you too. Have to go. I'll call you as soon as I can."

"OK, I understand. I'll be waiting. Good luck and love always."

Melinda was still smiling when she put the receiver back on its cradle.

She dropped into her chair and thought about what she needed to do next. She pondered the different avenues she could take and decided on a specific course of action. She needed two agents from her office to come and help coordinate the mission. She had to muster the special ops unit Secretary Broom had sent to Sana'a, Yemen, to protect them when Sam was to meet with Ra'id. And then, there was one more person she owed a chance to find some closure to the mission. She had people to meet, phone calls to make and little time to do it.

She reached over to her telephone and dialled for Gloria, her assistant. "Hi. Can you contact Lieutenant Jon and inform him he needs to get his team ready for deployment, pronto. And ask Agents Doyle and Stuart to meet with me immediately."

"Will do, boss," was Gloria's response.

****

"Hi, Dad. I just left the witch's office." It was John Doyle's turn to make a call. "Looks like I was volunteered for a mission."

"Isn't that what you were hoping for?" quizzed his father.

"Yes, it is. But, I'll be playing second fiddle to *her*."

"Remember what we talked about the last time we had this discussion: This could be the time she trips up. Just do the best job you can and keep your nose clean. I suppose I can't ask you where you are going and why?"

"Sorry, Dad. The most I can say is that it is over-seas, and that it's something to do with the mission she was promoted over. So it's probably as important as it is hush-hush."

"Then, all the more reason to play it by the book."

John dropped his head slightly, closing his eyes in resignation. "Yeah, you're right."

Looking up at the clock on the wall in his office and noticing the time, he said, "Gotta go."

"Take care and be safe," his dad added.

"Thanks. I will."

****

Twelve hours later, Melinda was exiting the rear hatch of the Boeing C-17 Globemaster III she had commandeered for the mission. She had swapped her black pant suit for a black swat-style flak suit.

Waiting for her at the bottom of the ramp was Agent Cohen, the Israeli secret service agent with whom she and Sam had collaborated in their pursuit of Ra'id Al-Eissa and the weapon he had created.

Arms outstretched, a huge smile on his face, Agent Cohen moved forward to meet her. "Welcome Melinda, or should I say Madame Deputy Secretary."

"Hello, my friend," was Melinda's response as she accepted his bear hug, tightly wrapping her arms around him as well. "It's so good to see you again. And don't you dare call me anything but Melinda."

Releasing his grip, Agent Cohen said, "In that case, don't you call me anything else but Shmu'el."

Melinda winked and replied, "How lucky am I to have two Sams in my life."

Agent Cohen looked up at the plane. "Quite the ride you have here."

She looked back to the cavern inside the plane where there were three sleek three-man stealth helicopters, neatly squeezed into the available cargo space. "Our *helos* are quite nice as well. We had to bring our own, not being able to count on the Lebanese for our search mission. Another stealth carrier, the type nicknamed "Airwolf", was borrowed from our carrier group out in the Mediterranean. You remember our ride to Kamaran Island?"

Agent Cohen simply grunted and nodded in the affirmative.

Melinda looked at Cohen. "As for you, it took a personal call from the President to get permission for you to be here as well."

Agent Cohen smiled. "I wondered what you had to do to get me out of retirement and into Lebanon."

As they both turned to walk toward the hangar which had been reserved for them in the cargo area of the Beirut–Rafic Hariri International Airport, being a head taller than he, she put her arm over Cohen's shoulders. As they strolled to the hanger door, she explained the situation to him.

Once inside, Melinda was met by the group commander who had been sent to Kuwait to help bring Ra'id in if Sam could convince him to give himself up.

There, too, were the three helicopter pilots and Agents Doyle and Stuart from her office. She had hesitated in choosing Doyle because of the resentment she sensed from him. However, she also knew he was a very capable agent and that he yearned for a chance to prove himself in the field. Agent Stuart was a competent field agent and was fluent in Arabic, which could be useful in this situation. The other two agents had been part of the teams Melinda had sent to various locations where Mohammed could have gone. They were quickly flown in to take part in the *takedown*.

After the introductions, Melinda laid out her strategy. Three agents had already been sent ahead to three cities in Mohammed's possible choice of routes to Damascus. They were to sit in waiting to identify the van and were to relay the sighting to Melinda. If Mohammed was indeed going in the most direct way, he would pass all three and be committed to a specific route. If, nevertheless, he did not drive by any one of the three agents, it would mean he had taken another direction: one that could more easily determine the actual route being used.

In fact, Mohammed had driven by the first agent in Aley and she was waiting for the call from the agent at Bhamdoun Al Mhatta.

The group commander would take his team in the Airwolf and act as the main assault group once Mohammed had been located. The other three helicopters, one carrying Melinda and Agent Cohen, the other Agents Doyle and Stuart, and the last carrying the two other agents would act as the spotters and backup when the prey was cornered.

Though not a foolproof plan, it did take the terrain into consideration. Another agent further up the road, Williams, counted on Mohammed going in the direction of the Dahr al-Baydar pass, in spite of the fact it was one of the highest at about seven thousand feet above sea level. But it was also the widest pass and the one the railroad takes to Damascus, making it the most likely.

Melinda, however, had serious doubts Mohammed would do so. She knew he had to know they were looking for him and that the obvious route would not be the safest. She bet on the fact that other directions would take him through some pretty rugged terrain, with hundreds of deep ravines, high ridges and switchback roads, most of which were covered with dense forests.

Coffee and sandwiches had been brought in while they waited for the calls to confirm Mohammed's passing. About an hour later, the call came through confirming he had driven by the agent in Bhamdoun Al Mhatta. If all went as planned, he would drive by the agent in Sofar in another two hours.

Melinda ordered the pilots to supervise the unloading of the helicopters by the airport ground crews and report back to her as soon as they were ready.

As she looked around at the group, she tried to guess what was going through their minds.

It was fairly easy to guess what was going through the minds of the attack team: They were sitting quietly, cleaning their weapons or challenging each other to see who could dismantle and reassemble their weapons the fastest. All fearless, single-minded and committed to the mission, Melinda thought.

Agents Doyle and Stuart were busying themselves with a game of cards and light banter for conversation. She knew their capabilities and understood that it wasn't that they weren't committed, but that this was just another mission to them. As well, they had the luxury of not having to carry the weight of responsibility she was carrying.

Then, there was Agent Cohen. She couldn't help but chuckle to herself. There he was, sitting on a chair up against a wall. His feet stretched onto another chair and snoring away, not a care in the world.

Time passed, and no call came. Melinda decided to check in with the agent in Sofar.

His phone vibrated, and he answered, "Yes."

"He should have passed by you a half hour ago."

"Yes, ma'am. However, he could have stopped to eat or *take care of business*."

Just then, the pilots re-entered the hangar, signalling that the helicopters were ready. Melinda gave them the *thumbs up*.

68

Getting back to her call, "You might be right, but call me as soon as you see the van, but no less than fifteen minutes from now."

"Yes, ma'am," and the phone went dead.

Melinda looked around, only to see everyone staring back at her. She knew it was time to act.

"OK, everyone. I think we have our answer. He has either taken a different direction, or he will pass by our agent within minutes. Either way, wheels up in five. I'll brief you on the way as to which route we will follow."

One last look at each one, getting the nod from them, they picked up their gear and walked out of the hangar.

The rotors of each of the four helicopters were already turning and gaining speed. The attack team was the first to board and strap in. Even in the sunlight, there was no reflection off the special light-absorbing charcoal-coloured paint. Long and sleek, with an odd radar-reflecting body shape, the craft nimbly lifted off with its load.

The other three teams walked to their respective helos and prepared to mount. Each was much shorter than the Airwolf, but they had some similarities. They too had the same paint and were oddly shaped as well. Even so, they could only accommodate three people. The pilot sat in his individual seat up front with windows above and on both sides, while the two passenger seats were located immediately behind, facing forward with their own set of windows above and to their sides for unimpeded views. Their seats were tight, leaving little room for moving or stretching their legs. This was made somewhat more uncomfortable for Melinda because of her height and for Agent Cohan because of the extra weight he had put on since his retirement five months prior.

The whoop-whoop sounds of the rotors were fairly loud as they lifted. Melinda spoke to the pilot in her helmet microphone. "What are the chances we could go silent all the way?" She was referring to the fact that these helicopters, including the Airwolf, could reduce their noise level by altering the pitch of the rotors in order to minimize the noise by seventy-five percent, making them next to impossible to hear until the machines were directly overhead.

"As soon as we reach fifteen hundred feet we'll be able to do so. We need full thrust to lift off to flight levels," was the pilot's response. He added, "Shall I relay the instructions to the other pilots?"

A little embarrassed for seeming a bit anxious, Melinda took a deep breath and in a more relaxed tone, she addressed the pilot. "Thank you, Captain. Pardon me for attempting to tell you how to do your job. I was simply hoping not to alarm the people on our flight path."

Agent Cohen patted her left hand, indicating everything was OK. The pilot took a quick look over his right shoulder at Melinda behind him and reassured her with, "Not a problem. I wouldn't lose any sleep over it." And then he calmly turned back and aimed the helicopter in the direction of Sofar.

She asked the pilot to open the channels to the other helicopters, which he did.

"Agent Doyle, how would you recommend we go about finding the target?"

Doyle was caught by surprise. Was she really asking him his opinion or was she baiting him for failure?

Taking a moment to look over the maps of the area on his navigational tablet, he checked for the possible alternatives to the route through Sofar. "Assuming he doesn't take the more direct route, he could take any one of three routes south, just on the east side of Rouissat Sofar, just beyond the ridge."

Pointing to the valley in which the three possible roads lay, Stuart nodded in the affirmative.

"I agree," said Melinda.

"Then he will need to go through Mreijat by way of the western route, or through Bmahray on the eastern route."

Looking over to Agent Stuart, he asked, "Did I pronounce those properly?"

Stuart smiled and gave the correct pronunciation.

Not taking any offence, Doyle replied, "OK, what he said."

"Either way, the two join up at grid number '4256' on the road to Fraidiss and Maasser al Chouf. From there he crosses over the mountain range to Kafraiya . . . " He glanced over at Oliver to see if the pronunciation was better, and indeed it was. He continued, " . . . and zigzags his way to Yanta, then over the border into Syria, and finally hooks up to Highway One, on to Damascus."

Melinda conferred briefly with Agent Cohen and returned to her com. "I think you're right. I want *you* to take the lead on this part of the mission. Tell us what you think we need to do to find him. I'll coordinate the Intel from the satellites I've had brought over the region."

Agent Cohen silently gave her the thumbs up.

Again Doyle was caught by surprise. But he quickly composed himself.

Uncharacteristically, he began with a sign of respect. "Thank you, ma'am. What I need, then, is to have chopper Two go on to Sofar over the main road, in order to make sure he hasn't somehow managed to evade the agent on the ground." Speaking to the pilot of that chopper, "Head past Sofar by fifty kilometres and if you don't find the van, return to us to help continue our search."

No sooner said, the helicopter was pointing its nose down slightly and accelerating ahead of the others.

"Chopper Three, take the most western road heading south, while Chopper One will take the middle route and Lieutenant Jon, you and your men will cover the easternmost road. If we don't find him, we'll regroup at grid 4256." "

From each of the helicopters came, "Chopper One, copy. Chopper Three, copy. This is Jon, copy."

The helicopters reached the crest of the high ridge Doyle had identified earlier and as if choreographed, the three, one after the other, banked to the right and headed toward different roads in the valley.

****

Approximately thirty kilometres further south, just five from Maasser Al Chouf, Mohammed was negotiating the last of the switchback turns in the road out of the mountains, down into the valley.

He relaxed his grip on the steering wheel and rotated his head to the left and to the right, trying to ease the stress of driving in such difficult terrain. He was buoyed up, realizing that just on the other side of the small town ahead, was the last of the mountain ridges he had to cross before descending into the valley leading to Syria.

Unaware of the danger swooping quickly down toward him, he allowed himself to smile, thinking about the fact that his task was almost over.

As he drove into the small town of Maasser Al Chouf, he recognized the same type of architecture found in the previous towns and villages he had passed through since leaving Beirut. Here, however, there were many more homes built of stone, with peaked terra-cotta roofs. And, for the past forty kilometres, he had noticed many more trees lining the roadway and the sides of the mountains.

He played a question and answer game, he being the only participant in the game. What could be the reason for the increase in trees and peaked roofs? Obviously, there had to be more rain here, he thought. He imagined that the terrain had to squeeze more moisture out of the wind than in other places. That made sense. And why was there a greater number of peaked roofs? To help the water run off into the cisterns. Right! And, that would explain the deep ravines he'd had to zigzag through. Then, looking at the valley in which the town was situated, he imagined the layers of rock and dirt that had once filled it. All this soil washed away by countless floods . . . That could account for the great Bekaa Valley just on the other side of Mount Lebanon, which he would be climbing shortly.

He had often played this type of game during his travels through the Middle East and Northern Africa, while moving as stealthily as possible, in order to find and kill the members of the Foundation for the Promotion of Islam. He had made a solemn oath to Ra'id, that he would use the weapon to terminate the life of each and every one of the members, before destroying it. No one should have access to such a weapon. Only God should be able to dispatch people in such a way. Although he far from compared himself to God, Mohammed did believe he was *His* agent in this sacred mission.

Looking at his watch, he saw that it was almost two in the afternoon and thought about stopping to rest a while before attempting to cross the last mountain barrier ahead of him.

He might even look around the town a little. He liked it, as it was just the right size and seemed to protect him from the world without. He could see himself returning to live there after his duty was fulfilled.

No, he thought, I need to get to the other side of the mountain range and then I can stop to rest for the night.

That's when he heard it.

A faint beating sound bouncing off the sides of the surrounding hills. Mohammed was unable to tell from where the sound was emanating because the echo resounded from everywhere. He knew this wasn't good.

The first of the helicopters, the one carrying Doyle and Stuart, had just come over the ridge behind Mohammed and was descending into the valley, the occupants looking for the vehicle through their binoculars. Then, the second helicopter flew over the crest of the ridge and followed the first. Even though they were flying in stealth mode, they were too low to fully eliminate the sound of the rotors, as the swoosh-swoosh sound reverberated throughout the valley.

Melinda's and Agent Cohen's helicopter was high above, along with the large Airwolf.

She was busy talking to a Sergeant Garcia on a military base somewhere in the Midwest of the US He was in control of the satellite that had been moved over the area to help with the search and was waiting to hear toward which grid he needed to direct the cameras.

It was Stuart who saw it first. He tapped Doyle on the leg and pointed ahead and to the right. Both acquired the vehicle through their binoculars.

"Ma'am, Doyle here."

"Yes, John."

"I believe we have him. About two kilometres, just leaving the town. I'd say grid 4380."

Melinda immediately relayed the coordinates to Sergeant Garcia. High above the earth, the satellite puffed a short burst of air, followed by another in the opposite direction, silently turning the spacecraft into position and then stabilizing it. The camera lens whirled as it adjusted the focus to see the town of Maasser Al Chouf, then the road through it before zeroing in on grid 4380.

And there it was. The roof of a black van, slowly working its way out of the town.

Melinda could see exactly what Garcia was watching, on her navigational tablet. "Can you confirm this is the van?"

Doyle responded, "That's an affirmative. I can see the side of the vehicle and the sign is the same one our agents in Beirut described."

"Good. Proceed," was all Melinda said to him.

She switched over to Garcia. "Sergeant, can you switch the visual to infrared, please?"

Instantly, the image turned to a shade of reddish orange. The heat signature of the vehicle was a bright yellow where the engine sat, with a smaller and somewhat cooler dot where Mohammed was situated.

Melinda returned to Doyle. "I can confirm he is alone."

"Thank you, ma'am."

Agent Doyle calmly issued his orders. "Commander Jon, can you descend and hover over the vehicle? I want to spook him in order to distract him."

"Straight away, sir."

Doyle scanned the area ahead of the van and spotted what seemed to be a large pond to the right of the road.

No, it was a quarry, cut out of the side of the hill next to it. There was a large open area surrounding the deep pit where the rock had been mined for material to build the houses in the area and which was now filled with water.

"Chopper Two, I want you to go ahead about two kilometres to where the map shows a hairpin turn, up the mountain. Drop to street level and work your way back. We can't let him start his climb over the mountain. Our choppers will be useless in that terrain, and with all the trees, he could stop anywhere and escape."

"Roger that," was the response from the pilot as he swung to the right and headed to the spot Doyle had identified.

"Ma'am, I see what looks like a quarry about a kilometre ahead. That's where we have to steer him. Can you tell if there are other exits I can't see from here?"

Melinda checked the tablet and superimposed a topographic map on the image. "Other than the back roads intersecting at the switchback and leading through some heavy growth in and around the quarry, there is only one way out, up the side of the hill, along what seems to be no more than a mule path."

"OK. Commander Jon, I need you to shoot just ahead of the vehicle to force him to turn into the quarry."

****

Mohammed was having some trouble processing what was happening. He didn't know how, but it slowly dawned on him that they had found him.

He looked around to see if there were vehicles following. There were none.

About then, the van began to rock and shake. Mohammed's heart leaped into his throat. Then a shadow darkened the afternoon sun around him.

What was that, he thought? He leaned forward over the steering wheel to glance up through the windshield.

He saw the underbelly of the Airwolf and its gun turret. He began to panic, searching for somewhere to escape.

No sooner had that thought crossed his mind than the M61 Vulcan cannon, mounted on the front of the helo, spewed out a burst of three hundred bullets in a matter of seconds, only metres ahead of the van.

Mohammed saw the road in front of him shred by the ammunition in the shape of a curved line across the van's path. Instinctively, he veered to the right onto a

driveway that had just appeared. He accelerated on the
gravel road, going where?   He didn't know.

****

"Great job!" blurted Doyle. "He's where we want
him. Commander Jon, allow him to move ahead. He
seems to be going to the other side of the pit. Sit down on
your side of it and have your men deploy undercover and
prevent him from returning to the highway."
"Bird Two, you need to return to us and position
yourself over the path to the left of the pit."
Speaking to his pilot, "Bring us to the right of the
pit and the van, just far enough to make sure he can't easily
use a weapon on us."
From the ground, the scene was impressive. The
Airwolf sat about three hundred metres from Mohammed,
its Gatling Gun trained on the van. If the orders came, the
van could be destroyed with a volley of thousands of high-
powered bullets per minute.
The other two helicopters were motionless about
fifty metres above the quarry, their rotors stirring up the
dust below, almost obscuring the view of the van.

****

Mohammed remained there gazing at the spectacle,
but from the ground up, acutely aware of the damage the
helicopter in front of him on the other side of the pit was
capable of inflicting.
He could try to get out and run. But where would
he go? He could attempt climbing the hill behind him or
running toward the small forest over to his right. Even so,
he knew he would be cut down in seconds by the soldiers

he saw leave the large helicopter. He had no weapon to defend himself with.

None but *one*, he thought.

His mind raced back to the moment he had decided to destroy the weapon on Kamaran Island, knowing it would eradicate everyone there, including himself.

Although there remained a few targets on his list, he knew his mission was over.

So what was the difference: Dying then, or now?

He had been a "Dead Man Walking" ever since his decision to kill himself along with the others on the island. His survival had simply postponed the inevitable. He only hoped he would have enough time to set the plan in motion, before the onset of the raid he knew was coming.

He bowed his head in prayer to Allah. Then, he leaned over to turn the weapon on. It would take about two minutes for it to come to full power.

****

Doyle was ready to tighten the noose. "Commander, have your men start to move in on both sides of the pit and flank him."

"Copy, that."

No sooner was the order acknowledged than the team members skillfully and carefully began to fan out around the deep watery pit.

****

High above the area, Melinda was watching the tablet and the infrared dots that were the men moving closer to the van. She could also see the van's engine and the single passenger behind the steering wheel.

She noticed something else. Something was happening in the rear of the van. Another dot appeared. And, it was growing larger.

"Sergeant Garcia, do you see this?"

"Yes, ma'am. Either someone else was there all along and *cloaked* somehow, or there's another source of heat there."

Melinda's eyes grew larger as she realized it was going to happen again. The heat source had grown in intensity in the Quonset Hut on Kamaran Island, just before it blew up, destroying everything within a kilometre and knocking the helicopter they were fleeing in out of the air and to the ground.

She turned to Agent Cohen who had realized what was happening at the same time she had.

"Jon! Get your men out of there immediately. If they can't get away, they need to take cover behind something large. Doyle, Chopper Two, put down now!"

"Ma'am, this is Garcia. The heat source has now overshadowed the other signatures."

Tapping her pilot on the shoulder, she ordered him to pull up and get as far away as possible.

****

In the van, Mohammed sat, quietly resigned to his fate. As he heard the familiar hum of the weapon in the back, he knew it wouldn't be long.

He looked up to the sky, spread his arms out upward and whispered, "Allahu akbar", God is great.

****

Commander Jon was sitting in the copilot's seat at the front of the Airwolf when he got Melinda's warning. He quickly called his men back, tracking their movements through his binoculars and coaching them as they made their way to the helicopter. He had them duck behind large boulders when they could and then sprint on to the next ones. The two men closest to the chopper made it and flung themselves inside.

Jon briefly focused in on the van and saw a strange sight. The driver was sitting within the front cab, arms outstretched. "What the hell . . . "

For the next few seconds, the commander was thrust into what seemed like a slow-motion action scene in a movie. He heard a loud whoop sound, followed by a wave of dust that emanated from the van, moving outward at close to the speed of sound.

He saw three of the other soldiers either in a crouched position or flat on their stomachs behind some of the large boulders which littered the area. The last member of the team wasn't so lucky. He was caught in the open between the rock he had just left and the next toward which he was running. When the wave reached him, he was picked up, much like a leaf in the wind, and flung at least thirty metres away.

That was the last image Jon witnessed. The wave reached the helicopter moments after the electrical circuits in the craft shorted out. His mind told him it was an EMP, or electrical magnetic pulse. Then the wave hit the chopper and blew out the windshield, sending small shards of glass flying inward. Several cut into Jon's face and hands, bouncing off the binoculars he was holding, as he watched his men. His pilot was luckier since he still had on his full helmet and visor over his face.

The cab of the helicopter filled with dust. Between bouts of coughing and trying to wipe the blood which had covered his face, he yelled out, "Count off!"

"Three, here. Two, here. The others were right behind us, sir."

Jon yelled back, "I think One, Five and Six are OK. But if you're not hurt, head out to help Four. I think he's about sixty metres to our three o'clock."

****

At the same time, the pilots of the two helicopters carrying the other agents reacted without hesitation to the orders they had received.

They forced their helicopters to dive straight down, catching the four agents by surprise, almost bringing up their last meals and rendering them seemingly weightless.

While the forty-metre drop took but a moment, the last ten metres were equally disturbing to the passengers. The pilots throttled up to maximum revolutions and levelled the helicopters out in an effort to slow the crafts in order to land.

Doyle's helicopter was about a metre off the ground and the other about five metres when the EMP occurred.

Not as well hardened as the Airwolf against such surges, sparks flew all around within the cabs, creating loud screeches in everyone's earphones.

Doyle's craft landed hard but safely on the ground. The second was less fortunate and crashed, crumpling their undersides, crushing the landing struts and wheels. Fortunately, no one was hurt.

****

High above, Melinda's helicopter had escaped the danger zone. She realized that the blast was much smaller than the one she had survived on Kamaran Island, due to the weapon in the van having but a fraction of the power of the original. And yet, looking back at the quarry from her window, she saw a similar, mini mushroom cloud rising from where the van had been.

She ordered the pilot to return to the site as quickly as possible, while trying to raise the other crafts on the radio, to no avail. She knew it was due to the wave which would have destroyed the communication equipment.

Then, a crackle in her earphones. It was Commander Jon reporting back. "Jon, here. Five confirmed alive, one unknown at the moment. The craft is flyable but it will be a slow ride back."

Melinda and Agent Cohen breathed a sigh of relief.

"And what of the other two choppers?"

"Unknown at the moment. I'll have my men check for them. Be with you in four."

"How are you, Commander?"

"I'm having some trouble seeing, but I'm alright."

Already knowing the answer, Melinda pursued, "And the target?"

"Well, ma'am, I can confirm there is a new pit in the quarry."

As her helicopter was approaching the area of the assault, she could see a couple of soldiers escorting Doyle, Stuart and the pilot over to the Airwolf. They seemed to be OK. A few more soldiers were pulling out the other agents and pilot from the second helicopter. They too seemed to be uninjured.

They landed close to the commander's craft. She and Cohen quickly exited and ran over to the others, making sure all were safe and sound. She asked for Jon. A soldier pointed to the rear of the helicopter, where she saw the commander crouched over a black body bag. She put her hand to her mouth and slowly walked over to him.

"We lost one?" It was more a statement than a question.

"Yes, Corporal Latimer, married two years, with a one-year-old daughter."

"I'm so sorry, Jon."

"Ma'am, it could have been much worse. Had you not realized what was happening, there could have been many more casualties here today. Thank you. My men and I owe you."

Agent Cohen came up behind her and put his hand on her shoulder once again. However comforting the gesture, nothing could lessen the sorrow she felt for this fallen soldier.

They turned to reunite with the other agents. The first to come meet her was Doyle. Looking none the worse for his experience, he extended his hand to shake hers. "Under Secretary Gordon, we all owe you our lives. Thank you."

Melinda was deeply touched by his overture. Perhaps it was due to the death of the soldier, or maybe he was showing his true feelings. "I'm glad there weren't more fatalities. Congratulations are due your way as well. You did a masterful job directing this mission."

Looking toward the highway, Melinda noticed people arriving from the surrounding area. They were curious to see what had happened.

"Stuart, could you go meet with the locals to defuse the situation? Tell them we are working with the Lebanese authorities, and that we were after a very dangerous man who decided to blow himself up instead of surrendering. Tell them he was responsible for a great many deaths of their kindred Muslims."

"Yes, ma'am."

As he walked away, Melinda asked the Airwolf's pilot if he thought they could take off soon. He said it would only take five minutes to clean the glass from the front of the helicopter, and that they could leave at any time after that.

"Good. In the meantime, I need to report in. I'll be in my chopper."

As she walked away, Agent Doyle was thinking to himself, maybe I was wrong?

****

Four days later, Melinda was sitting in Secretary Fleet's top-floor, corner office.

The space had been decorated by a close friend of his from New York: a designer for the rich and famous.

Though it looked sparse, there was more there than met the eye. The walls were clad in imported wood panelling made of fine Cabreuva wood from South America and normally used as flooring. In this case, though, it had been hand selected and matched to show only the soft tones of the lumber.

The two lone bookcases which framed the door into his office boasted clean straight lines and were made of the same lumber. They held his favourite novels and texts dealing with philosophy and were penned by a variety of authors from Tom Clancy to Socrates and Aristotle. The cabinets seemed to disappear into the wall.

The floor was of the same wood, but darker and more solid in colouring. At the centre of the room lay a large oval off-white carpet, contrasting the rest of the area and rendering whatever meeting took place there, more intimate.

The two off-white leather, low back sofa chairs matched the carpet, enhancing that feeling of intimacy.

But for the two large windows which gave Fleet an unobstructed view of the Capitol Building, the room could have been gloomy. However, the light they let in brightened the space, complementing the soft, warm tones of the walls and furniture.

The Secretary's desk was at once the ultimate in class and *nerdiness*. Sleek chrome legs, in the shape of curved X's supported a large, thick, glare-free plate glass desktop. There was nothing on it other than a simple crystal pen holder and a handmade Cabreuva fountain pen. You could think he never worked at his desk, but you would be wrong.

He had the one-of-a-kind top custom made, with multiple layers of paper-thin sheets of computer circuitry, connected to and by microfibre wires. In fact, the whole glass top *was* his computer. Simply applying a finger on the fingerprint sensor to his right brought the glass to life. A thirty-inch image would appear magically in the centre, along with a heat-sensitive keyboard just before it. The power to the computer was supplied by wires hidden in one of the chrome legs and plugged into a power outlet in the floor. For security purposes, he wasn't allowed, nor did he need hard drives: He was connected by wire to Homeland Security's mainframe computer in the basement.

Anyone invited to meet with the Secretary in his office was struck by the sophistication and the contrasting cosiness of the room, both reflecting his personality.

Today was not different. It had been several days since Melinda's return from Lebanon. Between jet lag, the debriefing and countless reports she had to fill out, time had been a blur.

She had gotten a chance to call Sam on several occasions to let him know she had returned and to check on him in the various cities where he was lecturing. Even so, she had little time for herself, and vowed to travel to

Toronto in the next few weeks when he would be back there, between engagements.

The Secretary had met with the President the previous day, and he wanted to let her know how the discussion had gone.

"Good to have you back. So, how are you feeling?"

"I'm doing well, sir. Thank you. I do have to admit, I think I spent more time in the debriefing process than I did in the actual operation."

Fleet smiled as he walked around the desk and sat himself in the chair next to Melinda's. As he crossed his legs, he absentmindedly picked a piece of lint off his pants.

True to his code of perfection, she thought.

"As you know, I briefed the President on your mission and he wants me to convey his congratulations on a job well done."

Melinda looked a little troubled. "Well, it wasn't the outcome I had hoped for. We tried to ensure that the *equipment* be taken intact. We didn't factor in the possibility that Dr. Al-Kammin would destroy the vehicle, along with himself."

"That was both a shame and possibly a blessing," responded Fleet. "It's probably for the best that the weapon no longer exists. I would hate to think what could happen if anyone, including ourselves, had such a tool at our disposal. And the President, as well, acknowledged that he was relieved at the outcome of the mission. Furthermore, *if*, and only if, we are confronted with the need for the weapon, we can build one based on the information from the laptop Dr. Buckner retrieved on Kamaran Island."

Melinda's expression softened somewhat with the knowledge she had done the best she could.

"As for myself," Fleet continued, "I'm pleased as well. I approved the letter of commendation you wrote for the members of your team, particularly for the distinct praise you gave Agent Doyle. I'm impressed by your willingness to delegate and share command for such a mission. Some of the agents in our employ would not want to do so, in order to take credit for any success."

A respectful smile came to her face. "Thank you, sir. He did a masterful job of finding the doctor in a short period of time, especially when you consider the terrain we had to cover. He deserves it."

Checking his watch, Fleet calmly said, "I'm afraid I have an important meeting on Capitol Hill. We'll have to cut our conversation a bit short."

He slowly rose from his chair, trying not to look as if he was unceremoniously dispensing with her. Melinda followed suit.

Fleet reached for her right hand and clasped it with both of his own. "The nation and the world will never know the service you have done them. We owe you a debt of gratitude."

"Thank you, sir," was all Melinda said, and she turned to leave his office.

Just before she reached the door, Fleet said, "I would recommend you take a few days off. You've earned it."

She turned and with a smile on her face, she quipped, "Already planned, sir. Sam's and my schedules just have to *jibe*. Don't worry, I'll leave the office in good hands." Then, she walked out.

Chapter 7

The plane was on the final approach from the Atlantic side before landing at the Daytona Beach International Airport. Sam could see the barrier island on which the hotel strip was situated. Just beyond was the Halifax River lagoon which separated the strip from the mainland. He didn't need the announcement over the PA system to know that they were within a few minutes of touching down. The flaps on the wings had dropped, and now he could hear the gears lowering the landing wheels.

He was excited at the prospect of spending a few days on the beach with Melinda. It had been quite the lecture tour to date and, now, he needed some R&R. He had missed her terribly and couldn't wait to be with her.

She had called him a few days prior, suggesting they have a little get-together to unwind. He was also anxious to get the lowdown on the mission she had completed, having spent days agonizing over her safety, awaiting confirmation that she was alright.

The tires squealed as they touched the tarmac and a few people onboard applauded in relief.

A half hour later, Sam was emerging from the arrival gates into the main reception area. Among the throngs of people awaiting the arrival of family and friends were several limousine service drivers, with name signs held close to their chests. Sam quickly identified the one held for him. It simply stated *SB*.

He smiled and shook his head. Leave it to the spy hunter. He felt as if he was in some covert operation being *handled* by Melinda.

He followed the driver who had gallantly taken his carry-on suitcase and walked to the pickup area.

There, standing seductively against the black, stretch limousine, was Melinda. Being the consummate male, Sam didn't even notice she was wearing worn, ripped knee jeans, a white T-shirt and a tan leather vest. All he could see was the woman he loved. He thought she was so cute with her hair pulled through the back of her baseball cap into a ponytail.

He walked over to her, and the two embraced for the time it took the driver to open the trunk, deposit the suitcase and then close the lid. When he looked up at the two, they were still holding each other tightly.

Sam finally stepped back and glanced at the car. "Nice wheels."

"I'm glad you like it. I'm not allowed to take taxies anymore. And by the way, don't pay any attention to the black SUV over there. They promised to keep their distance."

Sam looked over to the SUV with the black tinted windows she was referring to. "So much for a private getaway."

The two got into the vehicle, after which it pulled away from the terminal, with the second in tow about fifty metres behind.

As they turned left onto the S. Clyde Morris Boulevard, the driver took a quick peek in his rear-view mirror and saw that the two weren't looking at the surroundings, but rather, into each other's eyes.

As they reached the intersection to the W. International Speedway Boulevard, the limo took a left turn away from the beach area.

Sam pulled back a little, and with a puzzled look on his face, asked, "I thought we had a room on the beach strip?"

"Yes, we do. However, I thought you might like a little surprise. Sit back and it won't be long."

She was right as the limo only drove another several hundred metres before turning left again. Sam leaned forward to catch a glimpse of their destination through the front window. There, before them, was the superstructure of the Daytona Speedway complex.

"You're kidding! We're going there?"

Melinda chuckled and said, "Part of the reason for suggesting getting together this weekend was because of the Daytona 500. I managed to get some tickets for the two of us. I thought you could use a little excitement before we settle down to make our own this evening."

"This is great. I've never been to a big race event, ever. God, you're great." He hugged her and kissed her before looking around and taking in the hustle and bustle of the event.

The car pulled up to Gate 3, just behind the Main Tower. Immediately behind came the second vehicle. Three agents, dressed in the expected black suits, exited and began to scan the hundreds of people lining up to enter the site.

Melinda looked at Sam reassuring him, "Don't worry. They're here out of formality. Only the people at the office know where we are. We'll be fine." Then she added, "My life is a little different now."

They entered and started to climb up the stairs to the level where their seats were located.

Sam kept on looking at the size of the structure, with all its metal brace work and girders. "This place has the dimensions of a large cruise ship. It's monstrous!"

As they arrived several storeys above, they emerged into the bright Florida light. There, before them, appeared the famous race track and its seventy-three hectare infield with the twelve-hectare Lake Lloyd in the centre. The track itself circled the lake in the weird shape of a cross between a boomerang and an oval.

Sam thought the four-kilometre track was surprisingly narrow, at only twelve metres wide. Why, he wondered, aren't there more accidents on such a course, with so many cars?

Melinda led him to their seats in the Weatherly Tower, row N. Upon finding them, the two sat down.

All of a sudden, one of the agents appeared and handed them a soft-sided cooler bag. "Sorry ma'am, you forgot this." Then, no sooner had he arrived than he was gone.

"What was that?" Sam said.

Melinda laughed. "Just part of the service, I guess."

Sam looked inside the pack and found two pair of field glasses, a baseball cap in his size, sunscreen lotion, and in the thermal compartment, a six-pack of Bud Light.

Donning the cap, he reached for two beer cans and opened them. Handing one to Melinda and sipping from the other, he joked, "This is like drinking water. Wait until I get you back to T.O. I'll introduce you to real beer."

Melinda jabbed him in the ribs with her elbow. "Hey, when in Rome, do as the Romans do."

Wincing a little, he replied, "Yes, ma'am."

"And don't call me ma'am," she retorted, feigning insult.

They sat through the welcome speeches, the listing of the cars, their owners and drivers. Of course, sponsors had to be thanked. But the greatest audience response came with the traditional fly-over by the military.

This year, to the marvel of all there, the lead plane was a Northrop Grumman B-2 Spirit strategic stealth bomber, flanked by two F-117 Nighthawk fighter jets. The three planes flew at low level over the race track from the southeast and slowly banked heading back over the Atlantic to the northwest.

Sam turned to Melinda and tried to yell over the crowd, "I know it's a *guy thing*, but that was awesome."

Then came the national anthem followed by the moment everyone had waited for. This year, the Grand Marshal was Larry Yearn, seven-time Emmy Award winner. He had the honour of pronouncing those famous words: Lady and gentlemen, start your engines.

Lined up in the pit lane, the forty-three cars that had qualified cranked their engines.

The roar of the two hundred thousand people in the seats and the thousands in the infield easily overtook the sound of the engines of the cars about to do battle. Everyone was up and cheering, including the newbie, Sam.

Each in turn took their position behind the lap car slowly making their way onto the main race track.

Once around and then onto the second.

Into turn One and on to turn Two, down the super stretch to turn Three and into turn Four, the cars looked like impatient cats, ready to pounce on their prey.

As they approached the start line, the noise from the crowd intensified.

The cars began to speed up, hoping the pace car would get out of their way and let them run free.

The green flag was waved by John Lampman, another respected actor from the stage and movies. The race was on.

For a moment, the noise from the cars more than compensated for the noise from the grandstand.

Everyone followed the armada of cars careening toward the first turn . . . everyone, that is, but one person.

High above the bleachers, behind the glass windows in the Main Tower, reserved for a select few, stood one individual holding high-powered binoculars, focused on Sam and Melinda.

For half an hour, he ignored the crowd, concentrating only on the couple, but especially on Sam.

He watched his every movement and reaction to the cars racing and to Melinda. He watched for *tells* which would indicate habitual reactions, body language and movements, anything specific to Sam. No gesture or motion was lost on him.

And then he was gone.

Chapter 8

(Three weeks later)

The set was brightly lit. In the background you could see several large video monitors showing clips of current world events. Five individuals were sitting on high stools, surrounding an oversized oval glass table.

The programme director was linked to each of the cameramen and the moderator through his microphone and their earpieces. "Camera One, zoom in on Frank . . . Good, and hold. Two, pull back to get the group . . . OK. One, fade to black, and three, two, one . . . "

Looking directly into Camera Two, the host opened the programme with, "Welcome to Your Take. I'm Frank Jones and do we have a show for you tonight."

Then, with Camera One focusing on his close-up, he continued, "This programme tries to stay at the cutting edge of issues we feel you should be aware of, and we offer you, the viewer, the opportunity of hearing differing points of view about various topics. You, then, are given a venue to air your own thoughts and opinions on the matters discussed."

Again, turning to Camera Two, he proceeded. "This evening, we delve into the world of science. But rather than look at how it can impact on us with new inventions, toys and gizmos, we want to analyze how it can affect the realm of philosophy and try to answer the questions, 'Who are we?' and 'Where do we come from?'

"To my right is the author of The Divine Formula, Doctor Samuel Buckner, a biogeneticist at the University of Toronto. His book highlights the research he and his associate completed while trying to find evidence of how life evolved on earth and ultimately, how we became us."

Looking at Sam, "Did I get that right?"

Sam smiled and simply nodded in the affirmative.

"Next to him is another distinguished researcher and the Director of the Anthropology Department at the University of Seattle, Professor Donald Reece. Welcome."

Reece responded, "A pleasure to be here."

"To my left are two well-respected individuals who are critical of the research and some of the conclusions Dr. Buckner has drawn. First is Pastor Ian Trumbell of the Second Baptist Church of Charlotte, North Carolina, considered to be the largest megachurch in the US. Welcome to you."

"Thank you for this opportunity."

"Next to him is Father Patrick O'Connor, Director of Apostolic Formation for the Catholic Archdiocese of Boston. Good to see you again, Father."

"As always, a pleasure to see you, Frank."

The moderator turned again to Camera One, and flashing a smile, "Our programme tonight will be split into three segments. In the first, we'll let Professor Buckner give us an overview of his research. Then we'll have our other guests participate in the discussion with arguments, for or against Dr. Buckner's theories. And, as always, you, our viewers, will have the opportunity to wade into the fray by sending us your comments and questions through social media. For now, stay tuned, and we'll be back in sixty seconds, after these commercials."

The camera's on-light went out, and the wide smile on Jones' face faded as well. He turned to Sam and then to the others. "OK, I think that started well. How are you all feeling? Relaxed?"

Each guest smiled and nodded yes. Sam turned to Professor Reece and had a few words, while the other two engaged in their own discussion.

The programme director appeared before them and without saying a word, simply held his right hand up with four fingers extended, then three, two, one and pointed to Jones.

On cue, the wide smile reappeared. "Welcome back. Well, let's get this segment rolling."

Turning to Sam, "Professor Buckner, can you give us an overview of your research and in particular, can you describe the formula you have developed?"

Sam's heart started to beat a little faster, but nothing in his demeanour betrayed his nervousness. On the contrary, perhaps because he was used to speaking before large groups, or because he was confident in his research, he immediately gained control of the situation. "First, let me thank you for inviting me to your programme."

****

In her Watergate apartment, Melinda smiled to herself while watching the TV screen and thinking, that's my man. Go get them.

At the same moment, at a training compound in South Carolina, another was also watching and musing: enjoy your fifteen minutes of fame, buddy. You'll get what you deserve soon enough.

****

Camera One was in for a close-up of Sam.

"I can summarize my hypothesis this way: I believe gravitational fields have a much greater impact on the evolutionary process than we have ever given them credit for. We know the effect of the sun's and the moon's gravity on the tides of our oceans; that's on the macro side. However, what about their effect at the micro level?"

With a bit of a smile on his face, indicating he wasn't serious about what he was about to say, he continued, "Everyone has heard stories about the effect of the full moon on the mood of psychiatric patients and jail inmates. Just ask any nurse or prison guard." It was now the panellists' turn to smile.

"Stories of that nature are interesting and fun to talk about, but they are difficult to quantify. However, what got me thinking about the effect of gravity was the topic of astrology and its rationalizations of the effects which the moon, sun and stars have on human personalities. I thought that its longevity as a belief system required more research.

"That's when it hit me. Astrologists' assertion that the moment of birth determines an individual's nature, seemed too far-fetched for me. I did, though, feel that if there could be a moment when the genetic makeup of an individual could possibly be affected, it would only happen at the moment of conception. And the reason for that is gravitational in nature. So I surmised that astrologists possibly had a point, but that their calculations were nine months off the mark."

Jones jumped in. "So you are saying that I should believe what is in my future, based upon the astrology column in my newspaper?"

"No, no," Sam replied. "I'm not condoning the precepts of astrology. Astrologists propagate long-held beliefs that the position of the planets, sun and stars can affect one's personality and future. I believe *that* is impossible and just wishful thinking. One's personality is more a factor of your life experiences, and your future, of the decisions you make and their repercussions."

Sam looked into the faces of the panel members to see if he could discern any evidence of a positive or negative reaction. At this point, Professor Reece was nodding in agreement while the two religious members were listening stoically.

OK, he thought, just as expected.

"What my research has led me to believe is that gravity has the potential of influencing which of some of the millions of RNA molecules combine with which, or, which turn on or off, changing the genetic codes for blue eyes or brown eyes, blond hair or red hair. Most of the obvious traits would naturally be the result of the genes the child inherits from the parents.

"Nevertheless, geneticists have come to understand that the genes in our DNA are our genetic history, going back to the beginning of life on earth. These genes, remnants of our reptilian, mammalian and our early human links, are not simply dormant, but can be turned on or off, so to speak, and change the direction of our genetic mutation. They would have a tendency to change in roughly the same way over a set period of time, say that during which a strong gravitational object, such as a star, was flying by near our solar system.

"Get enough of these changes in any given species and you have a brand new group of individuals with traits that might allow them to survive more successfully than the previous group. They would then procreate and transfer the new genetic code to their offspring.

"For example, did you know that most humans living today carry anywhere from three to five percent of the genes found in our Neanderthal ancestors?

"My research shows that this whole process takes anywhere from one hundred fifty to two hundred thousand years to produce a new dominant species."

Sam could see this description was not sitting well with Pastor Trumbell.

Jones noticed the same reaction and said, "I'm sure our other panellists would love to jump in, but before they do, could you explain your formula for us? It might better help us understand your assertions."

Sam was happy to get to the less speculative portion of his research. He looked back to the monitors behind him and saw that the formula was up on the screen.

He turned toward the camera once more.

"Right. Let me take the formula and break it down for you. Then I'll get into how we came up with it."

Jones interrupted. "Doctor Buckner," to which Sam quickly responded, "Sam, please."

"OK, Sam. I'm sorry to interrupt, but what role did your partner play in your research?"

"Good question. Doctor Ulfayad was instrumental in my research. Though the basic premise is my own, I could not have completed the research without Jalal. He developed the software program that tracked the celestial bodies that have flown by our solar system in the past, as well as their trajectory and gravitational pull, which then allowed me to correlate the potential mutations in our DNA."

Seeing Jones was apparently satisfied with the answer, he quickly glanced at the few notes he had on his tablet and then continued, "If you look at the formula on the monitors behind us, it reads as follows: 'R' for 'result' equals 'N' over 1000, times the square root of 'M', multiplied by the result of 'T' over 'G', times 'I', times 'F', times 'W'."

Jones couldn't help himself. "Good heavens. Now I remember why I hated mathematics and science in high school," which prompted chuckles from everyone on the set, including Sam.

"Alright then, let me translate the formula for you. 'N' represents the estimated number of any given species at the time of the gravitational event. That is divided by a thousand, in order to calculate the statistically probable number of individuals who would be affected by any genetic mutation."

Sam glanced at Professor Reece and saw a nod of understanding, but when he looked at the other two guests, he could see they were having a hard time following.

"'M' stands for the number of genes in the species. The square root of this number would indicate the potential number of genes which could be impacted by the gravitational pull. I factored in the time passed between the events in one-hundred-thousand-year units, divided by the strength of the pull, multiplied by the number of celestial bodies which were involved.

"The last two items factored in are weighted numbers representing the estimated availability of food and the climatic conditions which would also impact on each species. So when we plugged the numbers into the formula, we found that it not only accounted for the number of new individuals in any given species, but also the timing when they became dominant within that species."

Jones turned to Sam. "When I first looked at the formula, it all seemed like gibberish to me. Now, though, I think I can see, if not fully understand, some of the logic behind your research. Can you summarize for the panel and our viewers, what it all means?"

"With pleasure. We tracked the paths of a number of stars and galaxies which flew close to our solar system in the past. We then compared *when* they were at the closest distance to us, with the known major changes in species on earth, in particular the hominids which led to us.

What we found was an interesting correlation between the two factors. Within one hundred to three hundred thousand years of each encounter, a new hominid species became dominant. Furthermore, the more massive the star, the sooner the shift in the species happened.

"For example, archaeologists recently began finding evidence of hominids controlling fire during the time of Homo erectus, several hundred thousand years after Gliese 710 passed through the Oort Cloud about one and a half million years ago.

"Zeta Leporis flew by about eight hundred and sixty thousand years ago, and Peking Man became one of the dominant species about one hundred sixty thousand years later.

"When Gliese 208 flew by about five hundred thousand years ago, Homo rhodesiensis and cepranensis emerged during the middle of the Paleolithic."

Sam turned from the moderator to look at the panellists. Professor Reece was leaning on the table, listening intently to his explanation. The other two still had that blank look on their faces.

Jones stepped in. "There are definitely a few coincidences in your findings which would seem to describe some possible links concerning human evolution, but what about other species?"

Sam returned his gaze to Jones. "I think the most interesting link, among many others we identified, was the beginning of the age of the dinosaurs. We looked for evidence of similar events at the time of the emergence of these animals. What we discovered was the fact that the Sagittarius Dwarf Elliptical Galaxy collided a couple of times with our Milky Way Galaxy. Ours, being the largest of the two, began cannibalizing the other of millions of its stars. The Sagittarius Galaxy is still passing through our own, but the main arm is now on the other side of our galaxy. Because it takes about two hundred twenty-five million years for our galaxy to make one revolution, it would mean that our solar system was flying through the intersection of the two about one hundred twelve million years ago, or about the time the dinosaurs appeared on earth."

That elicited a stir on the part of Professor Reece and of Jones, who commented, "And so, you believe you have credible proof for your hypothesis?"

"I'm not saying the research has contributed anything new to the world of science, other than to say it has given us proof that much of what we do know about the process of evolution is true. It also gives us answers as to how and why there have been such major evolutionary leaps in our past."

Sam peeked at the two religious panellists and noticed they didn't seem to be impressed. He wasn't looking forward to the next segment of the program. He thought about what he was about to say and decided he needed to be true to himself.

"The purpose of my research wasn't to try to discredit astrology or the notion of divine intervention. My intent was to explain and find proof of just how these major changes in evolution came about, though I sense the two religious members do not share my views. Nonetheless, as a scientist, I have to question all assertions, including the ones that state that there is or isn't divine intervention in human evolution."

There was a definite shift in the body language of the two panellists, and Jones' earpiece chirped with a message from the director: "Let him go on. This is getting good."

Sam continued, "If there is a supernatural entity involved, He, She, or It would have used a formula similar to the one I've described."

Immediately, Pastor Trumbell interjected. "I take offence to you calling God an *It*."

The comment was given a silent nod of approval from Father O'Connor, and the programme director whispered into John's earpiece, "Get ready to jump in if you have to."

Sam quickly responded. "I do apologize if I've offended you or any of the viewers. I didn't mean to. I'm simply saying that one should question or consider the validity of age-old tenets, but that it should be done within sound scientific parameters and not within pre-conceived, unproven assertions. And yet, I have to admit that the obvious fact that these assertions have been around for so many thousands of years also has to be taken into account."

Jones jumped in on cue, being told by the programme director through his earphone to turn to Camera Two for a close-up of himself and to go to commercial. "And on that note, we need to pay for this show. Let's take ninety seconds for our advertisers, and we'll be back with the next segment of our discussion. So, stay with us. You won't regret it."

"And fade!" barked the programme director.

****

Switching the connection from his microphone to Jones' earpiece, he added, "You won't believe the response we've had so far. There are forty-two people on hold on our phone lines, and we've already received seventeen hundred tweets and emails from our listeners. Interestingly, the majority of those from the South are against him, while the bulk from the North approve of his views. It's as if we were fighting the Civil War all over again. Great job."

The moderator turned to the panellists, only to see Sam sitting quietly, while the other three were in a hushed, but heated discussion.

With a smile, Jones said, "Gentlemen, keep some of that for this next part."

The three relaxed somewhat and resumed their positions for what they knew would be their crack at the bat.

Then, looking back at Sam, Jones said below his breath, "You've created quite a stir. Not only do you have them chomping at the bit, but you have the staff working overtime backstage, trying to sort out all the calls and messages from the listeners."

With a chuckle, he added, "Never thought science could be so much fun."

Sam calmly smiled. He looked down to his tablet laying on the table before him and noticed he had received an email. It was from Melinda. "Well done so far. Hot topic and I think it will get hotter yet. This should be interesting. Love."

He had no time to respond. The programme director was back, counting down the seconds.

****

The second segment began as did the first, with Jones staring into the camera, a huge smile pasted on his face.

"And we're back. I know our other panel members have been aching to get in on the discussion. Now's their opportunity."

As he continued, he turned to Professor Reese. "Let me allow you the first word and get your opinion of Dr. Buckner's research."

Sitting up straight and responding in a *professorial* tone, "Well, let me say that I am essentially impressed by the research."

With that, he looked at Sam and pressed on. "I read your study and I did take your formula to task. Several of my colleagues and I spent some time inserting estimated numbers for the various hominid species which led to our own and we found that your formula does allow us to come up with figures which correspond to our best estimates of the number of humans at the beginning of both the Palaeolithic and the Neolithic Age, as well as at the time around the birth of Christ."

Father O'Connor chirped in. "Still, these are only estimates."

"Yes, Father O'Connor, but, it is interesting how these estimates also correspond with the timing of the star flybies. The formula allows us to better map the changes we have seen in the size, shape and abilities of our ancestors. As a social anthropologist, I'm particularly interested in Dr. Buckner's chapter on one of the stars he mentions and its impact on the brain, or more precisely, the frontal lobe, during the Palaeolithic and how human society changed from that time on."

Turning to Sam, the professor asked him, "Doctor, it is your contention, isn't it, that the shift in the size of the human brain happened shortly after the time Gliese 208 flew by, expanding our ability to reason and think, and therefore, making us what we call, human?"

Sam thought for a second. "Well, yes and no. The *human* in us was with us long before that. It's that it has been changing and is continuing to evolve because of the *jump starts* the stars provided. It's difficult to condense the whole field of evolution in a few minutes, but in essence, yes, that is what I'm saying."

Jones jumped in at that moment. "Father O'Connor, what is your take on this theory?"

O'Connor sat back slightly, crossed his arms over his oversize belly, as if to pontificate. "Well, the Catholic Church has accepted the concept of evolution."

The look he got from Pastor Trumbell was not lost on the priest. He thought, O'Connor was supposed to back me up?

The priest continued, "Yet, nothing in what Dr. Buckner has said could not be explained through divine intervention. We believe it is the hand of God which has guided the universe to allow us to become man. If his formula explains *how* this came about, so be it. We feel *why* it happened is more important. God has a plan for us and is making it happen, using the universe to do His bidding . . . "

Trumbell was thinking this was getting better. Not what he wanted to hear, but better.

O'Connor continued, " . . . so, the Bible speaks of Adam and Eve as the first man and the first woman. There had to be a first at some time or another. Who is to say that the first true human wasn't created by God during the period in time the professor seems to be so taken with. No offence, sir."

Reese looked at him and responded with, "None taken."

"We believe what makes man special is his soul. When Dr. Buckner describes the dramatic change in these creatures that were to become human, we say it was God who infused Adam and Eve with a soul. That is why we are who we are."

Sam had been listening patiently, thinking this wasn't as rough an attack as he had expected.

In spite of that, he needed to add one comment.

"We may actually be saying the same things, using different words. If the hand of God is involved, I believe it would be called Time."

Father O'Connor looked pensive.

"That is an interesting comment. One I'll have to consider."

Sam was somewhat surprised by the remark. He may have dodged the bullet, but there was still the pastor.

Jones tried to intervene to pull the views together. "So, if I understand correctly, the Catholic Church does not have a problem with Dr. Buckner's findings?"

"Not with the concept of a formula which would explain general changes to animals and plants. As for us, we believe God waited patiently until the desired time in his plan to make us human."

Jones then turned to Pastor Trumbell. "Pastor, I would imagine you are not as forgiving as your Catholic counterpart?"

Trumbell had prepared himself for this moment. He felt he needed to redirect the conversation to expose Sam as a pawn, unknowingly leading people down the garden path.

He smiled and turned to face Camera Two whose light had just come on.

"I've been sitting here, listening intently to the discussion, and it struck me that almost everyone has missed the point. I would agree with my esteemed religious friend concerning the fact of divine intervention. But, I think he has not gone far enough. I believe in an almighty God, one who does not have to follow rules or formulas to do what He pleases. Divine intervention, as described by Father O'Connor, would lead one to think God has weaknesses. He has none!

"The Bible is clear on this matter. The earth, the heavens and man were created in six days, and He rested on the seventh. As learned as are Dr. Buckner and Professor Reece, they fail to see the truth. All the data they have pertaining to evolution is but an illusion. God created it all during that week but made it look like it took millions of years in order to make nonbelievers *think* they can understand His ways."

Off to the side, the programme director could see the astonished look on Jones' face. "Get a grip, man. The camera will be on you in a moment."

Both Sam and Professor Reece, also unseen by the viewers, had the same thought of having just been propelled back in time a hundred years.

The camera was back on Jones. Without skipping a beat, he picked up the topic and questioned the pastor.

"Pastor Trumbell, assuming the Bible is right, how old are the universe and the world?"

Trumbell smiled with an air of confidence. "Well, as a matter of fact, Bishop James Ussher published an analysis back in 1650. He followed all the lineages found in the Bible and was able to calculate the date of creation. Scholars and believers have used his findings ever since."

"And what is this date?" pursued Jones.

"His calculations led him to conclude the earth was created on the night before Sunday, October 23rd, 4004 B.C."

Looking now at Sam, he asked, "Doctor Buckner, is it impossible that God could make things like rocks *look* older than what they are?"

Sam had not seen this whole line of questioning coming. And yet, he didn't hesitate to respond.

"Pastor Trumbell, if I were a believer in the Bible, I could easily accept your premise. However, I find it difficult to put all my faith in just one book."

Trumbell felt he had Sam in a corner. "Could you elaborate for us?"

Catching himself after that question, he turned to the host and said with a meek smile, "I apologize for taking over your job as moderator."

Jones shrugged it off, but looked at Sam and added, "Sam, *could* you elaborate?"

Sam turned toward the pastor. "I consider the Bible, both the Old Testament and the New, to be the story of the Jewish people: their history book, per se. I also think it needs to be read and interpreted through their eyes, considering what they knew and how they lived, not through our eyes or from our perspective.

"Still, as a scientist, I need to rely on quantifiable evidence."

Trumbell stepped in. "But . . . "

"Yes, yes, I know," continued Sam, "you feel that evidence is not needed, or that it only leads to error. I find all the scientific and archaeological evidence refuting this approach to be overwhelmingly abundant."

Sam felt the direction this discussion was taking was leading everyone away from the night's topic, his research. So he took the offensive.

"Pastor, it is my understanding that you believe the Bible was divinely inspired?"

"Yes, that is true. It is as if God Himself put the words to paper."

"And, if I am correct, there are many versions of the Bible, are there not?"

Father O'Connor's eyes grew large as he realized where this was leading. But, he kept quiet.

"Well, yes, there are about seven major versions and a number of minor ones."

Sam knew his next line would be inflammatory, but he was willing to take the heat.

"If that is the case, can you tell me how God could be wrong so many times?"

The pastor's demeanour stiffened, and he was about to lash back. He saw the camera with the light on was pointed at him and he caught himself.

"Doctor Buckner, in some circles, that could be considered blasphemous. I will only say that the differences in the versions of the Bible are due to *human* misinterpretations."

Wanting to move away from this line of thought, he asked Jones, "May I quiz the doctor on another topic his research has raised, one which makes me question the value of his research?"

Jones had been listening to the programme director telling him, through the earpiece, that they were having problems. The number of emails and tweets coming in had gone off the charts and, along with the over 300 telephone calls on hold, they had crashed the server. They would have to ad lib the final section of the show.

Unfazed, Jones responded, "By all means. Is that OK, Doctor?"

"That's what we're here for."

Smiling once more, Trumbell tried a more subdued approach.

"In one of the sections of your book, you indicate that we should not be calling ourselves Homo sapiens, but rather Homo symbolicus. You allude to the fact that we are primarily symbolic creatures and that this is why we have religion and have created gods. You infer that we are evolving towards a time when we will be more thinking creatures than symbolic ones in nature. Is this correct?"

"In essence, that is what I've concluded. You've summarized my findings well."

"You, therefore, are saying that God is an invention on our part and that He does not exist. Do you not believe in religion? In God?"

This train of questioning peaked everyone's attention and Sam knew he needed to be careful.

"I'll try to be as succinct as possible answering you."

He took a moment.

Back in her apartment, Melinda thought, don't panic. You knew this question would come up. Be yourself.

"Let me tackle the first question. Do I believe in religion? As a vehicle to educate people in how to live our lives, religions have been a great benefit to mankind. Morality, on one hand, is a necessary principle: Laws and how our society works are based on it. I do find, however, that religions are, in general, exclusive and not inclusive. By that, I mean, they tend to differentiate *us* from *them*. If one does not believe in the religion's precepts to a tee, he or she is shunned, excluded or becomes the enemy. Religions tend to stifle questioning, which is the core of science."

Father O'Connor stepped into the fray. "But can that not be a good thing: To lead the flock toward the truth?"

"I'm sorry, Father, but if it wasn't for man's need to question, where would we be? Back in the Inquisition?"

That stung the priest, but he knew it was all too true and decided to let the pastor take the rest of the heat.

"As for my believing or not in God . . . "

The pastor leaned over the table onto his elbows, waiting intently for the answer. He knew that Sam's response would show him not to be a man of God and one none of his parishioners nor the students in religious colleges across the country should follow.

" . . . I came to science for much the same reasons I believe both yourself and Father O'Connor came to religion: To find the truth. The difference is that you have found your answers and I am still searching. You ask the *why* questions and I ask the *how* questions, in an effort to debunk or support the *whys*.

"Do I believe in God? I can say that I don't believe in the white-bearded God painted on the ceiling of the Sistine Chapel. On the other hand, I do think that there could be something there. I'm not saying God or gods, but something we haven't been able to define scientifically yet.

"I can't completely disregard the thousands of years' tradition of a belief in God. If and when we discover how the universe works, we might have a firm definition.

"I simply want the right to question and search for answers, without being labelled as sinister."

"Great! On that note, let's take a break," piped in Jones.

The camera lights once again died and Jones turned to the panel. "I need to tell you that we have run into a technical glitch. Our servers have crashed, and we won't be able to have live comments from our viewers. But, I'm told we can take a few of the emails and tweets we've received and have you comment on them. Then, I'll have you summarize your position on the subject. Sorry, gentlemen, but we have to roll with the punches and fill in our time. Are you OK with this?"

Each member of the panel nodded yes. Sam, in particular, was a bit relieved that he might not have to address 'live' people.

Pastor Trumbell smiled to himself, thinking their strategy to mobilize the troops might have worked. Yet, he was disappointed that Sam would not have to deal directly with some of his troops.

The programme director ran over to the moderator and handed him four of the several thousand emails and tweets they had received before the system crashed.

"Work with these and get the panel to make their final comments."

Jones looked briefly at the responses from the viewers and nodded to the director.

" . . . two, and one. The light on Camera One came on again.

"Welcome back. Well, this certainly has been one of the most controversial programmes we've had. The response has been overwhelming. So much so that our servers have crashed and we are unable to run our interactive segment. We did manage to salvage a few of your thoughts on the subject and we'll read them out for you and for our panel to comment on."

Turning to the group, he took the first email. "This is from George in Orlando, Florida. 'How are such ideas even allowed to get printed? How the hell can a star, passing by some million miles away affect us. Sounds like some left-wing pinko plot.'"

Sam chuckled at the comment.

"Well, this viewer certainly doesn't mince his words," responded Jones. "Any comment?"

Sam signalled he did. "I can understand how someone might doubt that something so far away could possibly affect us. But really, you only need to consider the gravitational pull of the moon on the oceans. As a child I often sat watching the tidal bore racing up the Petitcodiac River in New Brunswick, past our house. And yet the moon is almost three hundred and eighty-five thousand kilometres, or two hundred and eighty-five thousand miles away. Now consider a star which is a million times the size of the moon, or more, and you can better understand how it could impact on the earth, even if it was five hundred million kilometres away."

"Point well taken, Sam."

Looking at the others, and seeing no one intended to add to Sam's comment, he went to the second message.

"The next message is an interesting one. 'If Doctor Buckner is correct, and we are not Homo sapiens, how is it that we are capable of discussing his concept rationally? Isn't that what it means to be the *thinking man*?'"

"Professor Reece. Would you be willing to tackle this question?"

"Certainly. If I've understood Doctor Buckner's research correctly, he doesn't make the assertion that we humans cannot think or reason . . . "

Sam was nodding his head in agreement.

" . . . We all have the ability to govern our lives rationally. As a matter of fact, Homo sapiens translated literally from the Latin means 'wise man'. I think what the doctor is saying is that almost everything we do is either generated from symbolism or is translated symbolically. How we dress, how wear our hair, the hats we don, our languages, our art, etc."

"Sam, would you have anything to add?"

"Professor Reece is correct. We have a hard time divorcing ourselves from the images in our minds. Our perception of the world comes to us through our senses and history has shown that we tend to look for the obvious solutions to our problems. When we can't explain something, we also tend to invent an answer."

The pastor stepped in. "Is that why you jumped to your conclusions and questioned religion and God?"

Sam calmly replied, "I think you are correct," catching the pastor by surprise.

"In order to find answers, one must first ask questions and then do one's research. The answers are most often, unexpected."

Jones purposely took the third email and read it. "You might like this one. 'About time someone tells it like it is. Human interaction makes so much more sense when you look at it from the symbolic point of view and not the rational. History is understandable when you consider *what* truly motivates us.'"

Professor Reece put his finger up to get Jones' attention. "Trying to remain impartial on the matter, I put the question of the doctor's research to several of my colleagues, in a variety of disciplines. I was stunned to hear that several of them were rethinking some of the premises they had considered immutable and reconsidering them. Obviously, in the areas of social and physical anthropology, we need to rethink some of our conclusions. But, one or two psychologist friends of mine have told me that Yung's and Freud's theories could possibly be affected by this research. Another in marketing indicated that Doctor Buckner's conclusions reinforce the basis of all marketing: appealing to the *image* of the self as opposed to the rational."

"Fascinating," replied Jones.

Turning to the camera, he began to wrap up the show.

"We have about two minutes left in the show and I would like to get a final word from each of the panellists. Why don't we start with Father O'Connor.

"Father, you have been rather quiet during the last segment. Is there anything you would like to add?"

The priest smiled. "Well, I would simply repeat what I stated before, that the Church doesn't dispute the concept of evolution. Albeit, I would hope and pray that the viewers consider the possibility, what we consider fact, that there is a divine hand at work."

Jones turned to Professor Reece. "Professor, what about you?"

"I can't state that I'm in complete agreement with Doctor Buckner's conclusions, yet. The hard part will be the research to prove him right or wrong. But, it is promising."

"Thank you, Professor. Pastor Trumbell, your turn."

The pastor had taken quite the intellectual beating during this debate. He knew in his heart that he would eventually be proven right and he decided to take the high road.

"Firstly, I want to congratulate Doctor Buckner. His research has demonstrated how great God is and just how wonderful His creation is. Even the Doctor has to agree that the chances of us being who we are, are inestimably slim without the hand of God behind it. I will pray for him as well, hoping he will come to the same conclusion a large part of the citizens of these United States have reached, that the universe was created as is, for us."

Jones next looked at Sam. "You have the last word."

"I know a large segment of the show was devoted to some of the conclusions I have drawn, somewhat overshadowing the actual research. So be it.

"In deference to Father O'Connor and Pastor Trumbell, I too am searching for the answers to the questions around God, why are we here, or where do we go after death. I truly feel there is *something* there. By the same token, I'm not comfortable with the answers religions have given us, and the scientist in me is urging me to search on. Though I may not agree with the theology of religions, I have to admit, I find Christian morality and its premise, that we should love and help one another, as being unique and superior to others. I think it is a perfect example of the thinking of Homo sapiens; the philosophy of *an eye for an eye* would, I believe, be more that of Homo symbolicus."

For the first time that evening, both Father O'Connor's and Pastor Trumbell's holier-than-thou look seemed to soften.

"Now, I welcome the criticism of my research, and I see it as a healthy dialogue. Science is based on the premise that a theory needs to be questioned, over and over again, until it is shown to be unassailable or wrong. The research I've done is now at the mercy of others, to be poked and prodded. Thank you for the opportunity to begin that process."

With that, Jones again pasted that familiar smile on his face. Staring into the camera, he concluded. "There you have it. I would like to thank all of our panellists for their thoughts and opinions on the subject. We do apologize to our viewers for the technical problems we encountered. But, even that is proof of how much the topic was important to you and that so many of you wanted to express their opinions.

"Next week, another great show. We'll have Tom Hanks on to discuss his new movie and the charities he supports. Have a good night."

Part Two

Chapter 9

The door opened and in stepped *Hank* Evans. Sitting at the main console in the thirty-one-foot Classic Airstream trailer, George Harris, *Buzz* , a name he got from his flattop crew-cut hairstyle, turned in his swivel chair to see who was coming in.

"About time. Where have you been?"

Evans grunted as he heaved his duffle bag onto the floor, off to the left, and removed his camouflage jacket, which he threw on the dining table, a few feet further.

"Philly. I had some business to attend to."

Pulling a second chair and sitting next to Buzz, he stretched out and put his hands behind his head. He looked at a few of the twenty monitors spread into an L-shaped array on the corner walls of the trailer.

"So, how is he holding out?"

Buzz pulled out a clipboard and flipped through a few of the sheets attached to it. "According to the reports, Thornton has been solid for thirty hours now. He's eliminated six of the ten sent out after him. That's one guy who can hold his piss."

A devilish smile came to Hank's mouth. "He'll prove himself when he's up there another six hours. That's when he'll hit the *wall*."

The wall was a psychological and physical limit most snipers hit when on assignment. On occasion, a sharpshooter would need to position himself, sometimes in awkward places, for a prolonged period of time, in order to wait for his target to come to him. Only the best and most disciplined operative could last longer, before having to abandon his mission or feel the need to move. In some cases, this had deadly results for the shooter.

Evans had proven himself in Iraq, having sat basically motionless for forty-five hours, before seeing and dispatching his target, a high-ranking Al-Qaeda officer.

He received the Distinguished Service Cross for his actions. Though he wasn't in the grip of combat, his *kill* had forestalled the insurgents' offensive for months and saved countless American lives. Although his role in the war was a lonely and unglamorous one, the military was aware of its importance.

While in Iraq, he had rubbed shoulders with the then, Blackwater Worldwide *consultants* and had gotten to know them well. These mercenaries were contracted to protect American diplomatic personnel on the ground, and though they rarely mixed with the regular troops, because of his specialty, they saw Hank as different: almost as one of them.

The US administration had decided that the regular troops were needed for the active campaign against the insurgents. By hiring security companies like Blackwater, they could more discreetly *fudge* the official numbers of troops in Iraq, then at some one hundred thousand and forty.

The estimated range of mercenaries varied from twenty to thirty thousand, each bringing about four hundred forty thousand dollars to the coffers of the company, some six times the cost of a regular soldier.

Yet, because they had virtual immunity from prosecution and the ability to perform certain questionable duties which were forbidden to regular soldiers, they were considered invaluable to the US mission.

The dollars involved had struck Harold Evans as almost obscene, and he wanted to get his share of it.

When he returned to the US, he acquired a plot of land in South Carolina, about forty miles southwest of

Charlotte. He went about converting the twenty-one hundred hectare property to match closely the Blackwater Training Centre in North Carolina, in order to allow him to give whoever needed specialized training in client protection, hand-to-hand combat, and small-group search-and-destroy missions, the skills they needed and the required skills he wanted to instil in those whose names he would add to his database of mercenaries.

Still, his specialty rested in the sharpshooter training he provided. To this end, he reserved a major portion of the land which he divided up into three zones.

The first was a mock cityscape, the second a savannah-like area and the third, a forested area. Each setting required different strategies and a variety of skill sets the shooter would need to master. This would allow Evans to send his graduates to almost any combat zone in the world.

He also leased a plot of land, deep in the Smoky Mountain area not far away, in order to *harden* his clients. He would put them through a rigorous survival regime, using the terrain to challenge them to the breaking point. The deep ravines and almost vertical hills provided the ideal venue to prepare those who would be going to the mountainous areas of Afghanistan or Pakistan.

To help him in his enterprise, Hank made a point of hiring only those veterans whose experience best suited the various battle scenarios in his programme.

Buzz was such a man. He had fought in Iraq and then in Afghanistan, for a total of six tours of duty, accumulating an impressive twenty-nine kills in Iraq alone, second only to Hank's forty-two.

There were another sixteen men Evans had hired to help him deliver the training his clients needed. The issue of loyalty was paramount, each man willing to die for the other if need be. Although the salary was amazing, they did the work, not for the money, but for the *cause*.

Fiercely patriotic, they believed they had been given another chance to serve their country by producing the best *contractor* money could rent. They felt they were making a difference in the world and didn't mind the anonymous nature of their work.

Evans was intently watching a few of the monitors before him, switching some of the two hundred remote cameras on and off, in order to see the different areas on his property. He could manoeuvre them to follow the movements of the clients during their military-style exercises.

One camera was trained on a particular tree, which one would have to zero in on and watch intently in order to see Thorton's camouflaged body.

"He's done a nice job at hiding himself," commented Hank.

Then, switching to two other cameras, he followed the movements of a couple of trainees trying to find their prey.

"Are they Butler and Jones?" Hank asked.

Looking over to the monitor Evans was pointing at, Buzz responded, "The one to the left is Butler and the other is Lornes. Look up at monitors 6 and 8 and you'll see Jones on the north side of Thornton and Lewis on the south side. It looks like they might have an idea where Thornton is and are trying to outflank him. Even so, judging by their movements, they still don't have a precise location. By the way, Lewis tripped and fell on his chest laser sensor and rendered it inoperative. So if Thornton is going to take him out, it will have to be a head shot."

"We'll just have to add the cost of the sensor to his bill," was all Evans said, as he continued to manipulate the cameras to get a better idea of what was happening out in the field.

Harris inadvertently looked over to his left. The two monitors identified as nineteen and twenty were tuned to CNN and Fox News respectively.

His eye caught the *Breaking news* banner on the muted CNN screen. It wouldn't have meant anything to him, but the headline stated that a shooting had taken place in Philadelphia. He leaned over to raise the volume a little.

There, on the screen, was a female reporter, standing in the frigid cold, her wind-blown hair in disarray. As hard as she tried to behave in a professional manner, it was evident she was having some difficulty keeping her teeth from chattering while talking.

Behind her, corralled in police yellow perimeter tape, were two squad cars and an ambulance, all flashing their emergency lights. From the reporter's vantage point across the street, the cameraman could show her as well as the action taking place in the entrance to the building at the same time.

"Eleanor Learn here, for CNN. Behind me is the building at 510 Walnut Street in Philadelphia, which houses BDP International and the American Board of Internal Medicine, as well as luxury apartments on the upper floors.

"Our sources have told us that a man has been shot in one of the condominiums on the tenth floor of this building. He has been identified as Lloyd Crawly, fifty-two years of age and the police believe he was murdered twenty-four hours ago. He was found this morning by his cleaning lady.

"Crawly was a well-known professor and chair of the History department at Philadelphia University. He was also recognized as one of America's preeminent authors, having written several highly acclaimed biographies of the early US presidents.

"He had, nevertheless, created some controversy of late, with the revision of his biography of George

Washington, saying he had found it necessary to revisit his original premise concerning the President's military accomplishments. Further, Crawly said he needed to look at all the founding fathers through a new pair of glasses, as he termed it, in order to better understand their lives and what had motivated them."

The cameraman gestured for her to turn around. As she did, the coroner's staff was seen coming out of the foyer, with a wheeled stretcher carrying a black body bag.

Learn continued without missing a beat, "As you can see, the body is now being removed and will be taken for an autopsy, due to the nature of his death."

Turning back toward the camera, Learn said, "The police have labelled the death a murder, in that he died from a single bullet to the head from the outside, while he was sitting at his dining room table. If we look up at the windows just above us, I believe we can see what is thought to be the hole created by the bullet that killed him."

The image on the television set panned up to the tenth floor and zoomed in on one of the windows which sheathed the building. Clearly visible was a small hole, with a few cracks radiating from the centre, out toward the edges of the window.

"Luckily, the glass did not shatter and fall onto unsuspecting people below."

The camera returned to the reporter.

"The police spokesperson did admit that they were investigating two possible places the shooter might have been, in order to take the shot that killed Professor Crawly. Based on the trajectory the bullet had to follow to reach its target, the shooter would have had to be directly in front of the building. That would put them either on the roof of the Hall of Independence, behind where we are standing . . . " The cameraman pivoted to show the rear to the building, some hundred metres away " . . . or on the roof of the

National Constitution Center, which is on the far side of Independence Mall, almost a half mile away."

Back in the trailer, Buzz quietly turned to look at Hank, who was intent on watching the other monitors, ignoring the CNN report. Shaking his head slightly and smiling to himself, he returned to the newscast.

"Based on the police's preliminary investigations, if, and only if, the shooter could have gotten by security in the Hall of Independence and reached the roof without being seen with his rifle, the upward angle of the trajectory would have been too sharp to be able to hit the professor sitting at his table. As for a shot being taken from the roof of the Constitution Center, they agree the trajectory would be correct, but they find it difficult to understand how such a shot could have been carried out. They indicate that only a handful of sharpshooters in the world . . . "

Hank turned to Buzz and snapped, "Do you mind turning that off? I can't concentrate here."

Harris turned the volume down, leaving the monitor on, but muted.

Again shaking his head in disbelief, he simply uttered, "Just saying, man, some shot."

Chapter 10

Later that day, Hank Evans was driving his RAM 3500 Laramie Longhorn 4 x 4 Dodge pickup, up the long driveway to the baronial mansion he knew as home.

He found the house pretentious, but it served its purpose when he would invite potential clients to meet with him to close a contract.

Many of the people in need of his services did so because they wanted someone who could understand and appreciate their status in the world. Some of the individuals who had hired Hank's mercenaries were from Saudi Arabia, Switzerland, Paris and even Washington.

These contracts were but icing on the cake. His main sources of income were the military contracts he had acquired, just as he had hoped. With the US officially withdrawing from Afghanistan, huge opportunities opened up for his consultants to be hired to bolster the Afghani army and police forces.

He parked his truck to the side of the house, not to detract from the *scottishness* of the home.

He walked around to the main entrance and simply walked in.

The door was not locked. Indeed, that wasn't necessary since the grounds and buildings were protected by a state-of-the-art security system Hank had installed, over the objections of his adoptive father. Three full-time guards looked after the system on a 24/7 basis, with his *people* rotating on a monthly schedule. Hank thought it was a small price to pay for everything his adoptive father had done for him.

Dropping his bag next to the table in the centre of the foyer, he peeked into the parlour, then the den, to see if Oliver Doyle was there. He wasn't.

So, Hank walked to the rear of the house, over to Doyle's personal wing and knocked on the private living room door.

He heard his dad's voice call out, "Come in."

"Hi, Dad. I'm back for the weekend. How are you doing?"

Oliver Doyle deposited the glass of cognac he had been nursing and put down the business report he had been perusing.

He got up from his recliner and walked over to Hank and hugged him tightly.

"It's good to see you, Harold."

Doyle could not bring himself to call him Hank, thinking it somewhat beneath his position to resort to slang. That being said, he didn't mind being called *Dad* by Hank and was equally comfortable being called *Father* by John: Two different sons, both of whom made him proud.

Oliver pointed to the armchair just opposite his recliner and asked if he would like a cognac.

"No, thanks. If you have a beer handy though, that would do the job."

Oliver walked over to the walnut wall unit in his library and pulled on the panel door, exposing a tall narrow glass door, behind which were stored some of the bottles of his wine collection. At the bottom, in a separately cooled compartment, were a variety of beers from around the world.

"How about a Grolsch?"

"No, right now, I think I'd prefer a Bud."

Reaching to the rear of the refrigerator, Oliver pulled out a can of Budweiser, handed it to Hank and returned to his chair.

"So, how are the contracts coming?"

Hank beamed. "I have three proposals in the fire. "One for the President of South Africa. It seems people are catching onto his incompetence, and he's decided he needs to beef up his security with people he can trust.

"Then, things are heating up again in Lima, and I've been asked to provide some thirty trainers for their counterinsurgency programme."

Oliver stepped in. "And, the third?"

"That one is here at home. With the elections some eight months away, looks like Washington wants to increase the protection around the congressmen and senators up for reelection."

Doyle smiled slyly. "Glad you're in the mix on that one. I've spoken to some of my contacts, and I think I can tell you that you won't have a problem getting it."

"That's good to hear. I appreciate the support."

Very little of what happened in Washington was unknown by Doyle and he shared this information, firmly believing that knowledge was power.

His contributions to church leaders and his political cronies helped as well. Few people were better connected than Oliver Doyle.

Taking a swig of his Bud, Hank shifted in his chair. "To change the subject, how's John doing with the bitch?"

The comment didn't faze Doyle, although he seemed somewhat surprised. "Funny you should mention that. There seems to have been quite a change in John's opinion of the young lady."

Now it was Hank's turn to look stunned. "I thought he saw her as the devil incarnate. What happened to change his mind?"

"It would seem he did very well in a mission over in Lebanon. He was *volunteered for* by Gordon. At first, he thought he was being set up, but it seems she gave him the lead in the operation and he pulled it off. Not that I'm surprised at his ability, but she even got him a commendation for his efforts.

"Now, considering that John is still minding his p's and q's, he sees a little more merit in Miss Gordon."

"What about her professor friend?"

"Oh, his is a different story," continued Doyle. "He's still on his lecture tour, and in spite of our efforts to discredit him, his theories are proving to be a burr in our sides."

Hank muttered beneath his breath, "I know what you mean."

"What was that?" asked Doyle.

"Nothing. Just thinking out loud.

"So, when's John coming home?"

Doyle checked his watch. "He should be here within the hour. Supper will be at six-thirty. We can continue the discussion then. For the moment, if you'll excuse me, I have to respond to some of the questions which arose in the report I was reading when you came in."

Hank rose from his chair, finished the last sip of his beer and walked toward the door. But, then, he turned briefly to his dad.

"That's just fine. It'll give me a chance to talk to John about his problems over another beer."

He winked and then left the room.

Walking back toward the foyer to get his bag, he thought that he might have to do something about this intellectual pariah and the trouble he was stirring up. Perhaps he should be dealing with the *source* rather than the *effect* of Buckner's dangerous ideas.

Chapter 11

It was about ten o'clock in the evening, and Sam was sitting in bed in his Toronto condo, PJ's on, propped up against his pillows. He had poured himself a rum and Coke which he had set on his night stand and was holding his laptop.

On his screen was Melinda, in a similar position, in her apartment at the Watergate Hotel in Washington, but she, with a glass of white Burgundy next to her. The two had been on a Skype call for about half an hour at this point.

Every evening, when their schedules allowed it, they would spend hours talking about anything and everything. The distance apart was more bearable when they could at least see each other. Tonight's discussion was on the topic of psychics and mediums.

"You believe in them, right?"

Melinda knew Sam was up to something. "Yes, I do. I think they can communicate with the departed. There is so much proof. I gather you don't believe they can."

"Yes, and no," was Sam's answer.

He enjoyed the intellectual sparring and the bantering with Melinda. She was so much more conservative and traditional in her thinking than he, remaining well grounded in plain common sense.

He loved to play the devil's advocate in order to get a rise out of her. More often than not, however, she was quick enough to pick up on his attempt and direct it right back to him.

What he liked most, though, was the fact that on the more serious topics, she listened and was open to new ideas. She would give her opinion, never judging or disparaging his points of view.

She preferred the *why* and *what* questions in life, possibly because of her religious upbringing in the South or the nature of her job; regardless, she always searched for motives or reasons for things or people to be as they were.

On the other hand, she loved their discussions, because Sam brought so much knowledge to the table. His ability to dissect and analyse issues and to identify the flaws in the *obvious*, never ceased to jolt her into seeing things differently. She understood that Sam, being the scientist he was, was more comfortable with the *how* questions: how things worked or how they came to be.

Melinda also understood that both were searching for answers to life's questions, though both were coming at them from different directions.

It was like Sam had said to her once: each of them, in turn, played the role of *thesis* and *antithesis,* and the result of their discussions was the *synthesis.* As dry as that had sounded, Melinda was amused by the concept. So like him, she thought, to have come up with it.

"OK, so how would you explain *how* they do it?" exclaimed Melinda.

"I can't. Or, not with any certainty," Sam responded. "There have been so many people in the past, claiming to be able to speak with the dead. Many were proven to be con artists, researching their target's life story or simply asking very general questions to see which responses they could pursue."

"Well, how do you explain the likes of John what's-his-name, or that medium in Long Island?"

"You've got me there. I know who you mean. They are good!"

Melinda smiled as she felt she had cornered Sam, unable as he was to give her an answer. "The one in Long Island can simply walk into a grocery store, meet some stranger at the meat counter and pretty much tell her life's story. You have to admit that's eerie."

"Yup! It makes you wonder, alright. At any rate, assuming they are the *real McCoy*, and I'm not saying they aren't, then there has to be a way they are able to do it. Either they are really communicating with the dead spirit of the person they are talking about, or they are tapping into the mind of the person they are talking to."

With a skeptical look, Melinda pressed him. "OK, mister smarty-pants. Lay it on me."

"Where the first is concerned, I have no clue whatsoever how it could be possible, but I can explain how the second might be.

"Do you know how a radio or television works?"

"Sure. You take the remote and press the ON button, and it works," Melinda said sarcastically.

"Right. You're funny," Sam quipped back.

"OK, here we go. In a radio station, sound waves from a person travel into a microphone, which turns them into signals that are transmitted as electromagnetic waves over the air. The antenna on your radio then *cuts* the wave, in turn producing an electric current which is the mirror image of the wave. This current is then *tuned* by the radio and sent to the magnets in the speakers to reproduce the sound waves that were originally sent out at the station."

"I follow you so far, but how does that explain psychics or mediums?"

"Well," continued Sam, "your brain is much like the radio station. It's composed of billions of neurons, which are nothing more than wires through which your thoughts travel as electric signals. Around these wires are the electromagnetic waves which mirror exactly the current inside the neuron. Now, these waves don't just stay there. They too, travel outward.

"They can escape the confines of your body and can be intercepted by someone else's neurons, reproducing the electric current that was part of your thoughts."

Melinda responded hesitantly, "You're kidding, aren't you? Is that possible? So the words are transmitted in that way?"

"There's no reason why the principle of Faraday's law of induction could not work in the body, but I doubt actual words would be transmitted."

"Why do you say that?"

"Well, have you ever been in church and in a daze, absent-mindedly staring at the back of someone's head, and have that person turn around to look right at you?"

"Yes, I have. Just coincidence, isn't it?"

"Possibly, but have you ever listened to how the mediums or psychics describe things? They use words like *see*, or *feel*, or *sense* to describe images or impressions which represent something to them. All of these are at a lower level of communication. Forming words requires time and processing, while emotions are immediate."

In a moment of realization, Melinda commented, "You're right. Now that I think back, that's how they describe it. Even so, what about the spirit they say they are communicating with?"

"Well, either they are simply sensing the images from the person they are reading, or they are actually communicating with the thoughts and emotions of the dead person."

"OK, so how do we *tune* into the other person's thoughts?"

"That's the beauty of the human body. We all have the same DNA, even though our genes might be combined slightly differently. Our bodies are naturally tuned to the correct frequency. Some of us might be more sensitive to these radio or thought waves."

Melinda chuckled. She took a quick peek at her alarm clock. "Wow, do you know what time it is?"

"No."

"It's eleven and I have a seven a.m. meeting. Sorry, sweetheart. I have to crash now."

"That's OK," sighed Sam.

"Where are you off to next?"

Sam thought a second. "I'll be at Cal Tech on Monday of next week. So, it gives me a week here at U of T. I think I need to remind them I'm still alive, or they'll forget me. I plan on flying to Washington to see you the Tuesday following my stint in Pasadena. How's your schedule?"

"Looks good so far. We can firm things up tomorrow.

"Good night, babe. Love you." Melinda put a finger to her lips and placed it on Sam's image on the screen.

"Love you too. Get some sleep, and I'll talk to you tomorrow. Love."

Chapter 12

Melinda had arrived at the office early to prepare for the seven a.m. meeting she had called. She invited the directors of the five departments for which she was responsible: Cyber Infrastructure and Science, Production Management, Current Intelligence, Border Security and Homeland Counter terrorism. In addition, she had also invited the bureau chiefs from fifteen countries in the Middle East, Africa and the Orient. She had also asked John Doyle to sit in on the meeting.

Individual reports which troubled her were coming into Homeland Security. A few red flags had gone up and she wanted to either confirm her suspicions or put them to rest. If she was right, then something was indeed brewing, something which could have an impact not only on the US, but also on the rest of the world.

The meeting was being held in a large, windowless, soundproof room on the second floor, in the centre of the building: Homeland Security's equivalent to the White House's War Room.

Seated around an oblong-shaped table, all the participants were busy going through the documents Melinda had provided them in folders stamped *Top Secret*.

As she took the Chair's position in the middle and looked around, it dawned on her that she was the only female in the room: She had penetrated the old boys' club. She took pride in that, but knew it only put added pressure on her to work harder and succeed more often than her counterparts.

She began the meeting thanking everyone for coming and introducing each of the department heads to the bureau chiefs.

"Gentlemen, Homeland Security has recently seen a rise in the *chatter* from various terrorist groups around the world."

Looking at each of the bureau chiefs in turn, she continued, "I've been reviewing the reports you have all sent in to the office. My staff has analysed them, and we've been noticing trends that we feel show signs of a shift in their operations, suggesting that something new is happening."

Turning to Agent Darwin, Bureau Chief in Jakarta, Indonesia, "Could you summarize the conclusions you have included in your last report?"

"My pleasure, Madame Deputy."

Looking at the folder with all the reports, he began, "If you look at my report, Appendix E, pages thirty to thirty-two, I've listed all the issues our office has identified are happening in Indonesia and the surrounding area."

There was a flurry of pages being turned all around the table.

"As you are aware, the most dangerous period in Indonesia seems to have been in the early part of the millenium. Separatist groups such as Darul Islam in Indonesia, Fretlin in East Timor, Gerakan Aceh Merdeka and the al Qaeda affiliate, Jemaah Islamiyah, all were highly active and targeting Western hot spots, up to about 2010. The worst attack was in 2002 in Bali, when two hundred and two people were killed by Jemaah Islamiyah.

"Since then, the number of attacks has diminished and they now seem to target mainly government institutions, such as small police outposts. Indonesian officials credit the increased vigilance of their police force for the decrease in terrorist activity."

Melinda interrupted. "Do you agree with these experts?"

Darwin shook his head in the negative. "No, I don't. Yes, there are fewer attacks, and, yes, they now seem to be targeting the government operations, but if you'll look at issue 23, we have noticed an increase in contacts between suspected individuals. For a decade, most of the communications between these terrorists were vertical, meaning, within their own organization. They had different agendas and were jealous of their independence from one another. Lately, though, we have seen more contacts between the various groups, though we haven't been able to ascertain the purpose of these contacts."

He sat back in his chair, indicating he had finished.

Melinda then asked the bureau chief from Nigeria for his analysis of the situation there.

Bureau Chief Caldwell related a somewhat different scenario. Because of the efforts of the standing government to block any and all opposition, many groups and individuals had been branded as terrorists. Few truly met the criteria for the term except Boko Haram in northern Nigeria. Linked early on to the Taliban, they grew in strength through murder and intimidation. The government was unwilling or unable to stop them, fearing to send troops into the territory they controlled.

Each of the bureau chiefs, in turn, gave a summary of terrorist activities in each of their respective areas of responsibility.

When they finished, Melinda again took centre stage.

"Gentlemen, thank you for that. I believe your assessment of the local situation in your respective countries is accurate and has been the basis for the President's policies concerning the war on terror.

"Nonetheless, as I read through all the reports, I began getting the feeling we were missing something. I asked my team to dig deeper into one issue in particular: that of the number of possible contacts between separate and independent groups."

She signalled to Doyle to turn on the large monitor behind her.

As the logo of Homeland Security appeared, he aimed the remote control at it again and clicked. The image that came on next was that of the world, showing the borders of all the countries. In many of them, there were illuminated circles, both large and small, with a few of those circles having fine lines linking them to others.

Everyone turned to look at the screen.

Melinda went on. "What you are looking at is a representation of the chatter we have detected between suspected and known terrorists in each of the countries you see. This first image shows the activity in 2008.

"You'll notice the size of the circles over Afghanistan, Pakistan and Indonesia: No surprise that they show some of the most active groups at the time. No surprise either, that the communication between these three areas was intense."

She nodded to Doyle once more, and another image came up on the screen.

"At the moment, we have 2010. A larger number of countries now have quantifiable activity from local terrorist groups. The three areas we first saw are still quite active. You'll notice the new clusters show an expansion in terrorist activities across the world. A few of you were appointed to those areas at this time.

"I'd like to bring one thing to your attention. You'll notice that the connections between these groups are few.

"Let's look at 2012."

A similar map came up on the screen, but there were many more clusters, including some in the United States.

"If we look at a representation of the chatter as of one month ago, I think you'll see an evolution of sorts."

The map now showed the same clusters, with some having increased in size, while others having gotten smaller. What was remarkable and what generated a collective reaction of astonishment among the men were the lines linking the different groups to one another. The thickness of all the lines had increased significantly.

Responding to their amazement, Melinda said, "I agree with you, gentlemen. Though we have been generally successful in curbing terrorist activities, eliminating the top Al Qaeda and Taliban leaders, and keeping many of the others at bay, I believe it would be premature to rest on our laurels.

"If I am correct, the face of terrorism is evolving and morphing into bin Laden's vision. The huge increase in contacts between these groups, be they Islamic or not, is troubling. By not acting as independent entities, they may, in fact, be creating a new consciousness of what they can do as a world movement. As such, it means we would have to make a major shift on not only how we view their abilities to act, but how we have to deal with them."

The nodding of heads told Melinda she was on to something.

"Gentlemen, I would ask you to revisit your reports and analyse them from this new perspective. Take advantage of the department's infrastructure and resources.

"Let's meet again tomorrow morning to see if we can come to a consensus on the subject, and if you agree with my suspicions, we will then formulate some suggestions which we will make to the Secretary to take to the President."

Looking around the table, she continued, "If there is nothing more . . ."

As there was indeed nothing more, she closed the meeting.

Upon leaving the room, Melinda turned to Doyle who was in tow behind her. Letting him catch up, she quietly asked him what he thought of the meeting.

"I think you nailed it. If the decision is to take this to the President, we've probably just given ourselves a much harder job to do. Many of his policies will have to change to adapt to the new reality. Be that as it may, it could be an uphill battle to get him to buy into your theory."

Melinda raised her eyebrows and said, "I know. I'm putting my neck on the line on this one. Tomorrow's meeting will tell whether or not they think I'm crazy."

Her comment and situation were not lost on Doyle, who decided to lighten the subject.

"How's Sam doing?"

"He seems to be doing well in his lecture tour and should be in Pasadena at Caltech on Monday, then here in Washington for a two-day *layover*."

She immediately regretted using that term, but decided Doyle was a big boy, and he would get over it.

Chapter 13

Sam flew into Burbank Airport, or Bob Hope Airport, at six p.m. on the Sunday. He could have flown into LAX, but he preferred the less hectic and closer to Caltech airport.

He rented a car from Hertz and drove to his hotel, the Sheraton Pasadena, a mere ten blocks from the university.

After registering and taking a quick shower, he had supper in the hotel restaurant and then went back to his room where he settled in for a quiet evening. He wanted to Skype Melinda, and then get to sleep.

Early to bed, early to rise.

He was up by six, had a coffee and hit the treadmill in the hotel gym: He wasn't about to risk his life in the Pasadena early morning traffic. He had breakfast and was in the car by nine.

His lecture was set for ten a.m. in the auditorium at the Broad Center for the Biological Sciences. So, with a little time on his hands, he decided to tour the university grounds.

He felt comfortable driving around the campus. He realized that as different as colleges and universities might appear to be, they shared a common element in that they were all created to promote learning. Although he was a professor, he sensed a link with every person he saw on campus: the thirst for knowledge. Once a student, always a student.

Driving north on South Wilson Avenue where the Broad Center was situated, the GPS unit on his rental told him that he had reached his destination.

On the left was a large four-floor indoor parking garage, with a huge corrugated roof, supported by steel girders.

A quick question crossed his mind leading him to wonder why they would build a roof. Then he realized it was due to the summer sun and the associated heat. Not like Toronto, he thought.

Over to his right was his destination. From this approach, the Broad Center looked like an assortment of cardboard boxes, stacked side by side or a few on top of another.

He also wondered where he had seen that type of building before. He searched through the dozens of images that came to him. Ah, right! The Castel dell'Ovo in Naples, which, when he had visited the city probably three years before on holiday, had seemed like a structure built by a child out of Lego blocks.

As he reached the entrance to the ground parking lot in front of the building, he was struck by yet another image triggering yet another sensation of *déjà vu*. He was back at the Temple of Karnak in Egypt.

While in university, he had done some backpacking through the country, immersing himself in Egyptian culture. He had visited the temple and had walked through the great hypostyle hall, a collection of huge columns which used to hold the roof, approximately thirty metres above.

He shook his head a little, trying to figure out why he had had that flashback. Then it struck him that as he had driven past the building to the entrance of the parking area, an image had generated a series of memories.

The sidewalk by the street was expanded to a large twenty-by-sixteen-metre concrete area, perforated on each side of a five-metre pathway by two sets of nine, six-metre-high palm trees, each planted in three symmetrical rows of three. The pathway then continued all the way to the end of the building, shouldered on both sides by a long series of deciduous trees, shrubs and grass, creating a beautiful, shady canopy under which students could sit.

The palm trees had caused him to go back all those years and think about the hypostyle hall, through which he had walked, in awe of the architecture. He remembered that he had then made his way through the temple to the other side and followed the wide, 2.7 km Alley of the Sphinxes, displaying over eight hundred sphinxes and leading to the temple of Luxor.

By the time he had figured it all out, he was already pulling into a parking spot, just in front of the main entrance. He grabbed his briefcase, locked his car door and headed inside.

****

About fifteen minutes later, another individual parked his four-by-four pickup on South Catalina Avenue, a block away from the Broad Center. He, too, took a briefcase with him and walked along the shaded laneways between the single-, double- and triple-storey student housing complex. He loved the trees and the Spanish Mission-style houses, reminiscent of his college years, though today, he wasn't there to study.

He breathed deeply through his nose. Rain was coming. The winds had increased, and he could feel the rise in humidity. These were issues he would have to factor in.

Dressed to blend in with the student population, he walked through the complex to the rear of the large multifloor parking garage which served students and professors alike. Entering through one of the rear doors, he began assessing the situation.

He walked to the front of the building and looked across the street at the Broad Center and noticed the same trees Sam had seen. He, though, did not like what he saw. All the trees and shrubs were impediments to his mission.

He walked up to each level and reassessed his options. Because of the foliage on the trees, he was forced to position himself on the second level, giving him the only line of sight to his target, right up the centre of the long walkway. If Sam were to turn toward him or away from him, Hank would have an easy time picking him off. Even if Sam were to cross the wide sidewalk, Hank would still have enough time to do the job.

Hank was aware that the lecture would last about one hour, followed by an hour and a half of questions from the audience. That much he gleaned from the Center's Facebook page, describing the daily activities at the school.

The date and place, he had extracted from his brother during a phone call several days earlier. After a friendly brotherly chat over cars, their dad and work, he had asked about Gordon and Buckner. Not being a state secret, John had simply mentioned Sam's lecture at Caltech.

Evans waited until the front row was filled with parked cars, singling out two in particular, side by side, which had just been parked by what looked like two professors. As well, the area where they were parked was not monitored by the security cameras. He figured they would be there for the balance of the day, and all he needed was another ninety minutes.

Crouching next to the half wall overlooking the street, he kept a careful eye on the comings and goings in the lot. Traffic had dropped to a trickle, so he felt a little less concerned about arriving so soon.

He would not remove the rifle from the briefcase until he thought Sam would be about fifteen minutes from leaving the building. That he could determine by the number of people exiting the center. His research had revealed that Sam was to give his lecture in the ninety-seven seat auditorium. Counting on the fact he would not be the first to leave and anticipating a few residual questions after the Q & A, Sam would be about ten to fifteen minutes later than the bulk of the spectators.

Taking a seat on the concrete floor, his back against the half wall, he took a piece of gum from his pocket and popped it into his mouth. It was time to meditate and slow his heart rate, in preparation for the shot.

He heard footsteps, indicating someone was walking up the incline driveway, from the ground floor to the next level.

Hank waited to see if the person would continue up to the third level.

Oh no, whoever it was, they were getting closer.

Hank quickly slid the briefcase under the front of the car on his left. He then pulled his baseball cap a little lower over the sunglasses he was sporting and took a mickey of vodka out from the inside pocket of his jacket.

He hoped it wasn't the owner of one of the two cars hiding him.

As the person passed between the rears of both vehicles, he looked over to see what he regarded as a student, either at the end or the beginning of a drinking bout, or just taking a *swig* to get him through his next class.

The stranger smiled and gave Hank a two-finger salute, saying, "Hey, man. Party on."

Hank tipped the bottle toward the man and raised it slightly, in response.

The intruder walked to a car about ten spots further and left the parking garage.

If one were to think that the episode had elevated Hank's heart rate, one would be wrong.

As he put the cap back onto the bottle and into his pocket, he leaned against the wall, feeling the silencer-equipped pistol in the belt at his back. Had the stranger stopped to question him, it would have been the last decision he would ever have made.

****

Inside, Sam was reaching the end of his presentation and preparing for the question period.

He had concentrated on the mathematics behind his formula and the impact of the potential genetic mutations he theorized had occurred.

Based on the number of copies of his book belonging to the participants in the packed auditorium and the copious notes they were all taking, he felt good about his lecture.

For the next half hour, he answered a flurry of questions, thankfully about the science he presented and not the contentious topics he had to fend off during the CNN panel discussion.

The Director of Communications, who had greeted Sam at the door and introduced him to the audience, also thanked him at the end, eliciting a huge round of applause for Sam.

Many of the spectators walked down to the podium to shake Sam's hand and ask for his autograph.

When he was done, the director led Sam out to the entrance, congratulating him for his research and his presentation.

Hank was ready. He had removed his jacket, reversed his cap and taken a kneeling position, with the sniper rifle resting on the ledge.

He had spent the last five minutes adjusting the focus on the telescopic lens, using a dozen of the students as targets, as they left the building.

He had slowed his heart down to about sixty beats per minute and adjusted his breathing to counter the surges of blood through his arteries, all the way to the tip of his trigger finger.

His eyes took in the timing of the sway of the branches as they were tossed by the increasingly heavier winds. In his mind, he could see the airflow between the gun muzzle and the area in front of the main entrance . . .

****

Sam stepped out into the sun. He noticed that the wind had picked up since his arrival, but the warmth in the air was so much more pleasant than the wind in Toronto, rain or no rain on the way.

He took a quick look, spotted his rental car and thought, time to head out.

****

. . . and then, Hank saw Sam as he exited the building. This is going to be easy, he thought.

Not happy with the magnification and the resolution in his scope, he made an ever so slight modification and returned his finger to its position.

He took a breath and slowly released it in a steady exhale, while applying a little more pressure on the trigger.
. .

****

Sam walked beneath the first line of trees toward the long pathway. As he did, a shout from behind stopped him.

"Professor Buckner!"

****

. . . Hank could see Sam emerging from the protective foliage. First his feet and legs, then his shoulders, and now his head was visible.

The pressure on the trigger had almost reached the sweet spot where the hammer would be released, sending the high-powered bullet to its target . . .

****

Sam quickly turned to see who was calling him. It was one of the students who had attended the lecture.

****

A single crack sounded out. Regardless, a split second before, his scope had gone white, startling him.

A piece of newspaper, carried by the blowing wind, had whipped by, directly in front the lens, obscuring his view.

.   ****

Just as Sam was about to acknowledge the student, he heard a *whizzing* sound, followed by the distinctive resonance of something ricocheting off the concrete.

****

Hank reacquired his target as soon as he realized what had happened. Without losing a beat, a second bullet was off.

****

Sam's instincts took over instantly. Only one other time in his life had he reacted as fast as he did now: That moment on Kamaran Island, when he had stood, rifle at the ready, the mercenary coming around the corner, and Melinda's life in danger.

This time he had no weapon and Melinda wasn't there. Nevertheless, another person was.

Before hearing the second whizzing sound, which was followed by the thump of a bullet hitting the grass just past them, Sam had lunged forward, crashing into the student and bringing him down with him.

No sooner had they hit the ground than Sam realized he had knocked the wind out of the student, rendering him unable to move. Sam was in somewhat better shape and got up onto his knees. He grabbed the student by the collar and dragged him toward the closest tree, only now realizing that a shot, no two, had been fired from somewhere in the direction of the street.

He looked around and saw the dozen or so people who had been going about their business, were now all scrambling to find protection under the trees, some screaming, others looking every which way, trying to find the shooter.

****

Hank saw red and swore to himself but his instincts took over immediately. Within thirty seconds, the rifle was dismantled and reinserted into the briefcase. He found the two empty shell casings. With his hand touching the pistol in his belt, he peeked above the cars to see if anyone was around.

Seeing no one, he put his jacket on, turned his cap around the correct way and put his sunglasses back on.

He reached the rear entrance on the ground floor in a matter of only a minute.

Looking back to see if anyone had come into the parking garage, he quickly exited and moved away from the chaos he had caused.

As he walked through the housing complex, a student came rushing in his direction. "Hey, did you hear the gunshots?"

Hank shrugged his shoulders and said, "Hell no."

The kid kept heading in the direction of the Broad Center.

As he turned to watch the student racing ahead, Hank thought, what an idiot, running *toward* the shots.

****

Sam looked down at the student who was just now catching his breath. He had a pained look on his face.

Between bouts of coughing, he looked angrily at Sam and said, "What the hell was that about, man? All I wanted was your autograph."

It was obvious he had not realized what had happened.

"Sorry. You need to know someone took a shot at us; more likely, at me. You were at the wrong place at the wrong time."

Dusting himself off and looking around in the direction of the parking garage, he absent-mindedly muttered, "I'm thinking someone doesn't like me very much."

"Is he gone?" asked the student as he pulled himself up against the tree behind which they were hiding.

"I'm not sure, but there haven't been any more shots, and I doubt the shooter would want to hang around for too long."

Sam leaned over to look around. That's when he heard the sirens of the university security police. Thankfully, someone must have called 911.

Sam slowly got up and helped the student to his feet.

No sooner were they both up and making sure they were OK, than the police arrived.

Within minutes, Sam heard more and more police sirens, all heading in the building's direction.

Sam attempted to brush himself off again, then took his phone out to *tweet* Melinda.

****

He spent the rest of the day being interrogated by detectives at the police station and was released about three hours later.

Sam walked out of the station, only to be confronted by a throng of reporters from all the major news agencies.

Chapter 14

Melinda was frantic speaking with Sam on the phone.

"What the hell happened? Where are you? Are you OK?"

"Yes, yes, I'm fine. I'm on my way to drop off the rental, and I'll catch the six-twenty flight, local time, to Washington. I should be at the airport about eight o'clock, your time.

"Sorry I couldn't call you before now," Sam continued, "the cops kept me busy all afternoon and then the mob of reporters.

"Can you pick me up?"

"Like you have to ask!" growled Melinda, a little flustered.

Regaining some composure, she inquired, "Do you have any idea who tried to kill you?"

"None," Sam answered. "It's obvious it's because of my research. The thing is, I've had nothing but good feedback everywhere I've gone."

"Well, I think someone is attempting to tell you they are giving you a failing grade," Melinda quipped.

She went on, "I'm having my people look into what happened to you. I'll see if we can come up with a lead as to who tried to kill you. If they tried once, they could try again."

Sam's eyes widened a little. "I hadn't thought of that."

"I have a couple of agents coordinating the investigation with the local police in Pasadena."

Sam got a puzzled look on his face. "Why is Homeland Security involved? Shouldn't it be someone from the FBI or something?"

"The fact that you are a foreign national and *known* by the White House resulted in the responsibility being shifted to us. I was contacted as soon as the reports came in. That's when I got the ball rolling."

She paused for a second, took a deep breath and said earnestly, "Besides, you're my guy and I'll be damned if I'll let anything happen to you."

Sam got a little choked up. "I love you too, babe."

He was approaching the airport and saw the signs directing him to the Hertz Rental area. "Hate to cut this short, but I'm almost at the drop-off point for the car. I'll text you as soon as I land and you can pick me up just outside the arrival terminal."

Melinda sighed. "OK, not a problem. Be careful and don't take any chances. Get through security as quickly as you can. You'll be safe there."

She paused once more. "I love you, sweetheart."

He smiled. "Ditto."

Chapter 15

Secretary Fleet had been with the President for ten minutes, discussing the issue Melinda had brought to him after her meetings with the department heads and the bureau chiefs.

"You do know this would mean a clear departure from the policy we have been following for over fourteen years."

"Yes, Mr. President. On the other hand, we believe we are only at the inception of this unification movement of terrorist groups. For the moment, I'm not advocating a radical change. We will be monitoring the situation in light of this new insight."

The President was sitting behind the Resolute desk, as had so many other great men before him. Fleet had pulled up a chair to the right of the President, using the corner of the desk to hold the many folders he had brought with him.

Alexander was in a pensive mood, allowing Fleet to carry most of the conversation. Nonetheless, he asked, "How much credence to you lend to Deputy Gordon's theory?"

"I wouldn't have brought it to your attention if I didn't think it wasn't a plausible concept."

"What do you suggest we do?" questioned the President.

"We need to confirm our suspicions. I've given a directive to all our bureau chiefs to continue the investigation into this. We should have a clear picture in four to six months. So far, the chatter hasn't been about any threat of attack on the U.S. or its allies. We have detected conversations and emails, which would seem to indicate a further interest in broader discussions between the various groups."

The President looked down perfunctorily and pivoted from side to side on his swivel chair, seemingly a million miles away.

He looked up at Fleet after having come to a decision. "OK. I trust your judgment on the matter. This will give us a chance to formulate our response if your findings prove Gordon right. As well, it means I won't have to deal with it and the political fallout until after the elections."

He pushed back on his chair and rose to shake Fleet's hand.

"Good work, Wilson. And please relay my thanks to Deputy Gordon for me."

As Alexander was escorting Fleet to the door, he stopped and asked, "That was Melinda's young man who was shot at in California?"

"Yes, sir, it was."

"What do you know about the incident?"

Both men stopped before reaching the exit door.

"Not a whole hell of a lot. We surmise he has struck a nerve with someone who wants to stop him in his tracks. It looks like it was a professional and not just any *wacko* with a gun."

"Why do you say that?"

"Ballistics on the two bullets we found at the site indicates they came from a high-powered rifle, similar to the ones used by our own snipers."

The President's eyes got wider. "One of ours is trying to take him out?"

"We don't believe it's someone on active duty. Regardless, definitely a former military person *and,* the bullets also match the one which killed a Professor Crawly several weeks ago. That shot was special: from almost half a mile away."

The President could only remark, "You're kidding."

"No, sir. If it's the same person, our Buckner was indeed lucky. We can't figure out how the sniper could have missed his target, at a distance of a mere two hundred yards."

"Where is the doctor now?"

"Under wraps, so to speak, with Deputy Gordon," he answered with a smile starting to form on his face as he heard the *double-entendre* of his own statement.

The President shook his head. "Is there anything we can do in this situation?"

Fleet thought for a second. "We could assign protection while he is within our borders. It will take your OK to do so, sir."

Without a moment's hesitation, Alexander responded, "Done. I owe him and Melinda my life. And it wouldn't look very good in the media if he was killed on our soil.

"But before we do, I would like to speak to Sam myself. I need to get a better handle on whatever idea someone is ready to kill over. Check with Mildred to see what my schedule is like during the next couple of days."

"Will do, sir."

Fleet shook the President's hand once more and left the Oval Office.

As Alexander was walking back to his desk, he couldn't help but think how very crazy the world was: To try to kill another over an idea, especially here in the US, where the freedom of expression was one of its most coveted rights.

Chapter 16

The next afternoon, Sam was being ushered into the Oval Room.

Alexander was sitting on the sofa, a cappuccino in hand and a folder on his lap. When the door opened and he saw Sam, he closed the folder, revealing the words stamped on the cover: Eyes-Only.

The President got up, placed the coffee cup on the table before him and quickly handed the folder to Mildred, who had accompanied Sam into the room.

"Sam, it's so good to see you again, my boy."

He warmly shook Sam's hand with both of his.

A broad smile on his face, Sam returned the warm greeting. "I'm pleased as well, Mr. President. Thank you for having me here again, though I'm wondering why, sir."

Gesturing Sam to sit opposite him on the other sofa, Alexander offered him a coffee or tea, which he politely declined.

Laughing a little to himself, the President said, "Here it is, two in the afternoon, and I'm having a cappuccino. I'm told no self-respecting Italian would have one after eleven a.m."

Sam chuckled back. "I guess it's like white or red wine. There's no correct food to pair it with. It's what you feel like drinking at the time."

The President let out a hardy laugh. "Try telling that to the White House chef."

Changing the subject, Alexander continued, "First, how are you, after Caltech?"

"I have to admit I'm still a little shaken."

"I don't blame you," said the President. "Melinda?"

"She was upset at what happened, but it didn't take long for her to return to business mode. She is one *cool* lady."

"Yes, I'm rather impressed by her," responded the President. "Actually, I'm quite impressed by both of you. I probably would not be here if it wasn't for you and Ms Gordon."

"I don't know what to say, sir."

"I never told anyone, but, within minutes after Secretary Broom died before our eyes in the War Room, I began getting heat flashes and started to sweat.

"Then, suddenly, it stopped.

"I'm told the moment matched the one when the laboratory on Kamaran Island blew up. Another few seconds, and who knows . . .

"Well, enough of that for now. I've asked to see you in order to get a better idea why someone would want to kill you. This theory of yours seems to be pretty black and white. Why is it stirring up so much controversy? I had one of the White House aides brief me on it, and I think it to be a very plausible theory."

"Thank you for that, sir," Sam responded.

"The math and science are pretty straightforward. I think the controversy is due to some of the conclusions I drew and expressed. I have to admit, I'm starting to regret ever including them in my book. They seem to have taken on a life of their own."

"Tell me about them. Why do they provoke such emotions in people? How do they relate to me, for example, and my reelection?"

Alexander was in his element. He looked forward to talking to Sam in order to share ideas and have the opportunity to debate new concepts, without having the general public dissect every word, trying to trip him up. This was going to be fun, he thought.

"The core of the objections to my conclusions revolves around my assertion that humans are not the rational, thinking creatures we believe we are. Not that we can't *be* that. Still, it is in our nature to be more symbolic creatures than reasonable ones. The formula I have come up with shows the correlation between what we call rogue stars and the great evolutionary jumps we have found in our past. I contend the last one triggered changes which took our ancestors, creatures who fundamentally processed reality through imagery and not reason, and created a species which is more and more the rational type."

"That's a good thing, isn't it?" the President asked.

"I would say that, yes, it is, but that it does have its problems."

Alexander sat back on the sofa and crossed his legs, subconsciously stating he was open to the explanation.

Sam took note of the President's body language. "Sir, if I may. The very position you have just taken, speaks to my theory."

Alexander stiffened a little, not quite sure what he had done.

"Can you tell me why you sat back as you did?"

"Well, I guess I was getting comfortable while waiting for your explanation."

"And you did it without saying a word," responded Sam. "You were using symbolism to express an idea."

Alexander simply smiled, indicating he was beginning to understand.

"Let's take hats as a start," continued Sam. "People wearing certain hats convey a certain sense of authority, as do policemen or soldiers. Now take metal: Bend it one way to produce a car, and that car is worth ten thousand dollars. Bend it another way, giving it a different shape, and the car is valued at a hundred thousand dollars. Dress a man in a suit, and he's a businessman; dress the same man in jeans and a cowboy hat, and he's a farmer; well, at least in the minds of many."

Alexander stepped in. "I see where you are going with this, but how does it relate to your theory? This is more the subject of Psychology 101."

Sam continued on cue. "You are correct, sir, but more advanced courses get into the dichotomy of the human mind: for example, Freud's Id, Ego and Superego, and our inner struggle to make sense of the world."

"Now, you are getting a little *heavy* for me," stated Alexander.

"Sorry about that, sir. I get lost in the minutiae.

"Let me get back to my conclusions. My position is that the dominant human species which evolved several hundred thousand years ago was one which reacted to the world around it through symbols, including concepts such as who we are, why we are here and where we are going: The things of philosophy and religion. We found symbolic answers to these questions because they were easier for us to understand that way. On the other hand, with the passing of the last star near us, evolution triggered the frontal lobe of our brain, enhancing our ability to think and reason, allowing us to suppress that other side of us."

Alexander interrupted once more, playing the devil's advocate. "Are you saying that our symbolic side is a baser side of humanity, and that we are evolving into a purely rational creature?"

"No to the first question, sir, and I hope not, to the second.

"It may seem as if I am fixated on religion, but I only refer to it to show how this most symbolic of concepts has both good and bad. Think of the Spanish Inquisition, the present-day Islamic radicals, the religious wars of our past: How many people have died in the name of God? And yet, religion has been the single most important unifying institution, and the basis of all civilized society and of the foundation of our laws.

"As well, what is possibly the most beautiful side of humanity comes from our symbolic side: art, architecture, music, to name but a few. They are expressions of who we are, and perhaps our only redeeming qualities.

"I'm reminded of the gospel song, Amazing Grace. John Newton was a man tormented: Caught between his symbolic self as a slave trafficker and his rational side, questioning what he had done. He was able to *reform* his views and his life, some would say because of religion and not reason. Albeit, Amazing Grace boasts some of the most beautiful lyrics ever written and was due to the inner conflict caused by our evolving away from Homo symbolicus towards Homo sapiens."

"An interesting interpretation; even so, you paint a pretty bleak picture. Is there a future for us?" interjected the President.

"I suppose I do, and yes, I believe in our future. I believe we can take our symbolic nature and nurture it, tempered by reason when necessary."

Alexander was enjoying the brief respite from his own *grounded* world. Still, much as he liked the intellectual bantering, his position required him to be a practical man as well.

"OK, how is your theory pertinent to my situation?"

That caught Sam a little off guard.

"Sir, I don't know if I can give you an answer to that question. It's not easy for me, as a Canadian, to understand fully the responsibilities of your position, or the spirit of the American people."

He paused for a moment, trying to find a common thread between his theory and an application which could be useful to the President of the United States.

"If I were to sum it up in a brief statement, I think I would say that, in order to apply a Homo sapiens approach to politics, in contrast to the symbolic approach, one would have to *do the correct thing.*"

Alexander looked at Sam with an expression of surprise.

"Why would you say correct rather than right?"

Sam responded quickly.

"There's a difference between correct and right. Right implies a value judgment, meaning a symbolic or a morality-based approach. Correct would imply a reasonable or logical interpretation."

The President's eyes revealed a look of understanding. He then pressed on. "Granted, however, you'll have to be more specific about what you mean by *correct.*"

"Well, let me give you an answer based on your own history. Take President Lincoln: He was faced with a situation in which he knew the plight of slaves in America was untenable. Their predicament was created by a symbolic rationale, grounded in greed and justified by ridiculous logic and even ludicrous interpretations of the Bible. It was a quandary in which one race considered itself superior to another, giving it the right to do what they wished with the humans they kidnapped from Africa.

"Lincoln was confronted with a dilemma: Allow it to continue or do the correct thing and try to right the wrong. He chose to go against political expediency and compliance. It cost him his life, but he forever changed your history and, to some extent, that of the world."

Alexander looked pensively at Sam. "You know, we are still fighting that war."

"I know, sir. Your history and the human race are still in the process of evolving, which means the same type of conflict will exist for a very long time. That's *if* my formula is correct, and I believe it is.

"More recent history demonstrates more of the darker side of symbolism. Take Hitler. He believed he was part of the superior race, above the laws of others. He believed and stated that the masses were feminine and stupid, and that only emotions and symbolism could appeal to the German people while hatred of the Jews could unify them and help keep them under control. We know where that led."

The President sat back on the sofa and took a few moments to absorb what Sam was saying. He brought his left hand up and put his first finger to his lips. Then he moved forward a little and asked, "If I were to ask you to identify the one issue which most typifies what you think is wrong with the American culture, what would that issue be?"

It was Sam's turn to sit back into the sofa, but the look on his face was one of panic.

"Sir, if I may say, that's unfairly putting me on the hot seat."

Alexander smiled and responded with, "Yes. It is. Welcome to my world. So, what would your answer be?"

"It really isn't a difficult one to come up with, but it is contentious.

"OK, I'll go along for the ride. If I were to single out one issue which I, or Canadians in general can't understand and are flabbergasted with, it would have to be what we see as your unreasonable obsession with guns."

Alexander smiled. "Go on," he said.

"It seems everyone here has a gun. It is a foreign concept to me, to think that wherever I go in the States, the person next to me is likely carrying one.

"Growing up, I can tell you, no one locked their doors during the day and for the most part, they still don't. We felt, and still feel safe, *because* we don't worry about the person at the next table having a gun. Here, it seems you don't feel secure *unless* you have one on you."

The President chuckled a little. "You have a good point; even so, understand that our history comes out of a period when individuals needed to protect themselves to survive, even against their own government. The British ruled through brute force, making it necessary for everyone to take up arms in order to redress the injustice which they were enduring. We've enshrined that right in our constitution with good reason.

"As well," the President continued, "could not your sense of security at home be because, other than our attempt to invade you back in 1812, Canada has never been attacked? In part, because we have been there to support and protect you since then?"

Sam nodded in agreement, but added, "I was told something to that effect, by the young Ra'id, shortly before he died."

Sam continued, "I understand what you are saying, sir; in spite of that, I can't fathom the need, in this day and age, to guarantee citizens the right to own high-powered rifles, like the one which was used in trying to kill me."

The President's face saddened. "I can see why you would be particularly sensitive to that. It's unfortunate you had to live through such an event, here on our soil. As you know, efforts have been made to curtail the use of such weapons, but to no avail. The gun lobby is quite powerful."

Sam looked at the President and tried to quell the anger that had surged up in him.

"Sir, I get that your constitution gives each citizen the right to protect themselves. Right now, I think I'd like to have a gun to defend myself from the individual who tried to kill me."

Sam paused and asked the President, "Does the right to bear arms mean that, just because they can, someone could buy a tank and park it in their driveway, to deter anyone from harming their family?"

Alexander chuckled and shook his head. "No. It doesn't. Firstly, there are laws to prevent that specific situation from happening. You do, though, make a good point when it comes to defining what type of gun is reasonable to protect oneself. We haven't been able to. Some would argue we haven't wanted to come up with a better definition than the one we presently have.

"Contrary to your country, our independence came about through armed conflict. It was a grass-roots revolution, one in which small groups of individuals willing to die for the cause, had to come together to fight the mightiest empire of the time.

"So, if I were to apply your theory to our history, could I not say that the symbolic side was that of the British, who felt the colonies were inferior and there to be exploited, while our Minutemen were the sapiens side of the argument, doing what was correct?"

The look on Sam's face indicated he agreed, and he simply responded with, "I'd say you are a fast study."

He continued, "Sir, I didn't want to come across as a pompous critic of America, but you did ask, and I felt the need to be honest."

Alexander smiled tenderly, and then became more sullen. "I would ask nothing less of you. That being said, what would you have me do? My world, both at home and abroad, is a very dangerous place. Decisions I make affect the lives of millions. As Commander In Chief, my primary responsibility is the protection of the citizens of our nation and the constitution which guides us. This constitution may not be perfect, but it has evolved as one of the best sets of rules to live by."

The realization of exactly *who* he was conversing with, sank into Sam's consciousness. This was no longer just a theoretical discussion with a peer at the university, it was a discussion with the most powerful man on earth, one who could commit a country to war or peace, one whose life was not his own, but which belonged to the people who had elected him.

Sam felt very small at that moment and yet, he was incredibly grateful for the insight he had gleaned about the man and the country.

Alexander looked at his watch and made a motion of rising from his seat.

Sam knew his time was up. Taking the hint, he rose with the President, who walked over to him and extended his hand.

"Sam, this has been a delight. You have given me a lot to think about. I truly enjoyed using you as a sounding board. Thank you."

"No, thank you, sir, for taking the time to see me. I honestly think I'm coming away with much more than I may have left behind. As you said, much to think about."

The President turned to escort Sam toward the door.

"By the way, I would suggest you curtail your lecture tour for a week or so. I understand you are scheduled to visit MIT in four days?"

"Yes, Mr. President."

Alexander stopped in mid-stride and turned to Sam. "I've approved to have protection provided for you while you are on our soil. Unfortunately, it will take about a week, I'm told, to put everything into operation. Would it create too much of a problem for you to postpone your lecture?"

"I, I don't believe so. Regardless, are you sure this is necessary?" responded Sam.

With a huge grin on his face, Alexander said, "It most certainly is. How would it look, if during an election year, the President of the United States didn't protect the man who saved his life?"

Sam felt the comment was less one of political positioning, than a gesture of friendship.

"Sir, I'll do as you say. Thank you very much. I admit that I had reservations about my future lectures here, after what happened at Caltech. So, again, thank you, sir."

He exited the Oval Office, leaving the President alone, staring at the crest on the presidential carpet, rerunning in his mind, the conversation with Sam.

A look of resignation appeared on his face as he walked back to his desk.

Chapter 17

(One week later)

Back at the mansion, Oliver Doyle was in the main study, having a heated discussion with John and Harold; well, mostly with John.

Hank was somewhat quiet and morose, only adding to the conversation when pressed to do so.

Doyle was sitting back in his leather recliner and was unusually agitated. "I know it will be an uphill battle to get rid of him, but we only have a few months to hammer the man before the elections."

John took a sip of his Jack Daniel's on the rocks. "That may be so. But as you know, Alexander hasn't done anything contentious for us to focus on."

"You're right," Oliver responded, "which is why the *group* has decided to move in a slightly different direction."

The group he spoke of was the election action committee he had assembled, composed of some of the richest and most influential Republicans in the country. They had been meeting on a monthly basis for the past year and a half, developing strategies to bolster like-minded groups across the country.

Millions had been raised by them and strategically invested in the various Super PACs. Though they were essentially a PAC in their own right, they preferred remaining out of the limelight and channelling the money through arm's length organizations.

Doyle continued, "We think we need to stir things up and get Alexander to take a position we can use against him during the final months. So, we have decided to stoke the embers of illegal immigration, by backing a few of the Tea Party candidates who have been using the issue as a cross."

John asked, "Anyone in particular?"

"Well, there's Butler in Texas and Landsing in New Mexico."

The look on John's face was one of puzzlement. "How can you support them? They are as close to being Fascist as you can get."

Oliver smiled. "That's the type of reaction we are hoping to elicit. They are so far to the *right* that few will truly take them seriously. Alexander, as a result, will have to react and defend *his* immigration policy, which, as you know, is almost socialistic in nature. We think we can coax them into a filibuster over the issue. That's where our candidate will step in and provide a more palatable alternative to the two sides. We think it can be the main issue to winning us the White House."

John took another sip of his drink, shrugged his shoulders a little and cocked his head from side to side, indicating he thought the strategy could work.

Oliver turned to Harold and asked, "What's the matter? Cat got your tongue?"

"No. Just can't get too excited about politics, I guess." He returned to his pensive mood and took a swig from his bottle of Bud.

John interjected, "I may have something else you might be able to use against Alexander. Not that it's a huge deal, but it could strike a nerve in some of your supporters."

"And what would that be?" Oliver questioned.

"Well, you know Doctor Buckner, Gordon's *beau*."

Oliver nodded in the affirmative and, unnoticed by the other two, Hank's eyes began to show some interest.

172

"After someone tried to kill him at Caltech a few weeks ago, the Agency decided to ask the President for some protection for him."

Doyle looked a little puzzled. "Why would they do that for this guy? Why not simply tell him to stay home or let him take his chances if he insists on spreading his lies?"

By now, Hank was clearly paying attention to the discussion.

"There are rumours Buckner did something that the President is indebted to him for. We don't know what that is and it would seem Gordon was also involved. There are stories the President owes him his life."

Oliver still looked puzzled. "That doesn't make sense. How can some Canadian be mixed up in saving the President's life? Besides, I haven't heard a single whisper of an attempt on Alexander's life."

"No one has," responded John. "Even so, resources have been allocated for the doctor's protection. And, guess who's been tasked to be his baby sitter for the next couple of months."

That's when Hank blurted out, "You have to be kidding!"

John responded in a fatalistic tone of voice, "Nope. I have."

Oliver sat back into the chair, pondering what this could mean. Here was the President of the United States, possibly the target of some assassination plot no one has heard about, withholding the news from the American public, and using money and Homeland Security personnel to protect a foreigner.

Looking back at John, Doyle said in a slow and measured way, "Actually, I think you are wrong. This could be a 'huge deal' and strike a nerve not only with our supporters but with the American public at large."

He paused a moment and then added, "I'll have some of my people look into this, very discreetly. We can't have you implicated as the source of the information, *if* it turns out to be true."

John shot back, "I doubt you'll be able to find anything about why the President is protecting Buckner. But as for my part in protecting him, it isn't a state secret. Most of our department is aware of it."

Hank put his beer bottle on the side table next to him and leaned forward in his chair.

"Tell me more about your new baby-sitting job."

Chapter 18

At the request of the President, Sam had cancelled two of his lectures in the US and rescheduled them a month or so later. This gave him some time off, which he decided to spend back home in Toronto.

It was three weeks after the attempt on his life, and Melinda had flown in to be with him for a four- or five-day holiday.

Sam had planned several activities he thought would make it a great trip for Melinda. On the first day, he wanted an activity which packed a big wow factor. To do that, he was to take her up the CN Tower to get a view of Toronto and Lake Ontario.

They rode up the high-speed outside elevator, quickly rising above the city to the observation level, about three hundred forty-two metres up. Melinda was calm at first, but as they rose higher, Sam could tell she was starting to feel the effects of the height. He couldn't discern whether the smile on her face was from the thrill of the ride or that feeling of euphoria one gets just before panic sets in.

Arriving at the observation level, he took her over to the glass-floor section, where people could literally walk over the edge of the tower's column, allowing them to look all the way down to ground level. Sam took her hand and led her out onto the glass. Melinda walked gingerly, on her toes, as though she was trying not to put too much pressure on the glass. All the while, she covered her mouth with her free hand, to stifle any scream. Sam was chuckling to himself.

"How high up are we?" she asked.

"About three hundred and forty metres up which would convert to approximately, uh, eleven hundred feet."

Dead silence from Melinda.

It didn't take long for her to calm down and to start adjusting to the height, trusting the tower had stood for thirty-eight years and would safely do so for many more.

Seeing her relax, Sam thought it was time to take it to the next level: the SkyPod, another thirty-three storeys higher.

Walking around that observation level and peering out the outward slanted windows at the view, Sam could point to landmarks as far as one hundred sixty kilometres away. Melinda clung to Sam's arm and didn't let go, which suited him perfectly.

Looking down at the roof of the main pod below them, they saw a group of people walking out onto a narrow, 1.5 m ledge, tethered to the building by safety harnesses.

"What are they doing?" Melinda blurted out.

"That's the EdgeWalk," answered Sam. "Did you want to try it?"

Melinda turned and hit him on the shoulder. "Are you kidding? That would be my worst nightmare. Those people must be absolutely crazy. It's one thing to look out and around from the safety of this area, but to walk outside, in this wind . . . Oh, God! Look! Now they're leaning over the edge. Have they taken leave of their senses?"

By that time, Sam was laughing hard. He held her tightly, in part to help calm her down and also because he just loved experiencing life with her at his side.

He kissed her tenderly and suggested they head down to a lower level to 360, the revolving restaurant, for dinner. They were able to get a table next to the window for a better view.

As it was April, the sun still set relatively early, and it wasn't long before the lights of the city began to turn on, slowly at first, then spreading rapidly, in no logical sequence, much like a swarm of fireflies appearing in the forest.

It was easy to forget they were high in the sky, and the time went by quickly. Only once did the conversation touch upon the event in California. Sam asked if there had been any developments concerning who might have tried to kill him.

Melinda's mood soured a bit. "No, nothing. Whoever this person is, he, and we assume it's a *he*, is like a ghost. Even the ballistics reports have come back with nothing which could give us a lead, other than the fact that the weapon was a special gun, with high-end cartridges: possibly military.

"I didn't want to tell you this, but there could be a link between this attempt on you and a murder in Philadelphia several weeks ago. We've asked the FBI to send us a report on their findings. We should know something in a few days."

Sam looked at her with surprise. Then, he shook his head and said, "I'll bet it's just some nut with a gun and a grudge against Canadians."

He smiled meekly. Melinda did not.

"I'm concerned for you. And so are many others, not the least being my President."

Sam realized the discussion wasn't heading toward a warm and fuzzy place. "Sorry I raised a sensitive topic. I was curious.

"So, let's just switch subjects, and I promise I won't bring it up until you do. This is supposed to be a fun holiday, not a downer."

Melinda leaned forward and took his hand in hers. She was going to say something, but then decided just to smile softly.

The rest of the meal was spent discussing everything *but* the danger to Sam's life.

****

A few hours later, the two of them were sitting on the oversized sofa in Sam's condo, well nestled in the plush cushions, Melinda leaning into Sam, his arm over her shoulder, holding her close. They were listening to soft music and sipping a Cabernet Franc from a Niagara winery. By now, the two were feeling quite mellow.

Melinda happened to glance up at the top shelf of the bookcase off to their right. From the angle of the view she had, she couldn't quite make out what she was looking at.

It struck her funny that what seemed to be a complete disarray of wires was so unlike Sam, who was a neat freak.

"What is that?" she asked.

"What's what?"

"That, up there on your bookcase."

Sam turned to look in the direction she was pointing.

"Oh, that. Hold on. I'll get it."

He pulled his arm from around her and set his glass of wine on the coffee table in front of them.

He returned to the sofa with a strange sculpture. She could see now that it was a group of wire cubes connected to one another.

Sitting back next to Melinda, Sam held the strange object in both his hands.

"I've been working on an idea that I plan on taking to a physicist friend of mine, to get his take on my concept."

Melinda took the object and rotated it in different directions in order to get some idea of what it could be. She looked up at Sam with a skeptical expression on her face.

"'*Splain* Lucy'," she said, trying to mimic Ricky Ricardo.

Sam took the sculpture back.

"OK, I'll 'splain'," Sam responded, with a bit of a chuckle, "but it could get a little sobering."

"And in that case, we'll need a little more wine."

Sam topped up the two glasses and then got comfortable next to her once again.

"OK, go for it," Melinda said, "I'm all ears."

Sam raised the sculpture for a better view of it. There were actually four cubes made of different-coloured wires. One was twice the size of the others and acted as the base for the other three, which were attached to the larger one, but could each be articulated in a different direction.

"Have you heard of String Theory?" he asked.

"Sure I have," Melinda quipped. "I'm not completely science challenged."

Sam smiled and added, "Just checking."

She jabbed him in the ribs with her elbow.

"Ouch!" he said, wincing.

Rubbing his ribs, Sam continued, "So, the theory states that all matter and energy is made up of these little vibrating strings and depending on which way they spin or how energetically they vibrate, they are what makes up all other particles from quarks, to photons, to electrons, etc."

Melinda smiled and said, "That would be the unifying theory Einstein was looking for."

Sam looked at her with some amazement. "Not only is she beautiful, but she's smart too."

Melinda returned the look with a coy smile. "Now you're learning."

"You're right, though. But did you know that, in order for the math to work properly, String Theory requires the existence of at least nine physical dimensions and one time dimension?"

Melinda nodded and then said, "I've heard about that, but to be honest, I have a hard time wrapping my brain around it."

"Well, you're not alone, but that's where my cubes come in."

He rotated the cubes so Melinda could get a better look at the smaller ones.

"I had a bit of a time figuring it out as well. So, I decided to build this.

"Let's say the large cube represents the three physical dimensions, or places, we know: length, width and depth. The other three cubes, each attached to one of our three dimensions, would then represent the other six dimensions.

"Now, take a look at these dimensions," he said, pointing to two of the wires on the white cube. "Try to visualize the flat surface they create, and then, have it curve and travel to, let's say the same two dimensions, but on the blue cube: like a bed sheet connecting the two."

Melinda looked at it carefully and, in her mind, she saw the image.

"Yes, I think I can see that."

Sam continued, "You know what a ball of yarn looks like?"

Melinda nodded, yes.

"That is one thread of yarn all wound up around itself. Picture nine threads, each of a different colour, wound up in a ball of yarn, but make each thread a separate sheet, like the one you just imagined."

Melinda's eyes grew wide.

"Holy cow, I can actually picture it. Talk about a convoluted mess."

Sam smiled with satisfaction.

"The picture in your mind is what's called a Calabi-Yau manifold."

"A Cala what?

"I just see a twisted bunch of sheets."

He shook his head, smiled, and leaned over and kissed her.

"You really impress me. Not many people could so readily see that shape. We can talk about that topic another time.

"Now, can you guess why my three smaller cubes can move?"

Melinda thought for a second.

"Don't tell me."

She thought a little longer. Then she smiled and looked at Sam with a twinkle in her eye.

"If you move the cubes, the sheets move and the twisted shapes change."

Sam beamed with pride at her ability to understand so quickly.

"Amazing. Yes and what you have described is part of what I want to present to my friend. I believe that every change of angle of any of the dimensions makes the formula for that universe different. It would provide theoretical proof for the concept of *multiverse*."

Melinda asked, "OK, so where are all these dimensions?"

"Good question. They are incredibly small, but connected to each one of the three physical dimensions we live in. So if you take the cube with the white wires, you'll notice that one of its dimensions is attached to one of ours. So we share the same space along that dimension. Look at the cube with blue wires; you'll notice another of *its* dimensions is connected to a different one in ours. And, the same with the cube with gold wires."

"OK, I see that. I still don't see where they are."

"This is where it gets a little tedious."

Melinda could see Sam was in his element.

"The other three cubes are each about the size of a Planck unit, which is the smallest measurable length possible, compared to our universe or cube."

"So, they are too small to matter."

"Well, that's what's interesting. There are five String Theories."

"Five?" exclaimed Melinda.

"Yup, five. Each has a mathematical formula that explains the universe perfectly, but none works directly with the others."

"Now you're really confusing me," responded Melinda. "How can each be right and none agree?"

"It's like five blind persons trying to describe what an elephant looks like, by feeling a different part of the animal. In String Theory, it's called the M-theory, where the five math formulae are either the direct opposite of another or agree in part with one or two.

"For example, let's say our universe uses the numbers tens, hundreds, thousands. Another formula will be the direct opposite, using minus tens, minus hundreds, minus thousands. The freaky thing is that, let's say our universe or the large cube, uses the plus tens, then one of the smaller cubes uses the minus tens, and though we think our universe is big and goes on forever, the small cube goes on forever in the minus direction. The connection between all nine dimensions is like a minuscule portal, at every point in space that can take you into another place, but only if you are small enough to pass through."

Melinda thought for a moment.

"I think I see what you are trying to explain, but it's so much to try to take in. Why do you want to talk to your friend about this?"

"Just curious, I guess, to see if he thinks there's any validity to my concept. I think it would help explain so many things physicists are working on. I mentioned the theory of the multiverse or how a photon can run into a barrier, disappear and then appear on the other side.

"It could explain why twin particles can be millions of miles apart in our universe and be affected instantaneously by one another. Possibly, they aren't twins at all, but the same particle passing back and forth, using those portals between dimensions and being in two places at the same time."

"Whoa! That's mind blowing," Melinda exclaimed. "So, assuming you might have something here, what use would it be?"

Sam's shoulders dropped a little, and the look on his face expressed defeat and questioning.

"Honestly, I don't know. Just the fact that it could shed more light on how the universe might actually work, would be great. But you're right, probably nothing practical."

Melinda shook her head and chuckled.

"I don't know what world you live in, but it is really different from the one I know."

Melinda suddenly became pensive.

Sam looked over to her and said, "What?"

She hesitated a moment and then turned to him, with a questioning look.

"I know what you said while on CNN . . ."

Sam thought, uh-oh, here it comes.

". . . and, I'm not trying to start an argument here, but, do you believe in God?"

There it was. Not that he hadn't expected the question. But, here it was.

"What brought that on?" he asked.

"Hard to say. With all this talk about science, I was wondering if there was room somewhere in your theory for God."

She paused again and then continued, "I have to admit, I've always enjoyed going to church on Sunday mornings. Maybe not so much to pray to God, but to be with the rest of the congregation: Call it fellowship. It has always felt good to sing the old hymns and to see how everyone seemed to be united as one.

"I went then and still try to attend when I can, because I believe that if God exists, then there is life after death."

She looked up at Sam and her eyes started to well up a little.

"I need to believe there is something there after we depart. Somewhere where my mother and father are, my favourite dog when I was a young girl, and most of all, you."

That prompted a large flow of tears to run down her cheeks, and even Sam got misty-eyed.

"I honestly don't know," responded Sam. "I would love nothing more than being sure we could be together then. In fact, I can't help but think my research isn't possibly skirting the subject or is somehow coming at it from a different direction. It's almost like a ghost standing just at the edge of your peripheral view and when you turn to see it, nothing is there."

To emphasize the comment, he made the eerie sound they use in spooky ghost movies, *ooh-ooh-ooh*, with a high crescendo on the middle *ooh*.

Melinda poked him in the ribs again and tried to feign a look of anger.

Sam hugged her tightly and kissed her gently on the forehead.

"I want a lifetime of talking to you about this topic and all other topics you want to discuss. I think what is important is that we always stay open to each other's thoughts and beliefs."

Melinda looked up at him and whispered, "I love you."

Then she reached to kiss him on the lips.

After a long caress, Sam said, "On that note, why don't I get you a refill and we could put a movie on?"

With an air of mischievousness, Melinda smiled and said, "I can think of something else we could do . . ."

Chapter 19

It was six-thirty in the morning, three weeks later, and Sam was using a cherry tree as a brace, while stretching his legs before heading off for a jog in the Washington Park Arboretum, in Seattle. Close by, also wearing a jogging outfit, was John Doyle.

Since the President's order that Sam needed to be protected while on US soil, he had lost control of the schedule of his lecture tour.

Where he stayed, how he got around, what he did was now in the hands of John Doyle.

Though he hated being managed by Homeland Security, he had to admit that Doyle seemed to be up to the task if only because it made his life so much easier.

Doyle organized the limo service to and from the airports, selected the hotels they would stay at, and did all the driving in the cities where Sam was giving lectures.

While in Seattle, he had rented rooms at the Sorrento Hotel, on East Madison Street, giving them easy access to Highway 5 and its main arteries, which would take them to the University of Washington Medical Center, the next location for his presentation.

It was a charming, older hotel, which had been nicely renovated to maintain the *grand* hotel feel, but with clean, modern amenities. The dining room served gourmet dishes, and to Sam's surprise, John expertly paired them with the right wines.

The only issue Sam had with the hotel was that it had no sports facilities, which was the reason why Doyle had suggested the Arboretum Trail, not far from the hotel, for their morning run. The trail consisted of several kilometres of running paths spilling over rolling hills covered with a wide variety of trees which separated the paths in such a way as to make runners feel as though they were alone.

Once he completed his stretches and warm-up exercises, Sam took a deep whiff of the pine-scented air, pointed down one of the paths available to them and started his run, closely followed by Doyle.

What Sam didn't realize was that Doyle made his choices purely from a security perspective.

The cars he rented were relatively plain, leased under a false name and identification cards. When he drove, he kept a constant lookout for anyone following and approaching them.

The hotel was chosen because of its unlikelihood to be used as their base in town, and because it gave them easy access to the city.

Since he knew Sam could be vulnerable to a sniper during his runs, he chose the Arboretum Trail as well as the other parks they had used, for the simple reason that it afforded no high ground on which the killer could position himself nor any direct line of sight from which he could see Sam for more than a few seconds, let alone try to find him in this vast expanse of trails. Over and above that, the decision to go to a particular park was only determined by Doyle and always revealed at the very last moment.

Although there was a fair amount of research involved, it did make Doyle's life easier, in that *he* was in control. There was no way something was going to happen to Sam: not on his watch.

As they had done several times now, they ran side by side, in unison, talking as though they were old buddies.

Sam was surprised at the shape Doyle was in. After fifteen minutes of running, neither had broken a sweat. Though they were breathing a little heavier than if they were walking, they could keep up a conversation, without losing a stride.

"So, why did you accept to come to Seattle?" questioned John.

"The UW Medical Center is quite special. In my field, any interest on their part in a particular concept demands you pay attention."

Doyle continued his line of questioning. "Why so?"

Sam smiled as he kept on running and staring ahead, only now and then glancing at his partner.

"The Center is responsible for many of the basic science and technological advances in medicine."

He smiled to himself once more, knowing the next part might be difficult to understand.

"They've done pioneering research in areas such as cell replication and signal transduction, the biometrical structure of proteins and the development of medical ultrasound."

Doyle shook his head. "In English, please."

"Sorry. I was trying to bait you."

Doyle smiled, realizing he had been *punked*.

"They have done important work in the area of cancer research. They specialize in finding out how the cells replicate and become cancerous. Their makeup and how they affect other cells is critical in understanding how they might find a cure for the disease."

"Now, that makes more sense," quipped Doyle. "But, how does that relate to your theory?"

"Good question. I'm not sure. They haven't explained why I was invited. Someone there might have his or her own theory, one in which gravitational waves might have an impact on cancer cells. I'll be interested in getting more information about who was instrumental in inviting me.

"Did you know that at least five of their researchers have received the Nobel Prize in Physiology or in Medicine in the past two decades? That's impressive."

Doyle fell silent for some fifty metres, trying to decide if this was all some old boys' club of scientists, looking at getting their fifteen minutes of fame, or whether the practical results of their research made all the money spent on them, worthwhile.

Until now, he had had a less than favourable opinion of Sam. But, he was starting to understand that there was more to the world than the good guys, one of which he saw himself, and the bad guys, whose job was his to find and eliminate.

His upbringing had, to some extent, brainwashed him into thinking in black and white: no grey. How did former President *W* state it: You're either with me or against me.

His religious training reinforced this approach. It was so easy, he thought, to base most of your opinions on one single, never-changing book. After all, it had guided Christians for over a thousand years. Even so, here was Sam with ideas very foreign to the teachings of his church, ideas that confused him.

These concepts were being sought after by pretty smart people, some of whom had to be evangelical as well. And Sam seemed to be a nice guy, down to earth and passionate about what he did. He didn't come across like the Antichrist pastor Trumbell painted him to be.

The longer they ran, the more John began to think that having a beer and shooting the breeze with Sam could be a cool thing to do.

He was starting to regret the fact that Sam had only another three stops to make before finishing his tour.

Chapter 20

President Alexander had been pacing back and forth in front of the Resolute desk, hands clasped behind his back and looking vacantly at the floor.

He had been deep in thought for almost half an hour, appreciating the privacy this most famous room could give him, especially since he had told Mildred he wanted no interruptions whatsoever.

After what seemed liked his hundredth turn, he stopped. He looked over at the chair behind the desk, thinking about the many men who had occupied the seat and agonized over life-and-death decisions.

He turned right and walked over to the door leading to Mildred's office. He pulled it open and stepped into the doorway.

"Mildred, can you ring Ashley up to see if she has time for me?"

She called the First Lady's secretary and spoke for a moment.

"Sir, she's upstairs. She had no appointments this afternoon and decided to take a little time to catch up on her correspondence."

Alexander smiled and thanked Mildred.

He stepped back into the Oval Office and closed the door, only to walk left to the doors leading out to the L-shaped covered colonnade which framed the Rose Garden.

As he approached the main building of the White House, the Marine sentry manning the entrance to the building smartly opened the door for the President and saluted.

Alexander returned the salute and stopped short of passing through.

"Good afternoon, Ralph. How are you doing?"

Alexander knew every one of the Marines charged to protect the White House by name and often chatted with them.

The sentry smiled and responded, "Fine, sir. And yourself?"

"Very well, thank you. I heard through the grapevine that you are getting married in a month."

The Marine's smile grew even wider.

"That's correct, sir. I'm a lucky man."

Alexander reached over and gave him a pat on the shoulder.

"I don't doubt it. My wish for you is that you have as wonderful a relationship as I've had with Mrs. Alexander."

"Yes, sir. I hope so."

The President walked into the building, thinking that he would have to get something special for the young man. Who was he kidding? Ashley would be the one to come up with the perfect gift. He had no clue about such things but his wife did and he loved her for it.

Alexander often walked down the centre hall on the ground floor, to the Grand Staircase and jogged up the two flights to the Residence. Today, though, he decided to use the private elevator located in a small alcove, just off to his left.

As he reached the top floor, the door opened and he headed through the cosmetology room and then the President's Dining Room. Though more circuitous a route, it brought him more quickly to the West Sitting Hall and directly into the President's Bedroom.

Seeing the First Lady wasn't there, he walked left over to the door to the private sitting room.

Until 1970, this room had often been used by the Presidents as their bedroom, leaving what is now called the President's Bedroom, for the First Ladies, as was the tradition. Alexander had decided to revert back to Lincoln's example and use the latter as a bedroom for himself and his wife. The sitting area was remodelled to accommodate their more private times, reading, watching games on TV, or to allow them to do a bit of work, as Ashley was now doing.

The large room was tastefully decorated to reflect their approach to life: understated yet bold. The walls were painted in an off-white hue leaning toward a light shade of taupe.

The two tall windows on the south face of the White House, which many tourists erroneously considered to be the front of the building, looked on the Truman Balcony which was supported by the semi-circular portico. The curtains which framed the windows, were of a rich bronze tone.

The furniture was designed more for comfort than status. Two three-cushion, contemporary sofas and several plush chairs, one of which was a La-Z-Boy, were arranged facing one another in a cozy, discussion-facilitating pattern.

The La-Z-Boy, which was Alexander's favourite seat, was placed in order to blend in with the others if he was just talking with Ashley or with guests. All the while, its strategic placement also allowed him to clearly see the large sixty-inch HD TV hanging on the wall.

Since the missus didn't want it to look like a *man cave*, she had commissioned the design of a muted painting of the Mount Rushmore Presidents, all of whom were her husband's heroes, which magically separated down the middle to reveal the television behind it. When not in use, the painting simply blended into the decor of the room.

The coffee tables and end tables were Chippendale in design and made of American Walnut.

Ashley was sitting at the walnut slant-top desk with glass bookcase above, deep in thought. With her back to the President, he was halfway into the room before she realized she wasn't alone.

Turning to see who had entered, she perceived it was Felix.

"Hi, sweetheart," said the President. "I didn't mean to disturb you. You seemed preoccupied with what you were reading."

"Oh, it's nothing, love. Just a petition from a ladies' group in Chicago, hoping I might support their campaign to improve the quality of the food served to the kids in their school district."

Alexander raised his eyebrows. "It might sound like it's low on our priority list, but in the end, it all comes down to providing a roof over their heads and food on the table and isn't that one of the most important things we can do for the children of America?"

He put his hand on her shoulder and bent over to kiss her on the forehead.

Ashley looked at Felix with a slightly puzzled look. "What brings you up here in the middle of the afternoon?"

"Hum. Come and sit with me."

He extended his hand to help her get up out of her chair and led her to one of the two chairs in the most intimate grouping. He took the other.

Ashley knew her husband well. He was rarely dramatic, reserving this type of behavior only for life-changing moments. The first was when he decided to run for Congress, the next when he ran for the Senate and finally when he decided to take a stab at the presidency. She sat quietly, with a slight smile on her face, all the while wrinkling her forehead, as if saying, OK, out with it.

"I've been thinking a lot about what we talked about last night. I think I've decided to go for it."

"Seriously?" was Ashley's response. "You know the type of opposition you'll get, from all sides, on this."

"I know. But, we came to politics with one purpose. The two of us wanted to make a difference in this country."

She nodded in agreement but still maintained her quiet and composure.

"The more I think of it, the more I want my legacy to mean something. I believe that young Buckner might have been right when he said I should do the correct thing. I believe *this* is the correct thing for our country. If I have to go down in the upcoming elections, then, so be it. It will be for something I believe in and hold dear. Hopefully, I'll be remembered as a fighter and more so as a wise one."

Ashley leaned forward and put her hands upon his. "I love this side of you. It was there when we started this journey and it's what has made you special. Not sure how wise a decision this is," she said good-humouredly, "nevertheless, if you feel this strongly about it, then you know I'll be right there next to you."

As he smiled broadly, Alexander's eyes became a little teary. He leaned forward to kiss her, this time on the lips and said, "You know how much I love you. You've made me a happy man all my life. It's your strength that keeps me going."

Part Three

Chapter 21

The President's Chief of Staff, Patrick Dolan, was standing at the head of the long walnut table, framed by the sixteen leather upholstered armchairs which surrounded it.

Behind him, in the centre semicircular wall, was the mantled fireplace above which hung a painting of Theodore Roosevelt as a Rough Rider, mounted regally on his favourite stallion.

Two doors shouldered the fireplace. The one to the right opened onto the short hallway directly connecting to the Oval Office.

On the wall to the left, the south wall, was a smaller painting of Theodore Roosevelt, next to a large landscape painting. A seascape of tall ships preparing for battle hung on the opposite wall.

The off-white painted room had no windows, but was illuminated by a large false skylight over the table, which appeared to flood the area with soft, natural-feeling light.

At the rear of the room stood what looked like a large Chippendale walnut bookcase. In reality, the two large doors at the centre could be slid aside to reveal a large flat-screen television, often used by the recent President to make conference calls as needed to groups and individuals around the world.

Comfortably seated at the table were the President's chief campaign officers. These were the brightest and most seasoned group of strategists and spin doctors in the country.

They had worked individually with the President in his run for Congress and then for the Senate, and as a group for his successful bid for the presidency.

Experts in the fields of communications, psychology and *schmoozing*, they had been hard at work since the initial inauguration preparing for the second *go at it*.

With the elections only six months away, they were surprised to have been summoned to the West Wing, especially as a group.

"Ladies and gentlemen, let's get this meeting going."

Jonathan Moore, the chief speech writer, was the first to speak up and express what they all were thinking.

"Pat, what's this all about? We were all in the middle of some important campaign activities, and though I can't speak for the others, I'm coming to a critical point in the final phase of our strategy."

A murmur of agreement was expressed by the others around the table.

"I'm aware of that, Jonathan. You know you would not have been called in if this meeting wasn't important enough to take place face to face and in private."

This prompted a look of concern in the eyes of a few of them, but it also got the attention of the lot of them.

Looking at his watch, and moving aside a little, Dolan added, "OK, then. I won't be running this meeting."

As if on cue, the door from that short hallway opened and in walked Alexander.

Everyone started to stand, but the President gestured for them to sit back down.

"Don't worry about the formalities. This is going to be a working session, and I fear, possibly not a short one."

The comment caught the group as being ominous.

After sitting down at the head of the table, the President leaned forward and put his elbows on it.

Looking at each person in front of him, he began. "What I'm about to present to you is a radical departure from our initial strategy. It's one I will get tremendous opposition to and it might cost me the election; nonetheless, it is one I am adamant about."

The look of surprise was evident on all the faces around the table.

"Let me put it bluntly."

Pausing for effect, he added, "We're taking on the NRA."

It took the group a moment to have sink in what the President had just said. Then it hit them, each immediately evaluating how this would affect all they had done in their respective fields of responsibility and what they would be asked to do to implement this new element.

Almost all, at once, began to voice concerns about the President's revelation.

Alexander let the barrage of comments continue for a good thirty seconds. He was used to the firestorm he normally faced when meeting the Press. This, at least, was a much more sympathetic audience.

He sat back and put up his right hand, asking for calm. It worked almost instantaneously.

"I anticipated your reaction and you are right in doing so as such. You were hired not to be "yes" people, but rather to voice your opinions based on your areas of expertise.

"Now, I'm not asking you to try to convince me to do otherwise. It's a *fait accompli*. What I need to get from you are options for a strategy to implement this new piece of our platform. I need options, not obstacles. The obstacles are what you have been hired to overcome."

Looking around at his team, he noticed that some were gazing down at the table top, deep in thought, others were looking calmly at their president while others were in quiet conversations with one another.

Alexander had also anticipated this stage of the meeting and decided to leave it to them to make the first move, which came from Helena Lowden, the President's top strategist and the best spin doctor he had ever met.

"Sir, may I begin by saying that this is the boldest move in terms of policy since Kennedy's promise to put a man on the moon."

Done! Alexander thought as he smiled. This should be good.

The meeting with the President went on for an unprecedented two hours behind closed doors.

As he rose from his chair, he commented, "I love seeing you people at work. It's going to be a long evening and night, but I want your best options and proposals by morning. I think you should call your aides to bring a fresh change of clothes. I'll get the kitchen to work overtime and I promise you'll be fed and watered well."

There was a round of laughs from the team and before the President had crossed the threshold from the short hallway into the Oval Office, the group had already returned to brainstorming.

As the President walked into his office, followed by Dolan, he asked, "What do you think?"

"They'll do it, sir. I'm confident they are that good."

Alexander turned to look at his chief of staff and simply added, "I hope you're right. Both your job and mine are on the line."

He walked over to the door to his secretary's office and peeked in.

Mildred looked up, and unflustered by the President's appearance, asked, "Yes, Mr. President?"

"Mildred, can you call Tom and ask if he could join me."

Alexander knew that if he was going to move ahead on this, he would need the support of his vice-president above all.

Thomas Bragg was one of the few Democrats elected in the southern portion of the country. A direct descendant of General Braxton Bragg who had commanded the battles at Shiloh and Chattanooga, among others, he was able to straddle the delicate division between southern nostalgia and northern pragmatism. If it wasn't for him, Alexander would have lost critical southern states during the last election.

Thomas was a card member of the NRA. He loved hunting and thought fondly of the old American way of life and standards. Though not a strong supporter of the NRA, he had, nevertheless, rarely openly criticized the organization, knowing he could antagonize a good number of his North Carolina constituents.

Alexander understood that Thomas had to be his first convert. It wasn't going to be easy.

Chapter 22

It took the team two days to come up with a complete rewrite of the campaign strategy, in order to accommodate the new platform. When the President was advised they had the brief ready for his approval, he invited them to the Oval Office to make their presentation.

He had his secretary reschedule his appointments and sat behind the Resolute desk waiting for the knock on the door. As he sat, he ran through, in his mind, what he had put into motion.

His talk with the vice-president had not gone quite as well as he had hoped, but he had come back with a promise from his partner that he was in it for the long haul. Before fully committing, though, the vice-president wanted to have all the particulars about the strategy, especially the role he was going to be asked to play.

Chapter 23

The President and Patrick Dolan were discussing the plans for the inner cabinet meeting the President had arranged, in order to talk about the changes in the strategy for the upcoming election.

Alexander would have loved to have Bragg there to support him, especially with Lance Harper, the Attorney General. Not only was Harper incredibly knowledgeable about the law and the constitution, he was also, well, a Texan. Weren't they both born with a gun in their hands?

The meeting wasn't going to be held in the Cabinet Room around the corner from the Oval Office. Rather, Alexander had decided he would take them out of Washington to a plantation he and his wife had stayed at some years earlier.

The large expanse of land, the isolation, and the intimate setting could make it easier to introduce his idea of challenging the NRA. The Petit Pas Plantation was situated on Bayou Lafourche near Napoleonville, equidistant from Baton Rouge and New Orleans.

In order to reach it without drawing too much attention, Dolan had recommended flying everyone on Air Force One to the Marine Corps Base in Baton Rouge and then flying from there by helicopter to the plantation. Obviously, the President would be on Marine One, along with the other three decoy helicopters. The others would fly in an HMX-1 land Osprey, an odd hybrid between a fixed-wing plan and a helicopter: It could fly quickly and silently as a fixed-wing plan, but, when it was time to take off or land, the two engines on the tips of the wings could manoeuvre between the horizontal and the vertical position.

Their departure from the base would not raise any concerns from the locals but the landing at the plantation could create a little interest on the part of the neighbours. Only two helicopters, the President's and the Osprey would land, detaching themselves from the group at the last moment, deposit their passengers and rejoin the flyover and continue on. The plan was to have the stratagem over within three minutes.

Just then, there was a knock on the door leading into the room.

Both individuals instinctively looked toward the door, but it was the President who signalled to Dolan that it was alright and to stay seated.

Alexander walked to the door and opened it. There stood Wilson Fleet of Homeland Security.

The President held his hand out to shake his.

"Hello, Wilson. It was good of you to come so quickly."

Wilson broke out in a large smile and a well-practised response: "Not a problem, sir. I serve the President."

Alexander stepped aside to allow Fleet to walk by him and into the room. He headed over to Dolan and shook his hand.

"Please, grab a seat, anywhere you feel comfortable. Can I get you something to drink?" said the President.

"No, thank you, sir. I've already had my limit of coffee for the day."

When all were seated, Alexander looked briefly at Dolan and then began.

"Alright, Wilson, let's get down to why I called you here. I'm going to need your people to help secure two venues we'll be using during the election campaign."

There was a look of surprise on Fleet's face. "Sir, we are at everyone of your *sorties*."

The slightest smile came to Alexander's face. He was thinking, there he goes again, using a military term to describe the President's speaking engagements. Only Fleet would see campaigning as war.

"Yes, you're correct. Nevertheless, while you are aware of the second event at the Convention Center in New Orleans, the first, at the Plantation in only one week's time, needs to be kept under wraps."

Fleet's face remained blank. However, had one examined it closely, they would have noticed his pupils growing larger, revealing his curiosity and concern.

Alexander looked at Dolan again and then at Fleet.

"I'm calling a special meeting of the cabinet and I need to keep it ultraquiet and secure. Patrick will brief you on the particulars of the location and the transportation issues. As well, though my people usually look after the security at my sorties," he smiled and continued, "I'd like you to beef it up."

"That won't be a problem, sir. May I ask why the increase in security?"

The President hesitated a moment. "No, not yet. Actually, you'll be attending this meeting as part of the wider cabinet and you'll get all the information as the others will. You'll also be asked for you input."

"And New Orleans?"

Dolan stepped in at this point. "Sir, if I may?"

Alexander nodded his approval.

"As you are already aware, the President has planned a large fundraiser in New Orleans."

"Yes, we've been organizing since your campaign committee decided on the venue."

Dolan continued, "As you know, New Orleans is a focal point for the southern conservative element in the US. The President wants to take his campaign to the opposition, to the centre of their heartland. He will be making an announcement very shortly, which will up the ante a hundredfold."

Fleet leaned back into the sofa he was sitting on and let out a silent *whoa*.

Alexander gave Dolan a quick look and took over.

"I'm sorry I can't tell you more, Wilson, but all will become clear at the meeting next week and it is one of the reasons why I needed to see you in person and not inform you over the phone. By the way, sorry for springing this on you with just seven days' warning."

Fleet knew this was the cue that his session was at an end.

He rose and said, "Not a problem, sir. It isn't anything we can't take care of."

The President and his chief of staff rose as well.

"I want you to meet with Patrick in his office and he'll fill in the blanks."

With that, Dolan and Fleet shook the President's hand and walked over to their left to exit through the door that led directly into the chief's office area.

****

Exactly one hour and fifty-four minutes later, Fleet was back in his office. He touched his desktop at a particular spot and the names of each of his undersecretaries appeared on an iPad-size screen. He tapped on Melinda's name and a calling tone was heard.

There was a click and she spoke, "Yes, sir, what can I do for you?"

Using the silkiest of tones he said, "Could you spare a moment for me?"

Melinda knew that wasn't a humble request. The more silky his tone, the more serious the issue.

"I'll be right there: 'Beam me up, Scotty.'"

Fleet smiled. He loved the Star Trek franchise movies. He thought perhaps that's where he got the inspiration for his desk.

Three minutes later, Melinda walked into his office.

Fleet rose from his sitting position and gestured for her to take one of the two leather chairs opposite him.

"I need you to look after the fort next weekend. I'll be out of town . . . "

Chapter 24

The President's helicopter pilot allowed the rotors to slow down to the point of preventing dust from flying about. Marine One had followed the Osprey down to the private landing strip at the rear of the Petit Pas Plantation.

The cabinet members had all disembarked amid a cloud of dust. In spite of the reduced visibility, they were ushered to a safe area close to the small hangar on the property. Their transport had been able to land and take off in under two minutes, a tribute to the Marines who helped them out. Now it was up to the President to keep the projected time span down to three minutes.

As he stepped out of the helicopter, the President was quickly escorted by his Marine guard to just beyond the rotor length, where he was greeted by another, who led Alexander to the rest of the awaiting group.

No sooner had the first Marine guard returned to the helicopter than it lifted up into the sky to rejoin the helicopter convoy above, proceeding in a southwesterly direction. They would fly for about thirty minutes and then turn due north to head back to Baton Rouge to wait for the return flight to pick up the President and his cabinet two days hence.

As Alexander reached the group, Patrick Dolan moved ahead to greet him with a handshake and turned to the owner of the plantation, Leonard Marsh, motioning him forward to meet the President.

"Welcome to Petit Pas Plantation, Mr. President. It's such an honour to have you back. At the time of your last visit, you were, and I don't mean this with disrespect, just a congressman."

Alexander laughed warmly and patted Marsh on the back as they moved toward the group of secretaries. "Say, do you still offer those great cigars and wonderful brandy after supper?"

"Oh, yes, we do. It's one of our traditions."

"And," responded Alexander, "it's one of the reasons why we selected your plantation. Ashley keeps an eye out for my health, and cigars are a no-no. So, what happens here, stays here. Right?"

"Lips are sealed, Mr. President."

They walked toward the hangar where there were half a dozen limousines, including the presidential *Beast*, as the White House security team called it.

The President and Marsh got into that car while the rest of the group were led to other vehicles by the Homeland Security agents sent to bolster the President's own security people.

After a short drive of only two hundred metres, they reached the mansion. As they approached the house from the driveway on the southern side, Marsh was describing the different structures on the plantation, including the detached Captain's House at the rear of the main building, where Brad Pitt had actually sojourned.

Though the driveway ended at the rear of the building, the motorcade continued onto the grass to the front of the house, in order to give the guests a better view of the great white portico.

As all the guests were exiting their vehicles, they were greeted by the view of beautifully restored and very well-maintained Greek Revival architecture. The six tall Ionic columns which framed the front of the porch and supported the second floor balcony, as well as the roofing, were reminiscent of a Greek temple.

On either side of the main rectangular building were two smaller identical extensions, housing the offices and a private bedroom.

The group was led by the owner up the front steps to the large entrance door. As they stopped to appreciate the architecture, Harper leaned over to the President and said in his Texas drawl, "Is there any significance to the meeting taking place here at *Pedipaw*?"

Alexander smiled and corrected him. "It's pronounced Petit Pas, which means small steps."

Harper returned the smile and shot back, "I know what it means. I may be Texan, but I'm not illiterate."

Alexander laughed out loud, surprising the rest of the group, intent on soaking in the history of the mansion.

"Actually, there is a significance. I'm taking a small step toward what I hope will be as giant a leap as the one taken by Neil Armstrong on the moon."

"Cryptic," responded Harper, with a look of curiosity on his face.

Stepping through the door and into the traditional central hallway with its twelve-foot-high ceiling, they were guided to the library, immediately to the left and the sizeable living room just behind it. The parlour was to the right and front of the house, with the large dining room to its rear. At the end of the hallway stood the grand staircase, leading up to the second floor and bedroom area.

The owner turned to the group and said, "Ladies and gentlemen. The staff will escort you to the rooms you have selected. I invite you, at six o'clock, to the wine and cheese party we have prepared for you. Usually, it's the ideal time for our guests to get to know each other, but I would assume that isn't the case in this situation."

The group laughed and it was the President who chirped in, "No, that certainly isn't the case. They're together more than they are with their families, I'm sorry to say."

The staff, dressed in period clothing, approached the secretaries and having been briefed prior to their arrival, took each person to their respective rooms to freshen up.

The President was led to the Master Bedroom, while the Secretary of Defense had selected the Mrs. Marsh Room. The Secretary of State was assigned to the Mystery Lady Room, with its two four-poster beds. The only female member of the inner cabinet, the Secretary of the Treasury, was pleased to have selected the Honeymoon Suite in the Chalet, while the Secretary of Homeland Security took up the Proteus Suite, leaving the Brad Pitt Room for Patrick Dolan. Lance Harper, the Attorney General had opted for the Lower Floor Bedroom, due to his hip problems.

With everyone settling into their own room, Alexander needed a bit of time to himself in order to review the strategy he had planned for this marathon, two-day meeting with his key people. He noticed the large windows leading out to the front balcony of the house. He lifted the tall, almost floor-to-ceiling, double-hung window and gingerly stepped onto the balcony, only having to stoop slightly.

The view was not only beautiful but also serene. He walked closer to the banister and looked out across the large lawn with its huge weeping willows, to the small reed-lined river on the other side of the country lane in front of the plantation. Interesting, he thought: I call it a river and they call it a bayou. His mind went back to one of his meetings with Melinda Gordon, where she had related an interesting tidbit of information the young Buckner had given her regarding the origin of the word. The French had called areas such as this one, *bas lieu*, meaning lowland or swamp, but because the English couldn't pronounce it properly, they had simplified the term to bayou.

Looking down, he noticed the guards patrolling the perimeter of the property. It was only then that he noticed movement from his peripheral vision. Turning in the direction of the motion, he saw that he wasn't alone. Two agents from his security team were on the balcony along with him.

"Good day, gentlemen. Nice view, isn't it?"

"Yes, Mr. President," one of them said, while the other just nodded and turned to continue his vigil.

So much for privacy, thought Alexander, as he walked over to one of the rocking chairs on the balcony. He eased himself into it and began slowly rocking and thinking about the task at hand.

****

At six o'clock sharp, all of the members of the inner cabinet and the President arrived in the library. Lance Harper, though, was about five minutes late, explaining that the plantation was so relaxing and peaceful, he had fallen asleep and had only awaken some fifteen minutes prior. The group ribbed him about his age and the need for those power naps he was famous for.

After filling their glasses for a second time, the owner gave the group a short tour of the vast living room, which was customarily used for the large parties and dances the plantation had held, back in the day. They walked through the parlour and then into the dining room for supper.

The President had specifically requested that the staff not plan any special meals for them, only the dishes which they typically prepared for their guests. Alexander had fond memories of the meal he and Ashley had been served.

Tonight's feast would not disappoint: chicken and *andouille* gumbo, followed by Cajun shrimp pie or crawfish *étouffée* with green beans, and potatoes and ham; to satisfy their sweet tooth, dessert consisting of either bread pudding or pecan pie.

The cooking staff were asked to come into the dining room to receive the guests' many praises.

They continued voicing their compliments as they walked to the parlour for their after-dinner coffee and brandy, and to partake in that age-old tradition of cigar smoking, one in which Emily Chord, Secretary of the Treasury, did not participate.

After about thirty minutes of light conversation, the President signalled to Mr. Marsh that their first meeting was about to start. The latter respectfully thanked the group for choosing the plantation for their deliberations and reminded them that there were several carafes of coffee and plenty of brandy for them to enjoy on the side table in the room.

He left quietly and summoned the staff in order to send everyone home, leaving the house entirely to the guests.

The President knew that days before, the security team had been through and had scanned every inch of every building for possible bugs. Obviously, none had been found and with the nearest neighbour being half a kilometre away and the agents from Homeland Security and his own people on surveillance, he knew that anything that was going to be said, was going to remain safe and private.

Sitting in a rough circle, in a variety of chairs, sofas and upholstered settees, the group seemed mellow enough for the President to begin. Clearing his voice to get their attention, he started.

"I know you are all wondering why I've called this meeting, out here in the southern wilderness."

Though the group chuckled and nodded to each other, there was still some tension in the air.

"Well, I'm going to get right to the point. We are here because I've come to a decision that will impact on all your jobs. We are under six months from the November election, and I plan on throwing a twist into the campaign. I need to know who will be with me and who will decide it's too much of a twist to agree to."

The room went silent in anticipation. Each one of the secretaries was an old hat at politics and understood, better than most, the pitfalls of sudden and radical changes in a campaign race. But behaving like the professionals they were, they withheld their judgment until they actually heard what it was all about.

"I'm giving you the opportunity of talking me out of this, if you can," continued Alexander as he looked around to each one of them.

"I want to alter the election campaign to include the abolition of high-powered, military-style rifles for our citizens."

Luckily, the staff had left. The stir in the room seemed to come from a far larger group than was actually present, as each fired the first thoughts that came to them.

"Are you kidding?"

"At this time of the campaign!"

"You know who we'd be up against."

"There goes my job and all of yours."

"Felix, have you had too much brandy?"

The President let them all talk, allowing each one to vent their surprise. He could see the dynamics playing out before him: Every comment would be repeated by those who would criticize him in the up-and-coming campaign, nothing he hadn't anticipated.

He sat quietly, listening to the opinions being expressed and waited for the inevitable drop in volume and then the pause.

"Yes, you are all right, except for the amount of brandy I've consumed. I've been contemplating the issue for a while now and I've come to the conclusion that it's the correct thing to do, especially at this time in our nation's history."

It was Fleet who spoke up.

"Sir, you do know the type of opposition we are going to get from the NRA. They are going to pull out all the stops, fully aware they can topple this administration on this topic alone."

Alexander smiled and calmly responded, "There is no doubt in my mind that the NRA will try just that. But, they don't represent *all* Americans. I have faith in our citizens to see that we need to do this."

Chord stepped in next.

"Sir, why now. Why so late in the campaign?"

Alexander turned toward her, still managing to smile softly.

"I guess the old adage says it best: Why not now? I think our people have truly had enough of all these senseless shootings in our schools, on our military bases, in our post offices. There doesn't seem to be any place where they might feel safe from that crazed individual with an AK-47 or an Uzi.

"Look, I know all the reasons why I shouldn't be doing this. What I want to know is, what are the reasons why we should?"

Alexander looked around and sat back, giving them the required amount of time to digest the question. He knew their personalities and was confident they had already shifted from the knee-jerk reaction position, to one where they were analyzing the pros and cons of what the President had proposed.

Harper was deep in thought, eyes lowered, looking down at the floor. Slowly, he raised his eyes to meet the President's.

And so it begins, Alexander thought.

"Sir, on what authority do you propose to do this? You do know that only Congress can alter the constitution."

"You're right, Lance. You would know the law better than I. Besides, I am not suggesting we change the constitution. The Second Amendment is quite clear. It guarantees our citizens the right to own and bear arms and this cannot be infringed upon. I'm not proposing to go to the electorate and say we want to ban all guns: just the type that we issue to our soldiers and which are used to defend the Republic from without."

Unperturbed, Harper asked the same question again.

"Right. Let me try to answer more specifically. I don't believe the fathers of our country ever wanted to give the citizens *carte blanche* in deciding what type of gun they could use for their personal protection.

"The Second Amendment was passed in 1791. Though the Supreme Court has ruled that that right is vested in the individual and not just in the militias, I think the Militia Act of 1792 more clearly defines what they really meant by it."

Harper interrupted. "Yes, but that act was written in the event of an invasion or insurrection. This is not the situation we find ourselves in nor why the Supreme Court ruled as they did."

"I don't disagree with you. On the other hand, that's not the section in the Act I'm referring to. The Militia Act gives the President the authority to call up the militia in those two situations. It also states the type of musket the citizens or reservists called upon to serve needed to supply, the number of musket balls they were to have, a limit of no more than two spare flints, and the amount of gun powder they could carry in their pouches. These were to be provided by each citizen who was a member of the militia and could remain with him after the war, as was guaranteed by the Second Amendment.

"I hold that allowing the Presidents to determine the types of arms that had to be provided means the Presidents could also limit the types of arms a citizen could own."

Harper's eyebrows rose, and his facial expression indicated he seemed to think the argument could have merit.

"What about the Supreme Court ruling that the right to bear arms rested with the individual?"

"Again, I don't disagree with you or the Supreme Court ruling. Citizens do have the right to bear arms, but not the right to decide, without limits, what types they can own."

Lou James, the Secretary of Defense indicated he wanted to talk.

"Sir, I like that line of thought. I've always believed that the high-powered assault weapon should only be in the hands of the military and, in special circumstances, in the hands of law officers. However, the use of this type of weapon has proliferated in the past ten years, due in part to underground gun runners, the return of many of our veterans who used them in combat and the support of the NRA. If you want to tackle the problem, I see these three issues as being a priority."

Alexander nodded his head in agreement.

"You're absolutely right. I've indicated *what* I intend to do. I'm counting on you and others in our administration to help me determine exactly *how* we propose to accomplish it.

"As for the NRA, they are a formidable foe. They've muddied the waters a lot by trying to confuse the issue with court cases dealing with the Fourth Amendment and the right of protection from unlawful and unreasonable searches. They prey upon people's fears and the myth that we are trying to prevent them from owning guns. Countering that will be an important part of our strategy."

Ever mindful of the budget, Chord was next to question the President.

"OK, if we can't or won't search for these weapons, the only way around retrieving them is for the people to voluntarily hand them in. I really doubt that will happen. Which brings me to the following point: Several of our major cities have had success in buying them back. Are you proposing we do the same at the national level? If so, where will you get the money?"

"Good question. In fact, that was going to be my next question . . . to you."

That surprised her and she unintentionally looked to the other cabinet members seemingly searching for an answer.

Alexander smiled again.

"Look, we have spent billions trying to protect our citizens by fighting wars all around the globe. At present, we aren't involved in anything major. So, to protect our citizens here at home, could we not find and use a few billions to buy back these terrible weapons? If anything, Americans know money and money talks."

Seeing that the questions were slowing down and that most of the secretaries had settled back into their chairs and were more than likely musing about what the President was proposing, Alexander decided to end the discussion.

"I believe we all have a lot to consider and overthinking it, at this time, will not be that constructive. Now, I know several of you are from areas of the country where one could be strung up for even thinking what I'm recommending." The group laughed as he continued, "And I truly do not want you to go against your convictions.

"Don't take what I will say next as an ultimatum or a threat. I truly admire all of you for who you are and what you have accomplished. As well, I can only decide for myself if I want to put my job on the line. Whether you support my proposal or not needs to be your decision, without pressure from me. So, I planned that tomorrow's discussions would revolve around solutions to the problems you've raised. If you don't believe in this course of action, you can't bring me the best ideas on how to accomplish the task.

"Breakfast is at nine in the morning, and I will see then who is willing to finish out the day here. As for those who are not, I repeat what I said before: I respect you too much to bear any ill will. I will work with you to come up with a scenario which will help you leave with dignity and satisfaction.

"I'm sorry for ending this part of the evening this way. I do invite you to sit around and enjoy a little more brandy and perhaps ultimately finish the evening in a somewhat more convivial atmosphere."

Expecting one or two to head to bed, the President was pleased to see none did.

As well, in the morning, as he walked into the dining room, he found all the secretaries sitting, talking among themselves, as though they were at camp.

Alexander stopped at the door to the dining room for a moment and thought that he couldn't be prouder of the choices he had made in appointing these individuals.

Chapter 25

Fleet had barely been back in his office for fifteen minutes when he summoned Melinda to meet with him.

She came prepared to fill him in on what had transpired while he was gone. Her detailed report took about twenty minutes.

"And, what about the dossier regarding the terrorist groups you've been following?"

Melinda pulled another folder out from her satchel.

"Things have developed on that item. We've intercepted several communications between ISIL in Iraq and Darul Islam in Indonesia, which not only shows the growing ties they are forming, but that, for the first time, they are openly discussing the question of creating a united front. Sir, I believe this is the beginning of a worldwide union of terrorist groups. It's what I feared when I first brought it to your attention."

Fleet lowered his head as he tried to absorb what Gordon was telling him. The President wasn't going to take this well.

"I'll bring this to the President's attention, but I think even this issue might take a back seat to another."

Melinda looked at Secretary Fleet with surprise.

"Something happened at Petit Pas?"

Fleet nodded with an expression of resignation.

"Yes, actually it did. The President will be making a grand announcement shortly, one which we will be forced to focus most of our attention on, until after the election.

I'm not at liberty to say what yet, but I do want you to shift gears and start preparing a plan to work with the White House security team, the FBI and our own people, in increasing the security around the President and his cabinet."

"Does that include you as well, sir?"

"Unfortunately, yes, it does."

"Also, I want you, personally, to oversee the security at the New Orleans Convention Center, where the President will host a huge fundraising dinner. You have two months to prepare."

Melinda's eyes widened a little.

"Not much time, sir. But not a problem. For the moment, who can I bring in on this?"

"I'll leave that to you. Do keep in mind that, until the President's announcement, it should be contained, but after everything is out in the open, you can move as you see fit. Just keep me informed."

"Yes, sir."

Melinda started to get up, but Fleet gestured her to sit back down.

"Sir, there's more?"

"I was just curious. I understand your friend was in to see the President a few weeks ago."

"Yes, he was. It was a bit of a surprise for him, but he thoroughly enjoyed it. Why do you ask?"

Fleet looked at her with an air of curiosity.

"Well, all through the cabinet's discussions at Petit Pas, the President seemed different."

"Different, how?"

"Well, I know him as an intelligent man and a politically shrewd one. I know how he thinks and how he talks. But there was something different about his 'optics', as he called it, during the meeting. He wanted to have the nation see him in a different light.

"It crossed my mind that the change seemed to have come about shortly after his meeting with Sam."

Melinda now seemed truly surprised.

"Sam told me how much he had enjoyed discussing his theory with the President and that he had even been put on the spot by being asked . . . " she paused, as if getting a revelation, ". . . how his conclusions could impact on the President's position and the upcoming election."

As the thought sank in, she put her hand up to cover her mouth.

"So you believe this announcement has something to do with the President's and Sam's meeting?"

"As I said, the thought has crossed my mind. It could explain a lot. If so," he grinned, "your man's ideas are certainly dangerous. Definitely someone I'd love to meet."

He rose, walked around his desk and shook Melinda's hand.

"Thank you for holding the fort in my absence. And, a word of advice. If you have any time coming to you, you should take it sooner rather than later. I have a feeling we're all going to be extremely busy for the foreseeable future.

"On another note, rest assured that in spite of this redirection of our priorities, I will bring your concerns about the terrorist groups to the President."

As he escorted Melinda to the door, he added, "And, say hello to Sam for me, will you?"

"Yes, sir, I will. He's actually flying into D.C. tomorrow. I'll relay your best wishes."

"Good. Let him know that the President specifically requested his presence at the fundraiser in New Orleans. Do you think he will accept?"

A huge grin appeared on Melinda's face.

"Just try to keep him away."

Chapter 26

Melinda picked Sam up at the airport in her Toyota. Since it wasn't an official jaunt, she felt it better not to use the limo service to which she had access.

They hadn't seen each other in almost a month, so, arriving at her apartment, they headed directly to the bedroom. An hour and a half later, they emerged wearing housecoats, slippers and a look of happy exhaustion.

Melinda checked the clock on the wall in the hallway to the living room. It was five-thirty in the afternoon.

"Not too tired, I hope," she said with a wink.

"No, that was quite the pick-me-up, if you know what I mean."

Melinda responded with a grunt and chided him,

"Oh boy, that was lame."

Sam snickered as Melinda continued, "Well, I took the liberty of making a reservation for supper at a nice little French restaurant, for eight o'clock."

"Sounds great. Is it far?"

"No, only about an hour away in Great Falls, a small D.C. suburb. It has great food and it's quiet. We can have a nice conversation. There were a few other places that are a little more jet set, but they're all so loud."

They showered together, dressed and headed out to the restaurant. The traffic was incredibly light, so they arrived at l'Auberge Chez François about a half hour early, allowing them time to sit and order martinis.

As soon as their drinks were brought to the table and the waiter left, Melinda put her hand on Sam's.

Sam looked up at her curiously and said, "I love you, too. What's this for?"

"And I love you. I have some news for you and a question."

Now, that really piqued Sam's curiosity.

"First, you will be getting an official invitation to be part of one of the President's fundraising dinners, and you won't have to contribute."

"Are you serious?" he responded, smiling broadly.

"Yup, in New Orleans."

"Wow, that's great. It's one of my favourite cities. But, why am I being so honoured?"

"Well, that was my question. What did you tell the President when you met him last?"

"I, I don't know. I told you about our discussion."

"Well, it might have been important enough for the President to make some kind of decision that has the whole West Wing running. Homeland Security is putting a priority on something the President is supposed to announce in a day or so."

"You're kidding me. Let me think. We spoke about my research, my conclusions about Homo sapiens and symbolicus, and . . . Oh!"

"What do you mean, *Oh*?" asked Melinda.

"He asked if I could explain how my theory could make a difference in his role as President. And then he asked me to identify the one issue Canadians had with Americans."

"And you told him what?" quizzed Melinda.

"Your fascination with guns."

"Oh my God," whispered Melinda, as she looked around to see if anyone was close by.

"I don't get it. What did I do wrong?" questioned Sam.

"You didn't do anything wrong. You spoke from the heart, like you always do. It's one of the things I admire you for. But in this case, it may have precipitated something huge."

"Like what?"

Melinda was about to answer when the waiter returned to take their orders. Sam told Melinda that since she had made the arrangements, she should order for the two of them.

"No pressure, but, OK. I think I know what you would like."

Turning to the waiter, she ordered the mussel in butter and garlic starter for the two of them. For Sam, she selected the duck and for herself, the Dover sole. The waiter complimented her on her choices, indicating that they were longstanding classics at the restaurant.

"Alright, finish what you were about to say," Sam pressed.

"I don't know what it is, but we do know that the President is going to make this big announcement. My boss thinks you might have triggered it. If I'm right, it has to do with gun control, probably the single most divisive topic in America. I think the President is going to go to the electorate on a gun-control platform."

Sam sat, silent, with a shocked look on his face.

It took him a few seconds to sort out all the thoughts going through his mind.

"I find it difficult to believe I could have convinced the President to do something like what you're suggesting."

"Based on everything I see happening at the White House, it would certainly make some sense of the whirlwind of activity going on there. We'll find out in a few days, won't we. As well, it would explain why the President is inviting you to New Orleans."

She looked at him with a serious expression on her face.

"See? The whole thing is your fault."

Then, the two of them broke into laughter.

Melinda reached across the table and took Sam's hands between her own.

"All joking aside, you have no idea how proud I am of you."

That took Sam aback somewhat.

"I'm glad you feel that way. But, I see it differently. Granted, I can sway presidents," he said with a wink, "but I deal with ideas. You deal with bad people . . . really bad people. And, you take them down without breaking a sweat. You're like a superhero with me as your sidekick."

Melinda chuckled. Then, her face took on an earnest look.

"Don't be silly. It's just a job. I'm talking about our relationship which has deepened dramatically for me."

Sam jumped in. "I know what you mean. This is the first time a relationship has gotten so *heavy* for me and yet feels so right."

She sat back, still holding his hands and looked at him in a questioning manner.

"Just how many relationships are we talking about?"

Sam sarcastically responded, "It has to be about a hundred. No, two hundred."

Melinda pulled back from his hands.

"Oh, come on. I'm being serious here."

It was Sam's turn to take her hands in his.

"I'm kidding. Really, I've had very few. You forget how much of a nerd I am.

"Listen, I've come to a realization of my own and one I'm more than comfortable with: I don't know how I could possibly live without you in my life."

He squeezed her hands and then leaned over the table to give her a gentle kiss.

The rest of the meal was magical. It was as if a bubble had enveloped them, isolating the two from the goings-on of the restaurant and allowing them to finish their supper and conversation oblivious to anyone there.

The drive back to Melinda's apartment took place in almost complete silence, with Sam holding and massaging her free hand. When they finally arrived, not a word was said as they made their way to the bedroom, shedding every piece of clothing onto the floor.

Tonight had been a turning point for the two of them and Sam decided he needed to go shopping while Melinda was at work the next day.

Chapter 27

At about the same time Sam and Melinda were having dinner, Oliver Doyle was sitting at his desk in his home office, looking over some of the investments the Super PAC he had set up was making in the reelection campaigns of targeted Republican and Tea Party candidates.

His phone rang and he quickly picked it up.

"Doyle, here."

"Yes, I have a moment. Go ahead."

After about thirty seconds, Doyle's eyes grew large.

"And you have that on good authority?"

"Yes, I'm really pleased you called to inform me. This is amazing news. It's what we've been hoping for since the beginning of the election campaign. I think we have him now."

"Give my regards to our friends at the NRA. Tell them we'll need to coordinate our efforts."

"Great. Thanks once more."

He replaced the receiver on its cradle, sat back into his chair and let out a long, low whistle. He couldn't believe their luck.

The President was going to announce his demise and Doyle would be there to close the door behind him as he was leaving the White House for the last time.

****

Just as they were about to begin preliminary discussions over the tasks surrounding the fundraiser in New Orleans, one of the agents got a tweet.

He signalled Melinda that they might want to check the breaking news on CNN.

They turned on the large screen monitor on the wall. As the image formed, it was clear who was front and centre. President Alexander sat behind the Resolute desk, with his entire cabinet standing behind him in support. It would be pointed out afterward that the Secretary of Labor, Charles Donovan, was conspicuously absent, having resigned from his post just two days prior, due to health issues. The President's announcement would throw some doubt about the real reason this secretary from Georgia would decide to leave the cabinet, so close to the upcoming election.

Alexander smiled at the camera and began. "My fellow Americans. History brings us to a momentous occasion and, surrounded by the top leaders of my administration, I want to inform you, the citizens of the greatest country in the world, of a decision I have made, one which will bring us forward into a new era of peace and prosperity at home . . . "

Melinda looked at the agents around the table, then picked up the remote and clicked the television off.

"Alright, gentlemen, as Sherlock Holmes once said, 'The game's afoot.'"

She got a round of groans and a chuckle or two.

Melinda added, "This is no longer a theoretical exercise. This is for real. So, what's next on the agenda?"

Chapter 28

The following weekend, John Doyle travelled home to spend a few days with the family, before leaving to do almost a month and a half of security work beginning with a few of the President's campaign stops, then a major rally in Houston with the attorney general, and finally with Sam in New Orleans.

He and his father were in the dining room, waiting for Hank to come down from his room to dine with them.

Oliver had poured a couple of glasses of dry sherry. He seemed to be in exceptionally good spirits.

Hank walked in at that moment and took his seat opposite John, toward the end of the long, four-metre oak table.

Oliver was at the head of the table and reached over to pour his adopted son a drink.

Followed by John and Hank, he raised his glass and said, "Cheers to both of you. It's always a pleasure to have my two sons home. Especially at times such as these."

Both boys looked at each other, not knowing what to make of that statement.

"What times are you referring to?" asked John.

Oliver kept smiling and responded with emphasis, "Why, the times of the presidency being handed over to our party, along with the control of both Houses."

Slapping the table with his left hand while almost spilling some of his sherry, he continued, "Alexander has given us the win we've been working toward."

Hank nodded in agreement and added, "The *SOB* thinks that by simply making an announcement, his predictions will automatically come to be."

John had no comment, prompting his father to ask why he was so subdued over the good news.

"Father, it isn't that I don't agree with you, but my job requires me to be as objective as possible. At least until I hit the voting booth.

"I have to be careful about what I say and how I say it, when it concerns the President."

Oliver's face went sour.

"You're at home with us. You can be yourself here."

"Yes, I can. Sorry, Father. It's the *persona* I put on every day at work. It's difficult to drop the façade.

"You are right, of course. Alexander certainly has blundered politically. I haven't checked any of the polls, though, to see how the announcement has affected his ratings."

Oliver's smile returned.

"Let me tell you, the preliminary effect on the polls has been nothing short of spectacular. His ratings have dropped to forty-one percent."

"Which polls are these?" asked Hank.

"Our polls."

Oliver hesitated a moment before continuing.

"True, they have essentially been taken in the South, and though such a drop is to be expected there, it nevertheless points to the reaction the announcement has provoked."

He took another sip of his wine and then topped up each of the other glasses.

"His biggest mistake is having attempted to bring about this change so close to the election itself. He probably thought he could come in strong, stomp around the country shocking the population into thinking he was doing something great, and as a result, expecting them to mindlessly vote for him. He just doesn't know how quickly we can mobilize our supporters to counter his arguments and crush his attempt to hijack the election."

Chapter 29

Melinda had mentioned to Sam that she had about a week of holidays coming to her and that she should take them as soon as possible, knowing that otherwise, she wouldn't be able to take time off until well after the election was over.

With his speaking tour winding down, Sam decided to surprise her.

Several phone calls later, he announced that she should pack and bring her passport. The dress code was casual, but classy, appropriate for a Mediterranean climate. They would be leaving the following day.

As much as Melinda pressed him to tell her where they were going, he refused to say, and while fighting the urge to tell her, hinted only that she would be pleased with his selection of destinations.

****

The next day, the taxi dropped the two off at the departure area in the Washington Dulles Airport. Melinda still had no clue as to where they were heading, but felt excited to the point of giddiness.

Sam led her to the US Airways ticket counter and pulled out an envelope from the inside pocket of his blazer. He took the two tickets he had had delivered to him that morning and handed one to Melinda.

She let go of her suitcase and eagerly took the ticket to see what their destination was.

Her eyes grew large and she almost shrieked. The huge smile on her face told Sam he had chosen well.

"We're going to Barcelona?"

She flipped the page to the next destination and brought her hand up to cover her mouth, stifling yet another squeal. "And Venice, too?"

Sam was beaming by now, most pleased with himself.

They checked their luggage through and headed off to their departure gate.

They had about two hours to kill, so they looked for a bar. He thought a nice Martini or two would set a mellow tone while they spent some time discussing what they wanted to see and do in these most-incredible cities.

The flight left on time at four twenty-five and arrived, a long ten hours later, at eight forty-five in the morning, Barcelona time.

Melinda had a knack for being able to sleep on planes. Sam, not so much.

He barely ate any of the breakfast they served them in the morning. But he did have coffee. As they walked out to the taxi zone in the arrival area of the airport, he realized he could use a couple more cups.

He had booked a room at the Royal Ramblas Hotel, in the centre of the Gothic area of the city. It was perfectly situated to give them access to the many venues encompassing the sites they wanted to see.

Sam had selected Barcelona in part because of the beauty of the city and in part because he knew they would be there for the festival of La Mare de Déu de la Mercè, the patron saint of the city.

For the next three days, they were caught up in a whirlwind of activities related to the festival, as well as to the usual tourist itinerary.

From the parades featuring *Gegants*, tall human and mystical statues, to the fireworks displays, to the *Castells*, or human tower competitions, to the huge outdoor concert in Plaça Catalunya featuring some of the top Spanish singers and dancers, activities abounded and the two were part of the thousands of happy revellers in town to celebrate.

When they weren't at a planned outing, they used the HoHo, or Hop-On, Hop-Off tourist buses which took them to all the main points of interest in the city.

The most impressive of these had to be the Sagrada Familia which is the basilica conceived by Antoni Gaudi. The majesty of the church took their breath away. It was like walking into a man-made forest of columns, designed to look like huge trees, and roofs disguised as foliage.

They spent a fair amount of time just relaxing, sampling local Spanish wines accompanied by tapas. Whether the food was purchased in La Boqueria Market, just steps from their hotel, or in the restaurants of the Barri Gòtic area, they marvelled at how great it all tasted.

They even attended a Flamenco show in a theatre in Plaça Reial, about a ten-minute walk from the Royal Ramblas.

When it was time to depart for Venice, both Sam and Melinda regretted saying good-bye so soon to Barcelona. Sam, on the other hand, was very excited at what he knew awaited them in the city of canals.

After arriving at the Marco Polo International Airport, they took a short shuttle ride to the docks, where a water taxi was waiting for them. Sam had reserved the taxi online, during his day of *shopping*, while in D.C.

As the sleek vessel left the dock and moved relatively slowly out into the lagoon, Sam slipped to the rear of the boat and slid the large glass roof panel forward and out of the way. Then he extended his hand to invite

Melinda to come and stand with him, leaning on the roof, to get a panoramic view of the waterway.

The taxi soon picked up speed and was plowing through the waves, heading to the main island which was that of Venice, their new haven. The ride was as exhilarating as it was rocky. Melinda's hair was flying wildly in the wind. She returned briefly inside the cab and came back out wearing a beautiful silk scarf, à la Sophia Loren. Sam beamed lovingly and took advantage of the situation to put his arm around her waist and pull her in tight against him.

They passed dozens of water taxis and *vaporetti*, ferrying hundreds of locals to their various destinations.

After about ten minutes, the taxi slowed down and entered one of the canals, with the pilot expertly manoeuvring among the many gondolas with their starry-eyed tourists, and utility boats which serviced the city, transporting and delivering all the goods the local restaurants and hotels needed, from food, to beverages, to laundry.

The scene was like that out of a movie. The buildings, each connected to the other and lining the canals, were three or more stories high. All reached down, directly below the water level, and offered but small steps leading up into their respective *pallazi*, which provided only a few shuttered windows to peak out at the world.

There was absolutely nothing new or modern about them. On the contrary, the painted pale orange, beige and white stucco on the walls was old and faded, sections of which were peeled off, exposing the terra-cotta brick underneath. Many of the wooden doors looked as though they had been there for hundreds of years, some almost falling off their hinges.

But that was the charm of Venice and the two seemed overwhelmed by the history and beauty they were taking in.

The water taxi emerged onto the Grand Canal and turned toward the left.

As Sam and Melinda stood, leaning onto the roof of the boat, they both burst out with the same expletive, "Holy crap!"

As crowded and slow to manoeuvre as the narrow canal was, the Grand Canal was much wider and busier. Everywhere they looked were vaporetti, or water buses, gondolas, water taxis, and *traghetti*.

The water was choppier here than in the small canal, not because of the wind but rather the wake of all the boats crisscrossing the waterway.

They were rounding a bend and all of a sudden the Rialto Bridge came into view. This permanent stone structure had been built in 1591 and featured two inclined ramps, enclosed by six arches on either side of each ramp, supporting the roof structure, and culminating in one larger arch in the centre. The arches framed shops catering now to tourists. What was difficult to see was the wide-stepped ramp in the centre of the bridge, giving access to more shops. It would only be later, when the two visited the bridge, that they would realize why it was so wide. Instinctively, both Sam and Melinda ducked as the taxi sailed beneath it.

The best was yet to come. The taxi proceeded for another five minutes, when they spotted, looming ahead and to the left, the front of the Doge's Palace, indicating they were close to St. Mark's Square.

Sam and Melinda had seen pictures of the square a hundred times. But never taken from this angle and never in real life.

The taxi was moving too fast for their liking as they tried to take in the images of the tower, the cathedral and the square behind them. Oh well, they thought, we'll be there soon.

Just past the palace, the taxi made a quick left turn to follow another narrow canal.

High above them and about fifty metres in, they passed under the Bridge of Sighs, a beautifully sculpted crosswalk, used by prisoners who had been found guilty of their crimes and had to walk over to the dreaded prison.

They had to duck three more times while the taxi passed under the typical arched pedestrian bridges spanning the canal, before they turned left once more and headed to a small wood dock at the rear of one of the buildings.

Sam said, "I think we're here," pointing to the Hotel All'Angelo's sign.

The hotel staff came out of a large sliding glass door, leading directly into the lobby. After helping Sam and Melinda out of the taxi and gathering their luggage, the staff escorted them to the desk where they checked in.

While doing so, Melinda heard Sam asking about room 302.

"Were we able to get the room?" asked Sam.

The concierge responded, "Si, signore, your room is ready."

Sam responded without a moment's hesitation, "Grazie."

Melinda looked up inquisitively at Sam. "Don't tell me you can speak Italian too?"

Sam smiled and said, "Yes. But only one word and that was it."

They laughed as they headed to the elevator.

The porter led them to the room and pressed the magnetic key to the door lock. He stepped in quickly, wheeling the suitcases inside and went directly to the centre curtains covering the window. He pulled the drapes back, letting the light into the room. Then, he returned to the suitcases and stood, obviously waiting for a tip.

Sam slipped him a few Euros and he was gone.

Melinda looked around the room. It was typical of the older architecture of the city. High ceilings and rather plain in its decor. Sam said nothing, but went to the window area and simply pulled open the other two curtains.

Only then did it become apparent why he had asked for this room. The curtains hid three tall glass doors overlooking the canal behind the hotel.

Melinda walked over to Sam slowly, tears forming in her eyes.

"This is absolutely amazing. I can't believe I'm here with you, looking at this view. How did you know?"

"Long story short, I researched it on line and one review commented on the room. So, I thought I'd reserve it."

They ordered a bottle of Pinot Grigio from room service and spent the next hour just sitting by the windows, watching the Venetian world drift by.

This was Italy at its best: gondolas floating by with gondoliers singing old Italian songs, clothing hung out to dry on clotheslines attached to the windows of the homes nearby, a walled-in elementary school just beyond the small arched bridge.

Sam was trying to arrange the next few hours to work with the plan he had in mind.

They spent some time visiting St. Mark's Square and the Cathedral. He took Melinda into the centre of the square and let her feed the pigeons. The pictures he took of her, with pigeons perched on her arms and even on her head, were hilarious.

Sam suggested they return to the hotel, a mere five minutes away, to change for supper. He added that he had made reservations at one of the locals' favourite restaurants, the *Ostaria Boccadoro*.

When Melinda asked how he had chosen that restaurant in particular, he said he had watched a documentary on Venice, hosted by the great guru of tourist travel, Rick Steves, and had been intrigued by the stop at the restaurant. He had researched it and decided, if he ever went to Venice, it would be one of the restaurants he would visit.

They entered their room and immediately opened all the curtains again, poured themselves a glass of wine and sat to admire the view and enjoy the peace and quiet.

Sam checked his watch about forty-five minutes later and realized they needed to get ready.

He showered and donned his blue suit and white shirt. He would go without a tie, though.

It was Melinda's turn in the shower. Before she went in, Sam told her he had to go downstairs to make transportation plans. He would be back in about twenty minutes or so.

He did head down to the reception desk, only to confirm the gondola he had ordered would be there in about thirty minutes.

He then went to the hotel bar and purchased a bottle of champagne, arranging for it and two flutes to be bundled and transferred to the gondola when it arrived.

Absent-mindedly touching his left coat pocket, he almost panicked when he felt nothing. A frantic patting of the other pockets led to finding a small lump in one of them. He then willed his heart to slow down to about a hundred and fifty beats per minute.

He decided he had to calm down before returning to the room, so he returned to the bar and ordered a Cognac to help soothe his nerves.

Ten minutes later and somewhat more relaxed, he was back in the room, just in time to see Melinda coming out of the bathroom, dressed and ready to head out.

He stood there, hardly able to speak.

She was so beautiful, with her black hair pulled back into a single ponytail, highlighting her high cheekbones. She was wearing a stunning Dior chiffon dress she had purchased to wear at some Washington events. From the sheer shoulder panels attached to the soft white opaque V-neck top, the bodice transitioned to a four-inch elastic chiffon waistband. The off-white tone continued down into the skirt section of the dress, only to morph slowly into a soft light grey and on to a deep charcoal tone at the knee-high hem. Overlaid were petal-like patterns made up of sequins. The look was completed by a simple strand of pearls and black satin pumps which she had picked up at the Burberry shop on Calle Larga XXII Marzo earlier in the day.

Sam walked over to her, lovingly took her in his arms and kissed her tenderly.

He pulled back a little and asked, "Are you about ready?"

"Surprisingly, yes."

He took her by the hand and led her out of the room and to the elevator. Having descended to the lobby level, he went over to the desk to hand in the key. The receptionist looked up, smiled and winked.

Instead of walking out to the sidewalk in front of the hotel, Sam led her to the sliding glass door at the rear.

There was a puzzled look on her face, but she had learned never to be surprised by Sam and to just go with the flow.

There, waiting for them, was one of the sleek black gondolas they had seen earlier.

Melinda smiled and asked, "Is this for us?"

Sam answered with Victorian formality, "Yes, milady. Our coach awaits us."

He helped Melinda into the boat, assisted by the gondolier, and then slipped onto the velvet seat next to her.

The gondolier went around them to the front and took out a matching black blanket and gently laid it over their legs. He then lifted one of the forward seats and took out the bottle of champagne Sam had purchased. With the traditional pop of the cork, he prepared to pour their drinks in the two flutes sitting next to them.

Though she was smiling broadly and had slightly misty eyes, Melinda was speechless until the gondolier began rowing.

"Sam, this is surreal. I love it. I love you. Thank you."

She leaned over to him to kiss him passionately.

Just then, the gondolier began singing '*O, sole mio*'.

"Do you know what the song is about?" asked Sam.

"No clue, but I like it."

Sam explained, "It's about the beauty of a sunny day. But there is a brighter sun yet, that of my sun, or love, upon your face. Even when night has come, my sun shines upon you."

"That is really beautiful."

The two sipped their champagne, listened to the gondolier while he stealthily manoeuvred the narrow canals and corners.

The sun was setting by then. Only the tops of the buildings still caught some of the rays. Down below at the level of the water, the evening was overtaking the city and the canals were acquiring a magical and enchanting look.

They slid by dozens of other gondolas, some with couples like themselves, many with groups of six, riding together to reduce the individual cost of the trip.

Neither Sam nor Melinda paid any attention to them: They were immersed in each other and the ambiance.

Melinda noticed a slight change in Sam's demeanour. His hands were clammy and he was starting to sweat.

"Are you OK?" she asked.

She touched his forehead to see if he had a fever. No, that wasn't it.

Sam knew the jig was up and that it was time.

He got up from the seat and turned toward her, kneeling on one knee.

Upon seeing the goings-on in his boat, the gondolier knew what was about to transpire. He had witnessed it many times. So, he slowed the gondola to a crawl and stopped singing.

Sam looked up at him and smiled, recognizing the gondolier's efforts to make this easier.

Melinda looked at him, not understanding.

"What are you doing?" she asked.

Sam cleared his throat.

"Melinda, we may be from different worlds, but when we are together, every difference disappears. I've always analysed everything to death. But on the most important issue in a person's life, that of finding one's soul-mate, you've made it simple and a matter that doesn't depend on the mind but the heart."

Then it hit Melinda. Her hand was shaking as she put her glass down and then again when she brought both to cover her mouth.

Sam reached into his left inside pocket and found the small box. Taking it out, he opened it to reveal the contents.

"Melinda, it didn't take me long to decide I could never live without you in my life. I know our two worlds will make it challenging, but we'll find solutions to every obstacle.

"Melinda, will you marry me?"

Tears were flowing from those beautiful blue eyes and her hands were hiding the smile she had on her face.

Nevertheless, she took a moment to regain her composure.

Sam took the engagement ring out of the box, leaving the matching wedding band inside it. He reached for her left hand.

Slowly, she surrendered it to him.

"Will you say yes?" Sam asked.

She looked at him lovingly and responded, "Are you kidding? There's no doubt in my mind that I want to be with you and love you until the last day of my life. If I have to say it, then, yes, yes, yes."

Sam slid the ring onto the fourth finger of her hand and returned to his seat next to her.

They kissed long and passionately, oblivious to the five gondolas that had stopped in their tracks to witness and then cheer the lovers' moment.

Their gondolier resumed his rowing and the boat slipped away into the dark.

Melinda finally looked down to see the ring he had selected for her. Being a take-charge person, this was a new feeling for her. She didn't care what it looked like: *He* had bought it for her and that was all that mattered.

She could get a good look at it as they rode by the lit windows of the homes along the canal, or as they approached and left the small arched bridges on their way.

The ring was absolutely gorgeous and unique. She had never seen one quite like it.

Watching her trying to admire the ring, Sam stepped in.

"It's called the Riverwalk. It was designed by Bernard Passman, and if you look on one of the sides, you might be able to see that it's signed."

The ring wasn't the usual engagement ring. Melinda was trying to come up with how she was going to describe it to her sisters, who she would be calling that night, damn the time difference.

The ring was set in 18K gold and nothing was symmetrical about it. Inset in the gold was a seemingly undulating piece of black coral, reminiscent of the shape of an Egyptian eye, with a row of diamonds shouldering it on the one side, or lower lid, following the slow S-shape of the ring. Then, set on but above the black coral and slightly to

244

the right of the centre, representing the iris of the eye, was a brilliant one-and-a-half-carat diamond.

Melinda finally took her eyes off the ring.

"Is it legal?" she asked, to Sam's surprise.

"The coral? Yes. I was told it was harvested deeper than eighty metres below the surface."

Looking at her with a teasing look, he added, "I didn't know you were a *tree hugger*?"

"Not quite," she responded.

"It's so different. It's so me! How did you know?"

Sam took a sip of champagne and tried to explain.

"I didn't know for sure. I looked at so many rings that I was becoming jaded . . . pun intended. Then, I walked into this one jewellery store where they had the same old settings. I told the saleslady that I saw nothing which I felt was you. She hesitated a second and then asked me to follow her to the rear counter where she pointed out a collection they had managed to bring in. And there, in one of the small displays was this ring. One look and I was sold. I thought it was unique and so special. Of all the rings I had looked at, it was the only one which spoke to me, and it whispered *Melinda*."

She kissed him tenderly and then said, "I think I'm going to let you select all my jewellery."

By then, the gondola was lining itself up to dock.

Sam looked back at the gondolier and asked, "Are we there?"

"Si, signore. The restaurant is but a few metres through that laneway."

Sam had already paid for the ride while he had excused himself to go down to the reception desk.

He helped his fiancée out of the boat and holding her hand, led her toward the small square where Boccadoro's was located.

They emerged in a nearly empty square. In any event, there, occupying the first floor of a plain looking three-storey building, was the restaurant, with its black canopy and white frill on which was printed its name.

In spite of the sign, Melinda looked at Sam and asked, "Are you sure this is the right place? It seems as if we are alone."

Sam smiled and explained. "Don't worry. You're in Italy and people here don't usually come to supper before nine or so. We're two hours earlier than the locals."

As they approached the restaurant, one of the waiters came out to greet them. Seeing the weather was still relatively balmy, he suggested they try the tables outside. Considering Melinda's hesitance, Sam asked for one of the tables inside.

The restaurant was quaint but stylish. All the tables were covered in the traditional white linen tablecloths, but the walls were either exposed brick or painted in a chic deep grey, with large black panels within which were suspended pictures of Venice. The room they were seated in had but four tables, which added to the cosiness.

A moment later, a gentleman dressed in a white chef's jacket, introduced himself to the two.

"*Buonasera. Io sono Luciano. Benvenuti al restorante Boccadoro.*"

Sam realized the man was the owner of the restaurant and not someone he would want to meet in a dark alley. Bald, muscular, with a mustache and goatee that circled his mouth, he was quite imposing.

Seeing the two guests weren't too sure what he had said, the chef tried again.

"Bonsoir, good evening. I am Luciano."

The smile on their faces showed him they understood.

"Vous parlez français? Do you speak English?"

Sam responded, "Français et anglais. Je suis du Canada et ma fiancée est native des États-Unis."

Luciano took a good look at Melinda and said, "Ah, mais vous êtes un homme chanceux. Quelle belle femme."

Melinda looked at Sam, obviously wondering what they were saying.

Sam beamed back.

"He says I'm a lucky man!" He squeezed her hand.

"Vous venez du Québec?" Luciano continued.

"Non, je suis né au Nouveau-Brunswick et maintenant j'habite à Toronto."

Luciano seemed a little confused.

"Pardon, monsieur. Mais la plupart des francophones du Canada viennent du Québec."

Looking at Melinda, he continued in English.

"I believed your man was from Québec, as most Canadian francophones who come here, are. You on the other hand are not."

The three laughed.

"I will have the waiter come to look after you. I must return to the kitchen."

Before he could leave, Sam stopped him.

"Pardon me. But we have heard of your reputation and, trusting it and your skills as a chef, instead of ordering from the menu, could we ask that you surprise us?"

Looking and smiling at Melinda, he took her hand and raised it to show Luciano the ring.

"Tonight is a very special evening."

Luciano's face broke into a huge smile.

"But of course, it would be my honour to put something together just for you."

It had been a while since he had tourists give him *carte blanche* to show off his art. With a glint in his eye, he was off.

The waiter did come, shortly after , to take their wine order. Sam thought he would complete the circle by asking if the waiter could speak to Luciano to see what he was preparing for them and perhaps pair the dishes with a variety of local wines.

With Luciano returning several times to check on the two, the evening became a blur of great conversation, wonderful wines and a meal fit for royalty.

To start with, they were served what Luciano called *crudi*, a two-bite delight: tuna with blood orange and sweet prawn atop tart green apple slices. That was followed by spider-crab dumplings and black *tagliolini* with scallops and zucchini. Luciano apologized that he usually served this entrée with artichokes, but they weren't in season and he insisted on serving fresh vegetables. To finish off the meal, he brought a plate of small fried seafood bits to share and a decadent mousse made with five different chocolates.

Both Sam and Melinda had eaten their fill and craved an espresso although Luciano surprised them by offering them a snifter of cognac as an after-dinner drink.

"This will help you digest your food. I hope you enjoyed yourselves."

For at least five minutes, the two thanked Luciano profusely and praised his cuisine.

As they left the restaurant, they realized that both the inside space and the outdoor tables were now filled. The locals had arrived to claim their territory.

Sam and Melinda walked slowly back to the hotel along the dimly lit alleyways, guiding themselves by the church towers he had memorized, hoping not to hit too many dead ends, which they did, although only once.

Sam couldn't help but notice the number of times Melinda looked down at her left hand to see the ring.

I think they call it a heavy hand, he thought, as he smiled to himself.

Arriving at their room, the two sat for about an hour, sipping on a glass of wine and again watching the gondolas passing below their windows.

When it was time for bed, Melinda headed to the washroom, only to come out about five minutes later, wearing only her ring. Funny, but Sam was in bed under the covers, with not a stitch on as well.

"Great minds think alike," he said, as he patted the mattress next to him.

Chapter 30

Melinda was back at work three days later, jet-lagged and yearning for an Italian double latte.

She and Sam had discussed the whole issue pertaining to making their engagement public or not. They decided there was no reason for him not to tell his family and friends, but Melinda would only inform the secretary due to procedures within the department. By the same token, she would not inform the office staff, nor would she wear the ring while in Washington.

That part was killing her, as she found herself often looking down absent-mindedly at her left hand and being disappointed.

This morning, she had called her staff to brainstorm arrangements for the security measures they had to put in place for the President and the cabinet members. This would be her priority for the next couple of months.

The White House had sent over the campaign details the strategy team had come up with, in order to allow the President to sell his new platform.

Melinda's job today was to align the number of campaign stops and their locations, with Homeland Security protocols. They had a huge number of contingency plans for almost every imaginable scenario. Once the correct strategy for the occasion was identified, all the roles and tasks would already be described, and it was just a matter of assigning the personnel to follow the procedures.

When the time came to provide Sam with his protection, it was John Doyle who volunteered to look after that assignment, much to Melinda's satisfaction.

Chapter 31

"Larry, it's Hank."

"You sonofabitch! Why haven't you called before this?" was Larry Calhoughn's response.

Larry was one of the vets Hank had recruited to help him set up some of the security training at his compound. Hank had met him while in Baghdad for a debriefing session after one of his missions. Larry was responsible for security at the American Embassy there and had impressed Hank with the procedures he had implemented.

Obviously, the embassy was the one place the insurgents should not breach, from a political point of view, as well as for the protection of the high-level staff it housed.

The two had worked together to organize one of the top urban security training programmes in the country. Nevertheless, when approached by the people at the New Orleans Convention Center, Larry decided to settle down in one of his favourite cities and take the closest, most stable nine-to-five job he would ever know. The letter of recommendation from Hank didn't hinder him in getting the plum position.

"Sorry about that, man. I've been busy trying to keep up the standards you set here."

Larry smiled. "So, to what do I owe the pleasure of this call?"

"Well, I was thinking of spending a couple days in the *Big Easy* and figured I might be able to stop in to see you at work."

"That would be great! When are you coming?"

"I thought I would fly in on Thursday of this week and take a cab directly to the Convention Center. Would that work for you?"

Larry peeked at his calendar.

"Not a problem. Thursday's looking really good. About what time can I expect you?"

Hank picked up the reservation confirmation he had already gotten from the airline. "Looks like I'll arrive around fourteen hundred hours and could be there about an hour later."

"Perfect. What are you doing for supper?"

"I have nothing planned," responded Hank.

"Alright. Have you ever been to the Palm Court restaurant?"

"No, I haven't."

"Then you're in for a treat. Good live Dixieland music and the food isn't bad either, but the beer, just great."

"Sounds like a plan. Thanks. See you Thursday."

Larry was really looking forward to seeing his old boss and catching up on the gossip.

Hank was also pleased with how the call had gone. It was the first step in his strategy to finally take care of business.

Chapter 32

True to his word, Hank was in New Orleans and walking up the steps to the Grand Hall entrance at the Ernest N. Marial Convention Center, named after the first black mayor of New Orleans.

Passing through the main doors, he found a security guard nearby and asked him to contact his boss and let him know of his arrival.

While they waited for a callback from the security centre, Hank took a close look at his surroundings.

He was standing in a huge lobby. From the initial research he had done, he knew the almost fourteen thousand square-metre space was tiny compared to the general exhibition section far to the right. That one, totalling a staggering eighty-nine thousand seven hundred and forty square metres, could be divided into eleven separate rooms. Regardless, they weren't the surroundings he was interested in.

The guard got a double click on his walkie-talkie and was instructed to lead Hank up to Larry's office.

Larry was waiting for the two outside the office confines and after dismissing the guard, met Hank with a smile and a huge hug.

"How are you doing, big guy?"

"I can't complain," was Hank's response. "I see you've put on a pound or two since you took this job."

Larry chuckled and pinched his belly fat.

"I know. I have to do something about it, but I'm having too much fun putting it on. This city has so many great restaurants, I see it as a losing battle on my part."

He patted Hank on the back and said, "OK, come on and I'll give you a personal tour of the facility."

Noticing the small duffle bag Hank was carrying, he asked if he wanted to leave it in his office.

"No, thanks. I travel light and this way, we can head straight out to that restaurant you recommended. I'm starting to really crave some of that local beer they have here."

Larry handed Hank a guest security badge to pin to his jacket and led him to the elevator, which would take them down one floor to the main level.

As the doors closed on them and the lift began its descent, Hank asked Larry about the antiquated communication he was using in the centre.

"Ah, you took note of that, did you? It was the very first thing I decided to change. I've put an order through for some state-of-the-art com equipment. It should have been here a week ago, but was delayed because of some shipping SNAFU . . . "

Hank laughed at the comment, which meant *Situation normal: all fucked up.*

Larry continued, " . . . but we should have everything in place for the President's fundraiser in three weeks."

Hank tried to look surprised.

"Oh, you're having the big man himself stop by, are you?"

"Yup. Good for the cash flow, but one hell of a pain in the ass."

"I hear you there," responded Hank, all the while making a mental note of researching the com system Larry was getting.

254

The doors opened and the two walked out into the large lobby. They turned to their left and walked about fifty metres and then left again and through one of six large doors opening into the first of the exhibit spaces.

There weren't any shows happening that day, so the room was empty, adding to the sense of its size. Hank whistled in awe at the cavity.

"You could put a 747 in here and have room to spare."

Larry saw that his former boss was impressed.

"So," he added, "the hall beyond those large bay doors is as big, but the next nine are twice the size of this one."

"You're kidding. Wow," was all Hank could say.

"Come on. We'll head back to the Grand Hall. It's much nicer than these are."

They retraced their steps and walked down the long lobby room.

"Did you know that we can register several thousand people at a time for the various events we host?"

"No, I didn't. Is this where the guests at the President's fundraiser will come around?"

"Yes, and once they produce their credentials to security, they'll be ushered through there, to your right."

Hank looked over and saw several large openings leading into another space beyond. Larry led him to the other side of the portals and they emerged into another monstrous room.

Larry saw Hank taking everything in like a tourist and smiled to himself.

"What is this room?" asked Hank.

"This is the Pre-Function site. This is where we will serve cocktails prior to the main event which will take place on the other side of those doors.

The rectangular room had to be at least a hundred metres to the other wall and three times that wide, and about ten metres high. It was brightly lit, with some hundred tall, cylindrical chandeliers.

The ceiling had an interesting design. It seemed to begin just above the doors leading into the Grand Hall on the opposite side and reminded Hank of the old corduroy roads of pioneer times or the bamboo sheets used by Japanese chefs when rolling their sushi. The large oak beams ran the full length of the room and seemed to be stacked one on top of the other, creating a continuous ceiling which rose up along the walls. They then curved as they approached the top and crossed the ceiling, then curved back down again on the other side, to the top of the openings leading into the space.

Hank was intently observing it all, memorizing the position of each entrance point and door. He had noticed utility doors on either side of the large passageway which linked the lobby to the pre-event room.

"Interesting," he said. "Where do they lead?"

"Oh, just up to the catwalks above the cocktail area and over into the ceiling space in the Grand Hall.

"Let me show you the main event here at the centre. They walked to one of the six large double door entrances connecting the space they were in and the big room.

As they walked into the Grand Hall, Hank purposely commented, "Holy shit, man, this is humongous. How big is it anyway?"

"Glad you asked. It's over five thousand five hundred square metres. It can hold and feed up to sixty-five hundred people, legally."

Again, Hank was sizing everything up.

The ceiling treatment was the same as in the Pre-Function Room, but due to the fact maintenance people were working in the space above the ceiling, the lights were on there and you could see, through the space between the oak beams, a maze of catwalks, crisscrossing the entire space.

Paying particular attention to where the false ceiling curved down to join the rear wall, Hank thought to himself, yup, this will do just fine.

Larry guided Hank through the massive kitchen and the rear utility hallways, used by staff to move any equipment which was required for the various events held in the Grand Hall.

Having seen what he wanted to see, Hank thought it was time to have some fun with a good meal, a lot of beer, and live music to boot.

"Hey, man. Thanks a lot for the tour. This is just so incredible. I can see why you would have left the centre to come take the helm here. I envy you."

Larry was pleased, if not a little smug, at the comments. He knew he had made the right decision.

Hank looked around, questioningly.

"Uh, I think I need to go to the head. Is there one close by?"

Larry chuckled.

"Nothing here is *that* close by. We'll have to go back to the Pre-Function section. There are plenty of washrooms there."

They made their way towards the rear doors in the hall. All the while, Hank was checking out the false ceiling.

Reaching one of the washrooms housed in the wall between the pre-conference zone and the lobby, Larry stopped at the door to give his buddy some privacy.

No sooner was Hank inside, than he checked to see if he was alone. He was.

He plunked the duffle bag he was carrying on the sink counter and pulled out a handheld scanner. Then, he took a piece of white cloth out of the bag, laid it flat on the counter, pulled the security pass he had been given, and placed it on the cloth. He scanned both sides of the tag and then repacked everything, pinned his tag back onto his jacket and walked over to one of the toilets to show he had used it by flushing it.

He emerged from the washroom and walked over to Larry, who was talking to one of the security guards. When he noticed Hank, he finished his discussion with the employee, but told him to hold a second.

"OK, then. Are you ready to party?"

"You bet," responded Hank with a huge grin on his face.

Larry approached Hank and said, pointing to the security tag, "You won't need this anymore."

"Oh, right."

He removed it from his jacket and handed it over to Larry, who in turn handed it to the guard, asking him to look after it and to look after his friend while he ran up to his office to change into more casual attire.

Through the idle talk with the guard for the five minutes he waited, Hank memorized every detail about the man and his uniform.

He also ran through a multitude of scenarios he could put in place for his plan. He narrowed these down to three and would make a final decision once back at the training centre.

Chapter 33

"Hi, sweetheart."

Sam was on his daily evening Skype call to Melinda.

"How was your day?"

Melinda had just come out of the shower in her apartment at the Watergate. She looked at the clock on her night stand. It read eleven o'clock.

"I'm exhausted. I've been on the go since dawn."

"I'm sorry to hear that and I can imagine the pace you've been keeping."

"It's been a rough month and a half. We have close to a thousand agents following the campaign trail, both for the Democratic and the Republican party candidates. You already know, I've even had to be on several of the jaunts to help coordinate some of the events. There are so many details to look after.

"Mostly, I miss you. It was a shock leaving Venice and returning to the grind. Besides, not being able to *come out* about our engagement has also been stressful."

"I understand how you might be going through," responded Sam. "It's been somewhat of the opposite for me and I wish you could share the same feelings.

"Even today," he continued, speaking and laughing at the same time, "I got a phone call from Uncle Claude and he's already asking when the wedding is going to take place and how many kids we're planning to have."

"You're kidding!" exclaimed Melinda.

"Nope. They're presently conspiring to have us there again this coming Christmas. They all love you. So much so, that I'm starting to get a little jealous."

Melinda smiled and shook her head.

"I don't think you have too much to worry about there.

"Well, only four more days and we'll be together, finally."

"I can't wait," responded Sam.

"I have my tickets and my tux has been cleaned and pressed. By the way, what are you wearing to the fundraiser?"

"Oh, just a simple black dress like every girl has," she said, with a wink of her eye, "to match my ring."

"You're going to wear it?" Sam said, surprised and pleased all at once.

"I think it's about time, don't you? By then, everyone will be so busy with the wrap-up of the election, it will get lost in the chaos of the final days."

Sam was grinning from ear to ear.

"That's great! I'm so proud of you and love you so much. We'll have to celebrate all over again."

"You're on. I've booked a room for two nights, the night prior to and of the fundraiser, at the Marriott, just a few steps from the Convention Centre. I'll email you the particulars."

"OK. Now you'd better get some shut-eye. I don't want you falling asleep on me while I'm there."

As he flicked his eyebrows up and down a few times, he added, "It's been a while, you know."

Melinda laughed and quipped back, "You men. That's all you think about."

Sam feigned being shocked before admitting she was right.

"Well, yea," and he laughed, but then noticed Melinda's eyes. They were starting to glaze over due to her being so tired.

"OK, time to sign off, sweetheart. Contact me tomorrow, when you can."

He could see Melinda yawn and then smile.

"Hate doing this, but I'll hit the END button now."

Then with emphasis, he added, "Get to bed."

The computer image went blank.

Sam was left alone in his apartment.

A smile slowly came to his face as he thought about part of their conversation. He turned his Skype programme off and went to his Internet browser.

A half hour later and somewhat poorer, he turned his computer off.

It had been a good night.

Chapter 34

Two days later, around three in the afternoon, a security guard walked into the Convention Centre through the rear bay doors leading to the utility hallway behind the Grand Hall.

He wore a baseball cap and had on sunglasses, but, other than that, raised no concerns as he flashed his security badge to the guard. His moustache and goatee matched the picture on the card.

"Damn, it's going to be a long one today," he said, "I'm pulling a twelve-hour. How about you?"

The guard shook his head and said, "Naw. I'm off in fifteen. You poor sod."

The bearded guard continued on into the hallway, carrying a small duffle bag over his shoulder.

The decor was pretty plain where he was and almost industrial like. It ran the full length of the rear wall of the Grand Hall and was about twenty-five metres wide.

Above, there wasn't a ceiling per se. Only a string of off-white quarters, built over the main floor, each skirted by metal walkways and supported by steel beams which were covered with what looked like blown-on papier-mâché.

These enclosures, both on the right and the left, were separated by a large gap between them, allowing the guard to see, well above the second-storey structures, huge air ducts which were fed by the blowers and air-conditioners housed inside the utility rooms.

On the main floor were hundreds of collapsed, round tables and thousands of chairs, lined up against the two walls, in preparation for the President's fundraiser.

Looking around to see if anyone was there and seeing he was alone, Hank slipped between two groups of piled-up chairs and stashed his duffle bag beneath their legs.

He ripped the goatee off his chin, removed his cap and stuffed both in the bag on the floor. Then he pulled out another security badge and replaced the first on his shirt pocket.

Quickly walking to the doors leading into the Grand Hall and over to his right toward those leading into the kitchen area, he exited the Centre by means of the service entrance to the kitchen.

About ten minutes later, the guard at the rear bay doors who had just assumed his post, saw Hank walking up to him in a huff carrying another bag.

"Hey, man."

Showing this guard the new badge, he complained, "Crap, I'm late again. This is the second time this month. I'm going to be written up."

"No kidding," said the guard, "it happened to me last year and it took me six months to have the mark removed from my file."

Hank walked to the place where he had hidden the first bag. He put it over his other shoulder and walked about twenty metres farther, then over to the wall on his right.

There, he found a series of steel rungs protruding from the wall, acting as a ladder up to the gangway of the boiler room above. He climbed swiftly and stopped at the top, listening for any sound which would warn him of someone's presence.

None.

He walked around the room and then around the next, to another similar ladder, which led this time to a small opening, which, in turn, led into the space above the Grand Hall itself.

Stopping once more and letting his eyes adjust to the lower lighting level, he could see a maze of catwalks crisscrossing the whole section.

Just below, he could see the wall portion of the wood-latte ceiling rising toward him and then curving away toward the centre of the room, now forming a see-through floor, about four feet under him.

Quickly, but stealthily, Hank followed the catwalks toward the far side of the ceiling cavity. He stopped just before the opening which led into the ceiling space above the Pre-Function Room.

Below him, he saw the ceiling curving down to form part of the hall's rear wall and, over to his right, some one hundred metres away, he spotted another catwalk, it too leading through the wall into the other space.

He was searching for a dark zone, one which could afford him some degree of invisibility from any security guard's scrutiny. It also had to be far enough to help mask his scent from the security dogs he knew would be used to patrol the area.

He found one such locale, about twenty-five metres from where he stood, placing him in an excellent position almost directly opposite the site where the podium would be erected on the other side of the hall.

He took a rope out of one of the bags he was carrying, tied the two of them to it and slowly lowered them to the wood-latte ceiling. He then secured the rope to the arm rail of the catwalk in such a way that one length of the rope could hold his weight, while the other length could be pulled to undo the rope and let it drop to him, once he had slid down to the ceiling.

Again, he gathered his equipment bags and quietly headed toward the area he had selected for his vigil.

Using the spacing between the wood-lattes as a ladder, he carefully climbed down three metres into the crevasse created by the curved ceiling, as it met with the wall.

Peering through the gap between the lattes, he could see clearly all the way to the other side of the hall. He had chosen well.

He began making preparations for the marathon interval he had planned. First, he pulled out a series of fine see-through, non-reflective black mesh sheets. He stretched one out over the ceiling beneath him, in order to obscure him from anyone looking up from the ground floor. Then, he took two more and secured them to the wall and ceiling, creating a blind on either side of him, hiding him from anyone walking by on the catwalks.

He stretched another two sheets, about thirty centimetres in from the other two, as second walls for his makeshift *tent*. This way, if a guard used a flashlight to see into the dark confines of his hiding place, some of the light would pass through the first mesh to the second, giving the illusion of depth and continuous darkness, while effectively concealing him.

He climbed back up to the top of the arch to see if anyone was in the ceiling cavity. Seeing it was empty, he returned to one of the duffle bags and pulled out a canvas hammock and a small handheld drill. He attached two screws: one into the mortar between two of the cinder blocks the wall was constructed with and, on the opposite side, another to one of the lattes forming the ceiling.

If he was to survive the four-day ordeal, breaking his record, he would need to be able to rest with whatever comfort the hammock could provide.

He had provisions for the vigil: everything from rations to water, to waste disposal bags for his bodily functions.

In the second duffle bag, he had his favourite rifle, an Accuracy International AS50. Manufactured by British firearms producer Accuracy International, it allowed Hank to engage targets at very long range with high accuracy. It employed a gas operated semi-automatic action and a muzzle break, allowing for very low recoil and a fast target acquisition. The rifle was highly transportable, ergonomic and could be disassembled in less than three minutes, which he had shaved down to two minutes fifteen seconds. For this job, he had fitted a silencer on the end of the muzzle.

In fact, it was the gun he had used to kill the professor in Philadelphia.

He then removed the white security shirt he was wearing and donned a black long sleeve T-shirt.

Finally, he assembled his rifle.

He climbed back up to the top of the ceiling to check if anyone was about. Again seeing no one, he returned to his nest and stretched out in his hammock, laying his rifle across his chest. He would try to catch a few z's while he could.

He knew the President's people would be there the following day, three days before the event, to lock the centre down and set up their security umbrella. Once they were in the building, he would get very little sleep.

Chapter 35

Sam arrived in New Orleans at about three o'clock in the afternoon of the fundraiser. Taking a taxi to the Marriott, he checked in, but walked into an empty room.

Melinda was in the thick of overseeing the security side of the event and would only return to the hotel around five.

So Sam inspected the minibar in the room and retrieved a sampler bottle of Scotch. Finding the ice-making machine in the hallway, he took only one ice cube. Can't spoil a good Scotch with too much ice, he told himself.

Upon returning to the room, he located the remote and put the TV on tuning in to CNN.

The main story was about President Alexander, his aggressive move to ban high-powered military-style rifles and his fundraising event in *NOLA*.

He finished his drink, took a shower after which he unpacked and put on his tuxedo.

When Melinda arrived about an hour later, she was greeted with a huge hug and long kiss.

"My, aren't you handsome in your tux."

"Thanks," Sam said with a bow, "but you'll need to help me with the tie."

"Not a problem. How was your flight?" she asked.

"Actually, it was a non-event. I'm glad I took a nonstop flight, though. I don't know how you Americans put up with all those layovers along the way."

Melinda was in a hurry and already heading to the washroom when she responded.

"You probably paid a pretty penny for the privilege of a direct flight," and she was gone.

Sam chuckled and returned to his seat, consciously feeling the lump in the inside pocket of his jacket and another in one of his other pockets.

They were still there. Fighting the thought he might have forgotten them, he smiled again.

Melinda emerged from the washroom fully dressed about twenty minutes later.

Sam's jaw dropped and then he grinned widely.

"God, you are gorgeous!"

There stood Melinda: Her *simple black dress,* as she had described it to him, was an understatement.

She was wearing a full-length, sleeveless, body-fitting silk Dior dress. The pleated bodice seductively draped over her left shoulder and a wide black sash was pinched at her small waist. Patterns of black beads were sewn onto the skirt.

Only when she extended her left foot did Sam notice the long slit, exposing her shapely leg and her Louis Vuitton black evening pumps, accentuated by a gold leather heel.

She had pulled her hair back into a ponytail, knowing Sam loved the look, and only wore a single string of pearls and pearl earrings to complete the picture.

She smiled when she saw Sam's reaction.

"You like?" she asked.

Sam got up out of the seat and simply said, "How can I be so lucky?"

Then he took a step back, and rested his chin between his thumb and index finger, uttering a *Hmm* sound, as though he was passing judgment.

Melinda looked surprised.

"What?" she questioned.

"As perfect as it is, allow me to make the look even more so."

He reached into his pockets and took out the two velvet-covered jewellery boxes.

"I think these might go well with your little black dress."

Melinda hesitantly reached out and took the long box and opened it.

Inside she found a yellow gold Omega necklace and beautiful black coral pendant, framed in 18K gold, and shaped like a triangular sail. On the lower tip was a small flawless diamond.

"Sam, what did you do?" she asked, holding back tears.

"It's beautiful. Is it from the same collection as my ring?"

"Actually, yes. First, open the second box."

She did and found a pair of matching earrings.

Sam continued, "I saw them in that jewellery store where I bought the ring and made a mental note of it. The saleslady called the set the Tip of the Iceberg. The name stuck.

"When you said your dress was black, I immediately thought about these. So I got online right away and they still had them. I had the clerk express ship them to me and they arrived only hours before I left for the airport."

Melinda was still having a hard time speaking.

"You shouldn't have."

She returned the hug and kiss she had received walking in and quickly went back to the washroom to remove her pearls and put on her gifts.

When she reentered the room, Sam shook his head and said, "Stunning. Just stunning. And, am I good or what? They match your dress and your shoes."

Melinda leaned over to gently kiss him again and said, "What am I going to do with you? You're such a romantic."

Checking the clock on the bedside table, she indicated it was time to head to the Convention Center.

"Let's go. I want to show them all off. But first, let me help you with that tie."

Chapter 36

Hank had had little sleep over the last three days. The security patrols in the ceiling cavity had increased dramatically in the past forty-eight hours, running, now, about every thirty minutes.

Already, he could hear a low murmur of voices coming from the Pre-Function Room below and behind him. Guests had already started to arrive for the fundraiser.

His precautions seemed to have paid off, or was it the fact that over the entire duration of his stay, the guards had become somewhat complacent, due to the number of times they had walked through the area and had found nothing.

Either way, he was both exhausted and relieved that it would be over in a few hours. He had broken his own record, although it was one he could never brag about.

He needed to begin his final preparations. Check his security guard uniform and tag, thoroughly inspect his rifle, remove his hammock to give him the space he needed to set up, then cut into the sheet he had used to hide him from below. This last procedure would allow him to find the right space between the lattes, giving him the best angle of attack to take out his two targets.

Timing would be crucial. Once his deed done, he would only have thirty seconds to leave his lair and reach the catwalk, another twenty to get to the other side of the Pre-Function area and ten more to climb a set of metal stairs leading to an exit into a hallway on the third level of the centre.

At most, he had a minute to get to that hallway, before the centre was put on full lockdown and his buddy's security measures put into place. One minute of chaos in the Grand Hall was all he needed.

Chapter 37

The fundraising event had sold out within weeks of the announcement. Three thousand people had purchased a seat at one of the three hundred tables which were available. Each seat cost a minimum of a thousand dollars a plate, with the tables closest to that of the President's, going for up to ten thousand a plate.

The crowd in the Pre-Function Room milled around, sampling canapés and caviar hors d'oeuvres, sipping on champagne, trying to look as nonchalant as possible, all the while hoping to bump into someone of influence and wealth, capable of advancing their agenda: in other words, typical Washington lobbying.

Amidst the throng, Sam and Melinda roamed around, oblivious to the sheer magnitude of power the group represented. Not that they didn't get their fair share of stares, mostly from the men in the room and obviously intended for Melinda; regardless, they only had eyes for each other.

An announcement was made that the President had landed and would be there in approximately thirty minutes. The guests were directed to take their seats in the main hall and continue to enjoy themselves until his arrival.

As Sam and Melinda passed through the doors leading into the Grand Hall, it was evident by their facial expressions that they were as taken by the sheer size of it as was every individual walking in along with them.

Although the room was incredibly vast, the conveners had managed to create an ambiance of cosiness. The multitude of pod lights in the ceiling were dimmed low, giving the place somewhat of a nightclub feel. The main source of light came from the thirty-odd large crystal chandeliers which added a classy look to the space.

At the front of the room, a large wide platform with a podium was highlighted by spotlights hanging from the ceiling. Behind the platform loomed a ten- by thirty- metre screen, on which images and videos were shown of a variety of many beautiful sites in America. The videos were all accompanied by music interpreted by forty members of the United States Marine Band who played pieces by a number of composers such as Sousa, Grappelli and even Mancini.

At one point, Sam leaned over to Melinda and asked, "Do they always play this type of music at these affairs?"

"Pretty well," she replied. "It's expected. It adds that air of tradition, I suppose. And, check the people in the room. The average age has to be sixty-five."

They found their table at the front, just to the left of the one the President and his wife would be sitting at. Checking the name tags on the plates, they located their reserved seats which placed them somewhat with their backs to the screen on the wall. They would have to turn their chairs slightly in order to see the speakers at the podium.

Neither Sam nor Melinda minded. They were both aware of the magnitude of the gift the President had given them through their invitation and table selection.

Chapter 38

Air Force Two had arrived at the Louis Armstrong New Orleans International Airport twenty minutes before Air Force One. It had carried the vice-president and part of the cabinet.

A judicious selection had been made, to ensure the continuity of government, in the event of a catastrophe. Since the vice-president had insisted on attending the fundraiser, it meant that the secretary of state had to remain in Washington. The next in succession, after the vice-president, was the Speaker of the House. However, because he was a Republican, it was thought prudent to have the third in line, in the capital, to bring some balance to any issue that could arise.

The vice-president's plane taxied to a separate terminal on the north side of the airport, just behind the Signature Flight Support office. The government and the military often used this company's refuelling services at their many sites across the country. The locale afforded two more advantages: It was large enough to easily park both official planes and provided swift and direct access to Highway 10, which led to downtown New Orleans.

The motorcade was already waiting for the passengers and as soon as they disembarked, the five bullet-proof SUVs followed the double row of six police motorcyclists out of the terminal area, onto Aberdeen Street down to Loyola Drive. A right turn on the service road led them quickly to the access ramp and the highway.

By then, Air Force One's wheels were touching the tarmac and followed the same route to the terminal.

Because of security concerns, it was a rare site to see both planes sitting side by side. Throwing caution to the wind, the President had felt that, this time, the message he was going to deliver required a show of strength. His only concessions had been to split the group in two and to beef up security around the site.

He and his wife Ashley stepped out of the plane and down to the waiting limousines, followed by the other half of the cabinet. His convoy would be accompanied by two rows of ten police at the front and eight at the rear. It wasn't a question of ego, but the image of the presidency was an important factor in American politics.

Using the same roads to get onto Highway 10, the motorcade then careened down an empty road. Traffic had been stopped to allow both groups an unimpeded drive to the centre of town.

Ashley Alexander was looking at her husband going over his speech. She knew he had put his job on the line with his push to ban ownership of high-powered rifles by the general population. It seemed that everything he had accomplished in his long career in public life, as well as all the important sections of the election platform, were being reduced to this single issue.

Untold millions had been spent by the NRA and the conservative factions in the US. Since his initial announcement, Alexander had been maligned as a traitor and as un-American.

More than once, he had confided in her that, although this was the correct path to take, he worried the American public might not be ready for such a move.

He refused to run a negative campaign, preferring to present the facts about the number of Americans who had died violent deaths at the hands of cowardly or crazed individuals, wielding such weapons. The most painful for him were the references to the children all over the US who had met that fate. It crushed him that so many people believed in the propaganda promoted by the NRA and that these same people could not see the line between reason and insanity, between the type of firearm which was reasonable for their own protection as well as that of the constitution, and the type which waged war on their fellow citizens.

She reached over to him and touched his arm to get his attention.

"Are you alright?" she asked.

He smiled and softly said, "As alright as I can be. I feel good about this."

What was surprising was that a growing number of Americans seemed to feel good about his message as well. Polls indicated that, in spite of the drop in his ratings at the announcement, his popularity had risen steadily, indicating that his reelection might not be in doubt.

The motorcade had now taken the Pontchartrain Expressway which led toward the Mississippi. Shortly after driving by the Superdome on their left, the group took the 12D exit to St. Charles Avenue. Turning left, they drove under the highway toward Lee Circle.

As they rounded the circle, Alexander commented absent-mindedly to Ashley, "You know," while looking up at General Lee's statue at the top of the tower, "he almost won. Instead of becoming the president of Washington College, he could have been president of the Confederate States or perhaps the United States. Can you imagine how different history would be if he had been victorious?"

By then, they were passing the World War II Museum on Andrew Higgins Drive and fast approaching the Convention Center. No sooner had they taken a left turn on Convention Center Blvd. than they drove another hundred metres and veered onto a ramp leading to the entrance doors to the huge foyer next to the Pre-Function Room.

The car stopped and the door closest to the entrance opened. Before exiting, Alexander leaned over to his wife, kissed her and said, "Well, let's get this show on the road."

As he got out of the car, he extended his hand to Ashley and helped her exit the vehicle, before looking over its roof at the hundreds of people who had gathered to cheer him on.

The media from around the world were also represented and filmed every move the President and his cabinet made as they waved to the crowd and then entered the building.

They were quickly spirited away, directly ahead to a set of doors which led to a large cavernous exposition hall, now devoid of people, other than a dozen or so security agents.

Chapter 39

Sam and Melinda had been listening to a series of speeches given by supporters of the President and his policies. Future possible candidates for top government positions took their turn at the microphone, hoping to spark the attention of the crowd and the media and leave a lasting impression in the minds of the voting public.

The vice-president had been introduced as he entered the room and was cheered loudly as he took his seat.

Sam was taking it all in. Moreover, he was looking at the activities from a different perspective than the rest of the crowd. He was applying his theory of the importance of symbolism in human endeavours and saw this as a perfect example of what he had described in his paper.

He looked at Melinda, who was eyeing the room from an altogether different standpoint: that of security.

She looked over to her right. About twenty steps away and at the foot of the stage, stood Agent Doyle, dressed in a tuxedo, to blend in with the guests, but not succeeding very well. The fact that he was standing and watching the crowd while being all too obviously equipped with an earpiece made him stand out instead in the crowd.

Melinda caught his eye and he could see her mouth the words thank you.

The faintest, professional smile appeared on his face and was gone just as quickly.

Sam interrupted her train of thought.

"I find it interesting that the President can marry his new policies with this show."

Before he could get a response, the current speaker finished his speech and the Master of Ceremonies, the president of the Democratic Party, asked for everyone's attention. The President was in the house. The lights in the room increased in intensity.

"Ladies and gentlemen, it is my pleasure and honour to introduce the *man*, the reason why we are all here tonight, and one of the most patriotic and brave individuals I know, the President of the United States of America and the First Lady, Felix Ulysses Alexander and Ashley Alexander."

The President and his wife emerged from a door on the far right of the stage, to the applause and cheers of the guests in the room. The Marine Band struck up their version of Hail to the Chief. Everyone was up on their feet, including Sam and Melinda.

And even he, this Canadian, was being drawn into the drama of the situation, realizing the magnitude of what this type of event meant to the American electorate. Here was the most powerful man on the planet. You couldn't help but feel caught up in and intoxicated by the moment.

****

High above the crowd and to the rear of the room, the *ghost* had stirred and taken up his position. From the moment the guests had been allowed into the hall, he had begun his final preparations.

He had removed the black long-sleeve T-shirt to reveal the white shirt of the uniform he would need to blend in with the security crew, once the deed was done.

He checked his rifle one last time to confirm that the mechanism was working flawlessly and double-checked that any markings which could link it to him, such as production identification numbers, were filed off. It had been wiped many times to make sure no finger marks existed. He regretted having to leave the rifle behind, but he knew he could not take it with him. The price to pay for a successful mission, he told himself.

He had moved the hammock from a sleeping position to one where he could use it as a chair of sorts, in which he could station himself comfortably to view the events taking place below and steady him for the shot.

For twenty minutes, he had scoped the audience to see who was in attendance. With the Democratic big wheels present, including the vice-president and a number of cabinet members, the thought had occurred to him that he could cripple the administration by taking a bunch of them out, along with the President. And let's not forget Buckner, he mused.

He decided he needed to stick to the plan and not improvise on the mission he had given himself.

First Buckner, then Alexander. That had been the intent from the beginning and that was what he was going to do. Self-discipline was critical to a sniper: the mission above all.

Looking through the rifle scope, he focused on Sam, making slight adjustments to the optics. Then over to the podium and more adjustments, while memorizing the time it took to make the changes. He'd have to also contend with the three beam splitters shields, or teleprompters, in front and to the sides of the speakers, but he knew it would only take one bullet to shatter the critical one, with a delay of no more than two seconds for the second shot to fly.

He rehearsed his moves over and over again in his mind, while moving the rifle between his intended targets.

Good, he thought, one bullet to Buckner's head and before he hits the ground, a second bullet to take care of the teleprompter and the last one in the President's heart.

All Hank had to do now was wait for the perfect moment.

****

The President and his wife were beaming as they stepped onto the stage and walked confidently to the front of the podium, waving to the guests, every now and then pointing to a table or individual and giving them a thumbs up.

Sam thought, they are pros at this.

The applause and cheers continued for almost five minutes, with the Alexanders on several occasions signalling, though meekly, for the group to sit.

The cue to finally end the show of support was when the President kissed his wife and she was escorted down to her seat next to the vice-president.

Alexander pointed to her as she walked down the steps, sparking another round of applause, this one for Ashley.

The President took his place behind the podium, waved one last time, then began to speak.

"Ladies and gentlemen, my fellow Americans. Thank you so much for coming to our gathering and showing your support for my administration. Your presence here is a testimonial to our willingness to work together for the good of our republic and every citizen within it. It is a testimonial to your willingness to see what changes need to be made and having the courage to take the measures required to do so. And, let's not forget your contributions to our election campaign."

He paused and smiled for effect. The crowd laughed at the obvious reference to the cost of the seats they were now occupying while knowing the boost this event would give the campaign.

Continuing with his script and only occasionally looking at the prompter, he said, "The upcoming election is going to be like no other in the history of our country. When we win . . . " the audience broke into applause, with many rising from their seats in approval. " . . . When we win, we will reverse a negative trend that has plagued our nation since the inception of our constitution."

More cheers.

"When the Founding Fathers drew up our constitution and the laws that followed, they duly included the right for citizens to bear arms and fight those who would endanger our system of government. But they also had the wisdom to give the presidency the authority to define some of the limits to the types of arms they could bear."

Another standing ovation for the President, this one lasting almost a minute.

****

In his lair, Hank was thinking the President was digging his grave. Let him continue to talk treason. Your time is close at hand.

****

"Our opponents believe they have this election cinched, because they think Americans can be easily brainwashed into thinking their President is acting contrary to the constitution and to their interests.

"I say to you that they are not easily brainwashed. The American public has seen the lies expressed over and over again by fear mongers such as the NRA."

The crowd erupted once more, cheering loudly for a President who was on fire and ready to fight the forces of unsound reasoning and delusion.

They finally returned to their seats, confident that this was the man to follow and who would snatch the ball from the grasp of the opposition.

Alexander looked over at Sam and gave him a wink.

"A wise young man recently told me that I should do what was correct. And he was correct as well as right." Now, smiling at Sam, "So I made the decision to put my administration's life on the line, to correct the wrong, to save our citizens' lives, especially our young, and propose a wide-sweeping ban on high-powered, military-style rifles.

"Everywhere I have gone, citizens have told me that they approve of the platform we are running on and that these changes have been a long time coming.

"Even our allies, everywhere on the planet, have applauded the shift we are making, to the betterment of our image on the global scene, as well as to the betterment of the trust they put in us as the leader of the free world."

****

Hank's heart was starting to race a little. He checked his watch. It would be about one minute before the next patrol would pass through his area of the ceiling cavity. He would have to wait until after then to take his shot, giving him the maximum amount of time to make his getaway.

****

Alexander was enjoying the response and felt energized. This is what campaigning was about and though he didn't like the political games he was forced to play, he couldn't help but relish moments such as these.

Calming the audience, he continued, "What we will be accomplishing is nothing short of revolutionary in the eyes of the world and for our citizens . . . "

Throughout his speech, people had been taking pictures of the President. At the far right of the room, one gentleman got up and took a picture of the people at his table.

Sam was sitting with his chair turned enough to allow him to watch the President, Melinda in front of him and a good portion of the room.

When the flash went off on the man's camera, Sam's peripheral vision caught a small reflection coming from the back of the room, in the ceiling portion above the rear doors.

He didn't pay too much attention to it, but when the man took a second snapshot, a similar glint shone at the same spot. This time Sam looked more carefully and he realized the reflection of light had come from one of the spaces between the wood lattes forming the ceiling decor.

He took out a small digital camera from his inside jacket pocket and turned it on.

Melinda looked at him, smiled and turned once more to watch the President, thinking Sam was going to take a picture of him.

Instead, Sam aimed the camera at the rear of the room and used the electronic zoom feature to get a better view of the spot where he thought he had seen the reflection of the flashbulb.

****

Hank had his scope focused on the President, counting the seconds he would have before firing. He felt

Alexander had said enough to rile up the conservative army of voters, especially in the South.

****

"So why come here, to New Orleans, to make a final stand before the election . . . " continued Alexander.

Meanwhile, Sam was trying to make sense of what he was looking at. He could see what resembled a stick protruding from the ceiling and a faint circular glow just above it.

That's when it struck him. It had to be a gun. Thoughts raced through his mind in rapid succession.

A gun? Security agents? An assassin? For who?

****

Hank was panning back to Sam when he saw him actually pointing a camera toward his position.

It was his turn to have a series of questions running through his mind.

A camera? Looking at me or what? Shit, I have to take the shot. The game's on.

****

The President! It was an assassination attempt on the President.

Sam reacted quickly. He leaned over to touch Melinda's arm to warn her about what he thought was about to happen.

****

Hank put in motion the sequence of actions he had devised. He made a final adjustment to the scope, focused on Sam's head, breathed in and then out slowly. His finger gradually began to squeeze the trigger and he felt a slight recoil from the rifle as the bullet followed its trajectory.

****

" . . . So, together, we can bring new meaning to 'the land of the free and the home of the brave.'"
Once more, the audience cheered.
In the midst of the noise, Sam was leaning toward Melinda to tell her about his fears, when he heard what sounded like a soft whizzing sound just behind him. No one noticed the bullet bury itself in the steps of the stage.

****

What is it with this guy, that I can't simply blow the top of his head off, Hank swore to himself.
Immediately after he reacquired his target, another bullet left the muzzle of the rifle.

****

Sam reacted to the sound by jerking back and quickly looking at the far end of the room. No sooner had he done so than another whizzing sound passed him by on the left side of the head. This time, he felt the heat and the sting of what he now knew was a bullet, striking his earlobe.

It's me, he thought. That shooter is here and I'm the target. That can't be. I'm not worth the trouble. It still has to be the President.

But he could be after Melinda, too.

A surge of adrenalin coursed through his veins and he reacted instinctively, without thinking, to protect his fiancée.

In one smooth motion, Sam rose from his chair, shoved Melinda off her chair onto the floor and out of the shooter's sight while yelling, "Sniper! Stay down."

Few people took note of what was happening since they were still applauding the President's last remarks.

The vice-president, sitting at the table next to them heard the word *sniper* and turned to see who had uttered it.

At the same time, Doyle had seen Sam rise quickly and his boss being propelled to the floor. His first thoughts were, was she hit and where was Sam going?

He and three other of Alexander's security team realized Sam was heading toward the President. Why? Could he have been wrong about him?

****

Hank was cursing at himself for missing his target once more, thinking this operation was going down wrong. On the other hand, his real target was the President. Still time to take him out.

From the lower left area of the scope and as he was reacquiring the President, he had seen Sam who was now sprinting toward the podium and he thought he would never make it in time.

The hairline cross in the scope was now firmly fixed on the President's chest, right where his heart would be.

A final adjustment and he felt another thud from the muzzle of the rifle. A fraction of a second later, the teleprompter shattered in a hundred pieces.

Hank's finger was again starting to squeeze the trigger.

****

Sam was halfway to the President. Unfortunately, as he would soon learn, his manoeuvre to protect Melinda and the words he had yelled out, prompted the agents, including Doyle, to jump into crisis mode. First things first: remove the President from any imminent danger. At that moment, this seemed to be Sam.

Doyle sprinted toward Sam, but could not gain enough distance to overtake him, whereas the three agents on the stage, just behind the President were indeed near enough to do so. The one closest to Sam was able to tackle him about three metres from the President, while the other two were already grabbing the President to cover him and remove him from the stage.

Just then, the teleprompter exploded and a second later, the agent on the right of the President could be seen falling to the ground.

All of the action had barely taken five seconds. Many of the guests in the room were still applauding, not quite understanding what they were witnessing.

****

Hank had taken his second shot at the President and through the scope, he realized that the person struck by the bullet had not been the intended target.

A short curse and he then turned his anger off.

Now, a cold and efficient Hank began his escape. He leaned his rifle up against the back wall, confident it could not be traced back to him.

He put his security hat on, withdrew his Swiss Army knife from his pocket and neatly sliced through the two layers of meshing on his right.

A quick feel at each of his ankles to make sure two guns he might need were secure in their holsters.

He slid through the openings he had created and carefully climbed to the top of the curve of the ceiling to verify that no security guards had had time to get there.

Since none had, he quickly moved in a crouched position toward the first catwalk, twenty-five metres away.

He climbed onto the walkway and ran through the opening in the wall, over to the area above the Pre-Function Room and toward the far side.

There, a set of steps led down to a door which opened into one of the business sector hallways on the second floor.

He pulled the door open an inch or so, to see if anyone was around. Two of the centre's guards ran by and continued down the hallway.

Hank realized that the repetitive shrill sound of the alarm was muffled in the expanse housing of the ceiling, but here, and he assumed, down in all the halls on the first floor, the sound was quite loud.

He stepped out from behind the door and took a position in front of it, feigning to be guarding that exit area.

Checking both directions for more guards or presidential security agents, he saw the hall was empty for the moment.

Good, he thought, and began to walk quickly to his left, toward the end of the business office section.

****

Meanwhile, in the Grand Hall, all hell had broken loose.

The guests in the audience had begun to panic when they realized what had taken place.

An army of the centre's guards and the security team had converged in the room and had begun taking positions to gain control of the situation.

The President had been rushed out of the Hall, followed by his wife, the vice-president and all the cabinet members.

The security team was yelling for the crowd not to panic and to take cover under the tables. Most did, but a few hundred were already running for the closest of the dozen doors surrounding the space.

By then, Sam had been crushed by a total of four agents, pinning him to the ground.

Melinda had picked herself up off the ground and had regained her composure.

She saw the President and his entourage being escorted out, and had a brief moment of satisfaction at knowing that her people and those of the President were acting so quickly and efficiently together.

She turned her gaze toward the stage, saw the agent who had been shot and to the left, Sam, under a pile of agents.

She took her shoes off while on the run up the steps to the stage floor, yelling over to the agents on top of Sam that he was with her and not the danger. Rather, they needed to help the downed agent, who was now being tended by another.

She saw Doyle and yelled for him to look after Sam. She then turned and ran down the steps and toward the doors leading to the kitchen on the right.

She picked up the hem of her dress and hiked it up, folding it into the sash at her waist, knowing that with the slit up the left leg, she could now run unimpeded by her formal gown.

As she bolted past the kitchen, she signalled to several of the agents on the way to follow her.

Based on the building's blueprints which she had memorized, she planned to head to the stairs leading up to the upper floors, and begin a search from the far eastern side of the building, moving floor by floor to the west side.

The team of twenty burst onto the second floor level. Melinda looked at one of the agents she recognized.

"Luke, is it?"

The agent nodded, yes.

"Take half the group and do a thorough search of the rooms in this area. The rest, come with me. We'll head to the third floor. Oh, and give me your gun. I left mine at the office."

She continued down the hallway, now armed, and turned right. A door blocked the way to a service corridor which led to a set of stairs and up to the third floor.

****

Back on the main floor, Doyle was helping Sam get up.

"Are you OK?" he asked.

Sam was still feeling the effects of the pressure of being pinned by some rather stocky agents.

"Yes," he said, "I don't think anything is broken."

He took a quick look around and noticed the President wasn't there.

"Is Alexander safe? Is he hurt?"

Doyle responded with, "No, he's fine and so is everyone else in the room. It seems the President was the only target."

Sam felt his left ear and showed Doyle the blood on his hand and said, "I don't think he was the only target."

Doyle was surprised.

"When did that happen?"

Sam quickly explained the sequence of events, including pushing Melinda to the floor.

He looked around and in a panic asked, "Where is Melinda anyway? I heard her yell for me to be released but I couldn't see her. Is she OK?"

Doyle pointed to the doors off to the right.

"She thinks she's still in the ranks and in the field. She ran that way with a bunch of our agents. I'm assuming they're searching for the shooter."

"Can you reach her on your com?" asked Sam.

"No, she isn't wearing one. But I'll check with the agents who ran off with her."

Without a word, Sam took off in the direction Doyle had indicated, closely followed by the latter, determined to find her and make sure she was alright and would remain so. How he would protect her, he couldn't say, but he wasn't about to sit back and think about it.

****

Hank had taken the same path Melinda was now following. He had reached the upper level of the centre and was at the rear of the meeting room area. He had been slowed down while on the second floor when he had to stop and pretend again to guard an entrance or exit door, several times needing to use his buddy Larry's name to curtail the scrutiny he was getting, saying he had been sent there specifically by the boss.

He was about to pass through another set of doors which led to the service corridors around the upper level of the New Orleans Theatre, a large, four-thousand-person odeon, when he heard the noise created by a group of people he assumed were agents and guards, breaching the entrance to the other side of the cluster of meeting rooms.

****

Sam and Doyle had reached the second-floor level and were running down the main hallway with John holding his badge up and yelling, "We're team, we're team."

About halfway, Doyle was called over his com. One of the agents had found the sniper's hideout and he should come and see.

Doyle stopped and signalled to Sam to hold on while he explained the situation. Sam told him he should go and that he would be OK. After all, Melinda had a group of agents along with her.

****

Melinda and the rest of the agents accompanying her arrived on the top floor. She ordered all but one of the agents to check every meeting room on that level. With the last agent following her, they ran past all the enclosures toward the rear double doors leading to the corridor where, unbeknownst to them, Hank had decided to take a stand.

Melinda went through the door on the right, closely followed by the agent, and foolishly forgetting to look behind.

As the door closed, Hank raised the pistol he had at the ready, pointing it at the two people who had entered his space. He was holding the gun in both hands, in a police or military stance.

The agent with Melinda looked back briefly, now remembering to check the rear and saw a man pointing a gun at them.

He stopped and started to turn and raise his gun, but too late. One shot was fired and found its target in the agent's right temple, dropping him like a sack of potatoes.

The sound stopped Melinda dead in her tracks. She too turned in the direction of the noise and saw Hank moving two steps toward her, menacingly aiming his pistol at her head.

She quickly put her hands up in surrender, with her gun pointed at the ceiling.

The man didn't fire. Rather, a self-satisfied smirk came to his face.

"Well, well, look what we have here. You are a sight for sore eyes. A little overdressed to be an agent, aren't you . . . "

Then he noticed her bare feet and dress hiked up high, exposing her long legs.

" . . . or maybe not so much. I like the look.

"Now, put your gun down and kick it over to me."

Melinda started to lower the gun, stooping to slowly put it on the ground.

Suddenly and without notice, the door blew open, striking Hank soundly and sending him and his gun flying against the wall of the corridor, knocking the wind out of him.

Melinda looked up from her crouched position and saw Sam standing there, trying to understand what had just happened. Melinda was hunched over, her gun at her feet, an agent was on the floor in a pool of blood and a security guard was now stirring and trying to get up off the ground.

Hank looked up at the person who had knocked him over and realized it was Sam, the man he had twice tried to kill and failed. Not this time, he thought.

"He's the sniper," Melinda yelled.

"You're kidding!" Sam responded.

She shook her head, no.

Before she could pick up her gun, Hank had already rolled over onto his hands and knees and had lunged for Melinda's weapon.

He skillfully grabbed the gun while rolling over on his back and onto his feet.

Sam saw the move and instinctively looked around for something to protect them from what was about to happen.

A feeling of rage for the man, unlike any he had ever experienced, welled up in him. This man was going to kill the love of his life.

He saw the dead agent's gun just next to his feet. Quickly reaching for it, he rose and turned with the gun pointed at Hank.

He was a fraction of a second too late.

Hank shot once at Sam's heart.

Fortunately, as Sam was twisting his body to get a bead on Hank, he moved just enough that the bullet hit his left arm, but only grazed him.

Sam also pulled the trigger, but because of the injury he had just sustained, his hand dropped a little and when the gun fired, the trajectory changed and the bullet struck Hank in the thigh.

Melinda could barely believe what had just happened. She knew she needed to do something. The next bullet would kill Sam and she would be the ensuing victim.

She rose from her position and tried to tackle Hank. She managed to knock him against the wall forcing him to drop his gun.

As luck would have it, the gun Sam had used required small-calibre bullets and Hank's wound, though painful, was not entirely disabling.

He grabbed Melinda and used her as a shield from what he believed would be another bullet from Sam's weapon.

Seeing Sam was hesitating, he literally threw Melinda back toward him and began to run in the opposite direction.

Sam instinctively opened his arms to catch Melinda and in the process, dropped his gun.

"Are you OK?" he asked while helping her regain her stability.

"Yes, but you were hit."

Sam looked down at his arm and saw blood seeping from his tuxedo.

"It isn't bad, I think, just a scratch. I can still move it. Where did he go? We have to stop him from getting away."

Melinda looked around and saw her gun. Sam picked his up and they both stooped over the downed agent. One look and they knew there was nothing they could do for him.

The two started to run down the hallway after Hank.

The common wall to their right stood between the corridor and the upper portion of the theatre down below, which was shaped in the pattern of an octagon.

They ran about ten metres before the hallway veered to the right at a forty-five-degree angle, showing another thirty-metre segment.

As they reached the end, they heard what sounded like a metal door closing, somewhere around the corner.

They stopped and peeked. Ten metres farther was a set of metal stairs leading up to the door they had heard shutting.

"He's up there," Melinda whispered.

"Do you know where that leads to?" asked Sam.

"I think into the ceiling area above the large theatre," she answered.

"He's either cornering himself or he knows something we don't. Is there any way out of there?"

Melinda tried to remember the briefing she had received about the building.

"I don't know. Only one way to find out."

The two started to move as quickly and quietly as possible. They scaled the steps and reached the metal door.

They looked at each other to confirm they were ready to enter, took a deep breath and Melinda counted down from three.

They pulled the door open and rapidly stepped in.

It took a moment for their eyes to adapt to the low lighting. They were standing on a metal catwalk, about twenty metres above the dimly lit ground floor and theatre seats.

They tried to look around to see if Hank was there.

Sam tapped Melinda's shoulder and pointed up toward the centre.

There seemed to be some movement close to the ceiling.

****

Hank had entered the area and limped down the centre catwalk. Just below him hung support beams for the variety of spotlights and projectors used for the events and presentations in the theatre.

He had to cross over to another catwalk to his left. It led to a ladder which would take him to a hatch and allow him to escape onto the roof of the centre. He would then walk to the rear of the structure, to a set of metal stairs leading to the ground, next to the railroad tracks between the building and the river.

The climb was agonizing but his training had taught him to suppress the pain.

He finally reached the hatch and pushed on it. It didn't budge. He tried again, this time with all the weight and strength he could muster. Still, it didn't move.

He realized that it had probably been locked from the outside as part of the preparations for the fundraiser.

He whispered an obscenity and started back down.

Suddenly and for a brief moment, the area was filled with light.

He knew someone was now in the ceiling with him. He turned to look down toward the source of the light and saw the shapes of a man and woman silhouetted against the lit opening behind them. Then the door closed.

He started to hurry down to the catwalk.

Before he reached it, he turned to get a better look at Sam and Melinda's progress.

They were too close to allow him to get back to the centre catwalk and over to the far side to exit through another door.

He pulled the other pistol he had in his ankle holster and aimed at the shadows moving toward him.

He fired three shots, none of which hit their targets, but all of which sufficed to have the two stop and crouch to try to protect themselves.

It was all he needed to allow him to reach the centre catwalk and turn to move away from his two assailants.

****

Sam and Melinda ducked when they heard the shots. They could hear footsteps on the metal walkway and a moment later, a shadowy figure moving away from them, appeared about ten metres ahead.

Sam stood and yelled at the man to stop.

Hank turned and shot once more. This time the bullet hit the handrail about ten centimetres behind the hand Sam had rested on it to steady himself.

The door behind them opened and closed once more, shining light into the area. It had to be more agents coming toward the sound of the shooting.

They could see Hank turn again.

It was Sam's turn to shoot. He pulled the trigger twice, but only the first fired. He was out of bullets.

He yelled at Hank once more.

Hank turned to shoot yet again, but Sam had already proceeded to throw his gun at him, striking him in the head.

Luckily, it staggered him, giving Sam time to sprint in his direction and tackle him.

Melinda had tried to aim and shoot her gun, but couldn't get much of a target with Sam in her line of vision on the narrow walkway.

Sam's anger at Hank hadn't subsided in the least. So when he tackled him, it was with an extra amount of velocity.

Hank had never been hit as hard and falling on the landing of the metal walkway, with Sam's body slamming on top of his, almost knocked him out. He thought he might have even heard a slight crack somewhere in or around his ribcage.

Sam didn't come out of it totally unscathed. His nose smashing forcefully on Hank's forehead resulted in it breaking on impact. He saw stars and the pain drew tears from his eyes.

He struggled to get up off Hank and tried to punch him in the face.

In any event, being positioned on all fours and raising his right hand to strike, he exposed his torso to a solid knee from Hank.

Sam was thrown over to the handrail but lost his balance and found himself falling between the railing and the floor of the catwalk. Before going over and plummeting to his death far below, he managed to reach for the railing with his right hand and then his left, but his feet were dangling over an expanse of emptiness.

He heard Melinda shout his name in panic as she ran toward the two in front of her.

A cold chill ran through her as she saw Hank get up above Sam and point his gun at the helpless man.

Melinda needed to stop him.

She got into a crouched position to shoot, using her two hands to steady her gun and slowly squeezed the trigger.

****

There was only one set of footsteps clanging on the metal catwalk, behind Melinda.

John Doyle had managed to reach the entrance to the ceiling area well ahead of the others behind him.

He had heard the shots coming from inside the theatre room and hoped he wasn't too late.

When the door opened and flooded the area with light, he quickly appraised the situation and it wasn't good.

He saw that Melinda was stooped in a shooting position.

He saw two hands clutching the top rail of the catwalk and realized it had to be Sam.

But just then, the other man turned and looked back, glowering with almost demonic satisfaction as he pointed the gun at the man hanging on by a thread.

One look was all it took for John to realize the would-be assassin was his brother, Hank.

The blood drained from his face as he thought of the choices he was given: Shoot and kill Hank or let him finish Sam, and get away.

The dilemma was almost overpowering, but he knew he had but a fraction of a moment to decide.

He raised the hand holding his gun . . .

****

One shot rang out, surprising her, since it hadn't come from her gun.

Oh no, she thought. I'm too late. Sam!

But, as she watched in horror at the scene in front of her, the man stood, wobbled, took one step back and fell over the railing behind him down to the floor below.

She realized Sam had not been shot, but was still holding on for dear life.

****

As Hank had been pointing the gun at him, Sam had been looking up at his adversary thinking he was done for. His left arm was losing its grip on the handrail and he knew that if the bullet didn't finish him off, he would be fighting a losing battle.

He closed his eyes and heard the shot.

Feeling no pain, he looked up, only to see the horrified look on Hank's face and then his disappearance into nothingness.

His left grip was starting to slip, but before it let go, two hands grabbed it, then two more grabbed his right hand.

Steadying himself with the help of the other two, he forced his feet, one at a time, back onto the floor of the walkway and then his whole body.

He collapsed on his backside, only to be smothered by Melinda who had reached him first and had grasped one of his hands.

He looked over to the other saviour and saw John Doyle's face.

"Love you, sweetheart. And John, thanks for being there for me."

He glanced down through the steel grids that formed the floor of the catwalk and saw a body sprawled on the floor.

"Nice shot, sweetheart," Sam said.

Melinda looked briefly at Doyle and turned to Sam.

"It wasn't my shot. It was John's. He saved you."

She turned to Doyle and added, "Thank you. Without you, I might have been that split second too late."

She looked down to the body below and returned to Doyle.

"Any idea who the sniper was?"

Doyle hesitated for a moment.

With an air of despair in his eyes, he said gravely, "I'm afraid so. He's my brother."

The look of shock and horror on Sam's and Melinda's face could not have been more genuine.

Chapter 40

(June, seven months later)

Sam and Melinda were standing under a gazebo on the beach at Parlee Provincial Park in Shediac, New Brunswick. He was dressed in a white cotton shirt, open at the collar and cuffs rolled up. His slacks were of beige cotton and, they too, were rolled up, showing his sand-covered bare feet. Melinda wore a sleeveless, warm-white full-length cotton dress, cut in a slightly suggestive neckline. It was loosely fitted, flowing in the gentle wind, hinting at the amazing body underneath. She, too, was barefoot.

He had drawn her into him, gently caressing her neck from behind and holding her tight at the waist. The two were gazing out at the beach, reputed to be one of Canada's best and warmest saltwater beaches.

The past seven months had been nothing short of dizzying.

The attempt on the President's life had been foiled, in large part by Sam. Alexander and his entourage had been spirited from the New Orleans Morial Convention Center and whisked by limousine to Air Force One and Two, powered up and waiting for their arrival and priority departure.

The attempt on Sam's life had been provoked by the President's endeavour to ban high-powered military-style rifles within the United States. The fact that the weapon used in a plot to assassinate Alexander was indeed one of these rifles, wasn't lost on the electorate, who, a few weeks later, reelected the President with a sweeping majority.

The Democrats regained control of the two Houses, the first time since the 110th United States Congress.

The national wave of support for the new measures the President campaigned on also had its effects on the NRA. Their membership virtually dropped overnight by forty percent.

A sidebar to the tragedy at the convention centre was the fact that the meals which had been prepared for the paying guests had been distributed among all the soup kitchens in the New Orleans area, at the request of the President. Never had people in need eaten so well. Perhaps this too had some effect on the election results, in that the Democratic candidate for the House of Representatives as well as that of the Senate both won.

John Doyle was granted the Secretary's Exceptional Service Award, which honours remarkable leadership or service that is distinguished by achievements of unique national or international significance, reflecting great credit on the department. John's selfless deed of killing his adopted brother had profoundly moved the secretary.

He prized the award, but the guilt of his deed crushed him. The memory he had of standing there, behind Melinda, while suddenly recognizing Hank and being torn between brotherly love and duty, would mark him for life.

Not long after receiving his award, he submitted his resignation to Melinda who, at first, refused to accept it. She had pleaded with him to reconsider, stating that what he had done was the bravest and most patriotic act she had ever witnessed and that he deserved even more than a commendation. She would work at helping him get a promotion.

Tears almost welled from his eyes as he thanked her and resubmitted his letter.

Oliver Doyle, on the other hand, sustained both animosity and praise. Because he was the father of the man who tried to assassinate the President, his company suffered severe losses. Not enough to bring him to bankruptcy, but enough to have him lose his relationship status with many of the powerful men he had considered to be his friends. In hindsight, he realized that they had never been so: They were only people using others to their own advantage, much as he had done.

The praise he received came anonymously, through emails from individuals who were identified by the people at Homeland Security now surveying his every move, as originating mainly from the South and from some of the marginal, anti-government groups.

As for Sam's research, when the story about the assassination attempt and the part that he played in foiling it came out on every television news channel and radio station around the world, sales of his book went through the roof and the royalties from it brought in a tidy sum.

Melinda and Sam were again invited to the White House, to meet in private with the President. She too was given a commendation by him.

Sam was awarded the Presidential Medal of Freedom, the highest honour that can be bestowed upon a civilian, for, as the Act states, it is given for 'an especially meritorious contribution to the security or national interests of the United States, world peace, cultural or other significant public or private endeavors' and it is not restricted to American citizens.

The President and his wife, Ashley, welcomed the two after the award ceremony to a supper in their private quarters. The four spent that evening talking, joking and laughing, as though they had known each other for years.

Before Sam and Melinda left, the President and First Lady embraced them and told them they were considered family.

****

Today, though, was the day they were to begin their own family. It was their wedding day.

As Sam and Melinda stood under the gazebo, with the sun slowly setting in the western sky, they felt a wave of serenity and happiness wash over them.

Their families were either playing volleyball on the beach, sitting around the many campfires that had been set up, or as some of the kids were doing, running in the wet sand after the tide had gone out, leaving only small, gently rolling waves lapping at the shoreline.

They had agreed that their wedding should be simple and family oriented. Melinda had invited and flown her four older sisters and families up to Moncton for the event.

As for Sam, well, his family who hailed from the Maritimes had put together the feast of the century, right there on the beach. A huge, improvised kitchen had been set up to cook more Shediac lobsters, crab and scallops than an army could devour.

They had worked on the clam chowder for hours in the morning, and by the time the wedding ceremony was held, the makeshift tables had been set, the butter had been drawn and the homemade loaves of bread had been sliced.

Music was provided by Sam's uncle Marcel. Until about thirty minutes before the ceremony started, the music over the loudspeakers had been a mixture of French Canadian reels and jigs, Dixieland and Jazz. Suddenly, however, a version of *Hava Nagila* began to play.

Sam had looked at Melinda with a huge question mark on his face. No sooner had he done so, than over the sand dunes just behind the wedding party, a short, ruddy-looking man, accompanied by his wife, four grown children and their families, rose over the mound and came parading down to where the couple sat.

Sam looked again at Melinda and asked, "Is that who I think it is?"

Melinda laughed and then said, "Yes, it's a gift for you."

Sam got up out of his canvas sun chair and ran to meet Agent Cohen and his family.

"Shmu'el, how are you, old friend? This is such a surprise!"

By then, Melinda had joined the group and embraced Agent Cohen.

Introductions were made as well as promises to have everyone in the Cohen party meet everyone in Sam's and Melinda's families.

Then, a few bars of *Here Comes the Bride* chimed over the loudspeakers, announcing the time for everyone to gather for the ceremony, which was to be held in a gazebo, halfway up the dunes.

While the swimmers came out of the water, dried off and then went to the public change rooms to dress more appropriately, Sam led Melinda, hand in hand, to the place where their lives would change profoundly.

Melinda had asked her eldest sister to give her away, since her father had abandoned them when she was four and her mother had died fifteen years earlier. Sam, in turn, asked his uncle Claude to do the honours as his best man.

It took about fifteen minutes for everyone to make it to the gazebo and circle it. The four main players stood before a Justice of the Peace and the soon-to-be newlyweds were to pronounce their vows before the eighty or so family members who had come to celebrate the occasion and to display their solidarity and support.

The judicial officer cleared her throat, prompting everyone to hush. There were smiles of anticipation on the faces of all in attendance and even an uncharacteristic thumbs-up from Agent Cohen.

"Let us begin, shall we," said the Justice of the Peace.

"In the names of the betrothed, I welcome you all to this wonderful juncture in their lives. This setting couldn't be more perfect than, I would guess, the relationship enjoyed by Sam and Melinda."

Sam contemplated Melinda's face lovingly, but said nothing.

"We are gathered here to witness the union of these two individuals in matrimony."

Pretending to survey the group, she added, " I don't imagine there is anyone here who would have an objection to this union, but if there is, now is the time to speak up."

This brought a round of laughter from the assembly and two of Sam's uncles waved their arms telling the JP they objected to the union because they were also suitors seeking Melinda's hand.

Sam found them in the crowd and pointed at them saying, "OK now. Let's not get carried away. She turned you down gently, remember?"

Again, laughter from the group and the two uncles nodded in mock sadness and acknowledged they had nothing to add and to get on with the ceremony.

The Justice of the Peace turned to Sam and Melinda, smiled and said, "Seems you dodged the bullet."

Sam and Melinda looked at each other, remembering the events at the convention centre and the close calls they had lived through.

The Justice continued, not knowing why, what seemed to her a smile of complicity had been exchanged between them.

Scanning the assembly, she carried on.

"Sam and Melinda have requested a moment to share their feelings for each other in the form of their vows. Melinda, would you be the first to do so?"

Melinda turned to Sam and took his hands in hers and peering directly into his eyes, she began.

"Sam. My whole life has been one of competition and struggles. I've had to be strong and logical at all times, not letting anyone know the real me. Then I met you. I can't say our first encounter was conducive to falling in love, . . ."

This brought chuckles from everyone, but they quickly quieted down to hear the rest.

" . . . but there was something about you that was incredibly attractive to me. Your thirst for knowledge and truth, your humility and sincerity touched that part of my being that allowed the walls I had built around myself to crumble.

"I felt I could open up to you without worrying about being questioned or judged.

"We may come from two different worlds, but there are no borders between us. We are one. *I* am one with you. I offer you my mind, my body and soul, now and forever."

The smile on Sam's face could not have been broader.

Melinda's sisters were crying by that time, as were half the people in attendance, including all of Sam's uncles.

The Justice of the Peace beckoned to Sam.

"Sam, would you pronounce your vows?"

It was Sam's turn to clear his throat.

"Melinda, what can I say that would do justice to how I feel about you. If it wasn't for you, I would never have almost been blown up, shot at and tackled by secret agents."

That had the Justice's eyes grow large and elicited more laughter from the group.

Melinda shook her head and nodded, yes.

Sam continued.

"However, I would not have it any other way. With you, I am more than I was. With you, I am complete. With you, I am a better man. I have never known anyone like you.

"At first, your piercing blue eyes took me in and I felt my soul meld with yours. I know of no one more capable, intelligent and strong than you. When I'm with you, no matter what the circumstance, I feel safe and totally happy.

"I, too, give you my mind, my body and soul, now and forever."

All eyes were still misty and a few guests were blowing their nose.

The Justice paused a moment and then turned to Sam's uncle Claude.

"We have the rings?"

Wiping a tear from his eye, Claude reached into his pocket, pulled out the two rings and presented them to her.

The Justice handed one of them to Sam and asked that he place it on Melinda's finger as a symbol of his love and commitment The term *symbol* was not lost on Sam and Melinda, but in this situation, he felt it was most appropriate.

Then, Melinda placed a ring on Sam's finger and the two were declared married. With joyful enthusiasm, they were asked to seal their covenant with a kiss.

Sam slowly pulled Melinda to him and wrapped his arms around her while giving her a gentle but prolonged kiss, to the applause and cheers of the crowd.

Then the Justice of the Peace cast her gaze over everyone and said, " Family members and friends, I am proud to present to you, Mr. and Mrs. Buckner."

Amid the cheers, the Justice of the Peace managed to say that they could sign the certificates and the register later.

They stepped down from the gazebo onto the sand, to hugs, handshakes and good wishes from the group.

It was now time for more music, beer and a memorable Acadian feast on the beach.

The day had been simply perfect. Sam and Melinda felt surrounded by and immersed in love.

A few hours later, as the two again stood in the centre of the gazebo, Sam held onto Melinda while the sun was setting, as they reminisced about their day and how blessed they were.

Melinda turned slightly to glance back at Sam. He leaned his head forward to get a better view of his wife's beautiful face.

"I wish this could last forever," she whispered.

Sam smiled and kissed her cheek.

"It can, if we want it to and work at it."

She squeezed his arms, which were wrapped around her waist.

Sam whispered, "Look at what we've been through in the past year. We've beaten all the odds. So, I ask you, what could possibly go wrong? . . ."

About the author

Leo Audette is the author of *The Osiris String*, the first of the Sam Buckner trilogy. He lives in the Niagara Region, Ontario.

Correspondence for the author should be addressed to: laudette2@leoaudette.org.

In the sequel to *The Divine Formula*, Leo Audette continues the Sam Buckner saga. He brings together intriguing and controversial themes, and a cast of characters that come alive on the pages of the novel.

SlipTime

A Sam Buckner Adventure

By

Leo J. Audette

Turn the page for a special advanced preview of the third instalment of the Sam Buckner adventures.

Prologue

The patient was lying on a narrow bed, in what looked like a hospital room. He couldn't be sure of that, or for that matter, of anything else.

As he gazed at his surroundings, the fog in his mind prevented him from fully focusing on the details, such as the single, small window perched up high; or the stainless steel toilet in the far corner; or the metal door with a peek-through window.

He could only move his head from side to side and seemed to be paralyzed from the neck down. Every few moments though, he felt the restraints on his wrists and ankles, which were the reasons for his immobility. Then back into the fog.

The patient had been found wandering on a country road, delirious, making little sense of who he was or where he had come from. The police did not consider him to be a vagabond, in that he was well, but strangely, dressed. He had no identification on him and no form of currency in his pockets.

With no reason to charge him with any crime, they had decided to take him to the hospital for observation and to determine what was wrong with him. The doctors checked him over and diagnosed him to be healthy and uninjured. Knowing they should not simply release him onto the streets, they called in a psychiatrist to evaluate his mental state.

Five days had elapsed since he had been found and, still, the doctors could not make heads or tails about the condition of the man whom they called Patient Joe.

The most remarkable thing about the situation was that, on the same evening, they had found a woman with identical symptoms, wandering down the same road. She had been sent to another hospital and it had taken two days for the health system's medical database to correlate the two incidents. She was then moved to the same hospital in order to simplify and compare their evaluations and treatment.

Patient Jane was now in a similar room and suffering the same delusions as the male patient, two floors below.

In the cafeteria, down the corridor from Patient Joe's room, two psychiatrists were drinking coffee and discussing the corresponding occurrences.

"Yes, I agree with you. The two cases are definitely related, but I'll be damned if I can explain their symptoms," said Doctor Young.

"Simon," added the Head of Psychiatry, Doctor John Lawson, "I believe the way they were dressed when found and the strange vernacular they use, has to be the key to understanding what has happened to the two."

Doctor Young responded, "You make a good point. We're going to have to think like detectives as much as doctors to solve this case."

He paused a moment and continued. "There is a little light at the end of the tunnel, though. Patient Joe has had an ever-increasing number of lucid moments. Though they are short in duration, I feel his mind is slowly reasserting itself and will begin to make some sense of what he is going through. Has your patient displayed the same signs of returning to clarity?"

"Yes, she has, but her moments of reality have only begun to exhibit themselves today. Hence the reason for our meeting now."

"How would you propose we proceed with these two?" asked Young.

"I believe we need to continue monitoring their progress and keep each other informed about the frequency and duration of their moments of lucidity. Then, when they both have reached the thirty-minute threshold of clarity, we should introduce pictures of each one to both of them and assess their reactions. If they prove to be positive, and, if and/or when they fully recover from their state of stupor, we will bring the two together. Perhaps the pictures or their meeting will jog their memories and we might be able to understand what has happened to them. Then, and only then, will we be able to help them with the correct course of treatment."

Young considered the suggestion for a moment.

As he rose from the table, he nodded in the affirmative and said, "I agree with you. There isn't much we can do for them until they are in a position to give us some feedback on any of our questions. Thank you, Doctor." Then, with a grin, Lawson added, " Might I suggest that the next time we meet, we discuss it over a Scotch."

"That's a great suggestion," responded the junior psychiatrist.

Doctor Young returned to his wing and looked in on Patient Joe. As he watched the man on the bed, he wondered what type of trauma could have produced his bout of psychosis.

He then headed off to his office to continue the detective work he had spoken of with his colleague. He went to the closet and pulled out the clothing Patient Joe was wearing on the evening he had been delivered to the hospital.

Looking at the style of the articles and material they were made of, he walked over to his desk and sat down, depositing the clothing on its surface.

He then waved his hand over the right corner of the desk and the hologram of a computer screen appeared before him. He touched a few virtual buttons and a search page came up.

He uttered a command, "Display twenty-first century men's apparel."

He sat back into his chair and began watching the images and videos that materialized before his eyes.

Chapter 1

The door to the Roosevelt Room, in the West Wing, flew open and then crashed behind President Alexander as he stormed out, walking angrily to the door which led directly into the Oval Office, on the opposite side.

He was quickly followed by the Chairman of the Chiefs of Staff, General Baxter. As he entered the Oval Office, Alexander turned to him and growled, "Why did you wait until now to inform me about this?"

The general didn't flinch.

"Sir, it was a need-to-know issue, and until we knew you weren't going to be a one-term president, there was no need to chance that too many people would become aware of it: national security and all. No first-term President has known or been told of the situation. Orders not to inform them were given by President Eisenhower himself."

The general had never seen Alexander in such a state of rage. He had always been a cool, calm and collected individual. Nothing ever seemed to phase him. This briefing, however, had burst the dike. Even the veins on the President's forehead were visible.

The general understood the President's reaction. He, himself, almost had the same reaction when he had learned of it, some ten years before. There were only a handful of people who were privy to the information: himself, the Executive Director of the President's Council of Advisors on Science and Technology and the Executive Director of the National Science and Technology Council, both sitting in the Roosevelt Room. And now, President Alexander.

Three other Presidents had also been brought up to speed on the issue, but they had all passed away, taking the secret to their graves.

Alexander wasn't finished. In a less threatening tone, he continued.

"Harry," addressing the general informally, "What do you mean, an issue of national security? This extends way beyond our borders. It could affect all of mankind. How and why would the people involved keep this a secret, and for so long?"

Before the general could respond, Alexander gestured for him to sit down.

He was regaining his composure and was ready to discuss the briefing and the revelations which had been disclosed to him.

"I want to see the *thing* myself."

The general nodded, yes.

"I assumed you would, sir. Whenever you want, I'll make the arrangements."

Alexander rose from the sofa and walked over to the door leading to his assistant's office.

Mildred looked up at the President as he peeked in.

"Yes, Mr. President?"

"Do I have anything pressing tomorrow?" he asked.

She quickly brought up the President's schedule on her computer monitor.

"You have a meeting with the secretary of state at one o'clock and one with the ambassador of Ecuador at four."

"Reschedule both. I'll be out for the day. And, inform Captain Graves that I'll need Air Force One ready to go by seven in the morning, tomorrow."

Mildred was used to these sudden changes in routine and simply replied, "Will do, sir. Any preferred date for the new meetings?"

Alexander pondered for a moment and responded, "No, not yet. I'll know better when I return tomorrow evening."

Chapter 2

Sam was just walking to the new apartment he and Melinda had been able to secure, but still at the Watergate Hotel. Her first apartment there had been a one-bedroom, and though larger, as was each one in the complex, than the average unit found in other buildings, it was still better suited to one person than to a couple.

This one happened to have been previously occupied by Placido Domingo. Situated on the top floor and in the centre of the C-shaped South Watergate building, it provided the new tenants with a fantastic view of the Potomac River from its expansive living room, as well as from its master bedroom. Large floor-to-ceiling windows allowed for the unobstructed vista.

The apartment, though, was more expensive than the allocation Homeland Security could give Melinda, at her pay scale. On the other hand, the royalties Sam had begun receiving for the sale of his research paper, The Divine Formula, were more than enough to afford them the amenities and space this apartment provided them. When the world learned about Sam's involvement during the assassination attempt on the President's life, his became a household name and the sales of his book went through the roof making it a number one bestseller on the New York Times list of *must-reads*.

Above and beyond this, because he was now married to an American citizen, he was able to apply for and obtain a Marriage-Based Green Card, giving him permanent residency in the US.

He was also granted an H-1B visa, allowing him to work in the US. Cambridge University had given him a tenure-track position, in part because of his contribution to science and in part, unbeknown to Sam, because of a few discreet phone calls made by Secretary Fleet to some of his former colleagues at the university. It meant he had to share his time between giving lectures at the University of Toronto and at Cambridge, but his schedule was more than manageable.

Sam was both starved and sweating. He had just returned from the complex's health club, where he went every day he was in town. The amenities offered by the Watergate were amazing: everything from full-time concierge service and twenty-four-hour room service, to restaurants, rooftop terraces and swimming pools.

Life could not get better, he thought. Well, not quite, was his internal reply. The fact he was coming home to Melinda propelled his state of happiness and contentment to a whole different level. How could he be so lucky?

"Hey, where are you, Ms. Gordon?" he called.

Sam and Melinda had discussed the issue of her taking his name, but they had decided, due to her position, that it might be wiser to leave things as they were. They knew they were married and that was all that mattered.

"Where else? I'm in the kitchen, where a proper lady needs to be while preparing dinner for her man," Melinda responded with a tinge of sarcasm.

Sam hurried to the kitchen area and poked his head around the corner.

There was Melinda, standing over the stove, wearing a red kimono-style silk housecoat, stirring a pot of Beef Bourguignon.

"Wow, that smells good," Sam said, as he walked over to her and held her from behind, caressing her neck.

"It should," she replied. "It has half a bottle of Beaujolais in it. But it won't be ready for at least half an hour."

Sam let her go and started making his way to the hallway which led to the bedroom section of the unit.

"I need to take a shower. I had a good workout in the gym."

Melinda tasted the stew and thought it might need a little more salt. She then covered the pot and reduced the heat to simmer. Turning the timer on, a mischievous smile came to her face.

As she headed down the hallway, she caught a glimpse of a naked Sam entering the bathroom and disappearing to his right.

She couldn't help but think what a nice ass he had.

She heard the shower door open and the faucets turn on.

Melinda strutted to the bathroom, slowly undoing the belt on her kimono and letting the cloak gently slide off her shoulders, exposing her Nubian skin and her curvaceous and slender body. She too was naked by the time she reached the opening to the bathroom.

The whole shower cavity was filled with steam and she could barely see Sam for the mist. She opened the door, allowing cooler air to flow in, magically revealing Sam who was leaning, arms outstretched against the wall, his head under the rainfall shower fixture.

It was her turn to embrace him from behind, pressing her breasts against his back.

The shower filled with steam once more, and the two disappeared from view.

Twenty minutes later, they emerged from the stall, patting each other dry with their towels.

"I could almost use another shower after that," Sam commented, "but I think I'm really hungry now. The stew smells amazing.

"You know," he said with a grin, "it's nice when we can have dessert before the main course."

Melinda laughed and tapped him on his behind.

"Who says *that* was dessert? More like an appetizer, don't you think? Wait until after supper."

The two kissed as they walked out of the washroom.

Chapter 3

Later that evening, Melinda's cell phone chirped. She and Sam were sitting with a bowl of popcorn, watching a movie they had rented.

She reached for a napkin, quickly wiped her hands and picked up her phone. She looked at the number of the caller and turned to Sam.

"It's my boss. I wonder what he wants."

"Hello, sir."

"Hi, Melinda. I hope I'm not calling at an inopportune moment?"

"No, sir. Sam and I are just chilling out at home."

"I'll get right to the point. I've just spoken with the President and he would like to see you first thing in the morning."

Melinda had a surprised look on her face as she tried to cover the microphone with her hand and mouthed to Sam that it was concerning the President.

It was his turn to look surprised.

She returned to her call.

"I'll be there. Did he say why?"

"No, he didn't. Actually, he said he could not even tell me, but that I would be brought into the circle before long. All very cryptic."

"And he wants to speak with *me*?" Melinda added, totally puzzled.

"It would seem so. He said I would understand when briefed.

"Now, if I was an insecure man, I'd start worrying about my job. Nevertheless, I trust the man and won't read into this. Oh, and he asked that Sam come with you."

Melinda's eyes grew even larger as she looked at Sam.

"That won't be a problem. I'm sure he will be looking forward to seeing the President again."

Now it was Sam's turn to mouth *what*?

Melinda gestured for him to hold on a moment.

"At what time and where, sir?"

"He wants you there at seven a.m., in the Roosevelt Room." He paused a moment and then added, "This sounds important. He usually doesn't schedule meetings before ten. My curiosity is peaked with this one."

"As is mine, sir," responded Melinda.

"OK, so I won't hold you any longer. Fill me in with whatever you are allowed to, when you are able to. Good night."

The telephone went dead at the other end.

Melinda turned her phone off, putting it down slowly, deep in thought.

"What was all that about?" quizzed Sam.

"I'm not sure? We've been summoned to the White House for a meeting with the President."

"It sounds like something big is up," responded Sam, "And your boss isn't in the loop. Is that normal for Washington?"

Melinda thought for a second.

"No, not really. Someone at my level isn't made privy to information the boss doesn't know. I can't figure this one out."

Sam looked at his Emopulse watch.

"It's getting late. Why don't we hit the sac. Morning will come soon enough."

Melinda looked at Sam and added, "I have a feeling it's going to be a long night."

All Sam could say was, *yup*.

www.ingramcontent.com/pod-product-compliance
Lightning Source LLC
Chambersburg PA
CBHW061537170626
46811CB00001B/11